**Shashi Warrier** was born in 1959 and studied economics at BITS, Pilani. He then drifted through several occupations, including consulting, journalism, computing, management, and teaching, before he began to write seriously. His output since has included fairy tales, thrillers, and literary fiction. He finds writing for children the hardest, and hopes to return to it one day. He was invited to the International Writing Program, University of Iowa, in 2001, and is an honorary Fellow of that university. He likes beaches, motorcycles, and cooking.

He lives in Mangalore with his artist-writer wife Prita and two dogs and a cat.

ALSO BY SHASHI WARRIER

*Night of the Krait* (1996)

*The Orphan* (1998)

*The Hangman's Journal* (2000)

*Sniper* (2000)

*The Orphan Diaries* (2009)

*The Last Hangman* (2013)

# The Man Who Wouldn't Be God

SHASHI WARRIER

SPEAKING TIGER

SPEAKING TIGER PUBLISHING PVT. LTD
4381/4 Ansari Road, Daryaganj,
New Delhi–110002, India

First published in India in paperback by Speaking Tiger 2016



ISBN: 978-93-86050-27-4

eISBN: 978-93-86050-31-1

10 9 8 7 6 5 4 3 2 1

Typeset in Adobe Garamond Pro by SÜRYA, New Delhi
Printed at Sanat Printers, Kundli

*This book is for Dad's elder sister, Ammu Valiyamma,*
*the wisest lady I ever knew.*

## Chapter One

I TAKE THE Metro to work. My wife takes the car.

Not that she minds letting me have the car. Except I'm an alcoholic, you see. Driving to work is safe enough, at eleven or thereabouts every morning, but I have a few discreet swigs of rum during the day and she doesn't like me driving back home in the dark with all that sloshing inside me. Not in Bangalore's peak-hour traffic, with irregular lighting and only inches to spare on each side. So I take the Metro, and she takes the car.

I tell her I don't mind but I do, at least until the third large rum of the day, which generally happens by half past noon, so I'm no longer grumpy at lunch. On a typical working day, I have a couple with lunch, and a quiet little nap afterwards, leaning way back in the comfortable swivel chair in my room at the office. Back to the grind at three, a few calls, a meeting or two, a little writing, and it's time for another couple of pegs instead of the cup of tea my colleagues have. And then it's time to go home.

So when do I work, you might ask. Well, the straight answer is, not very often. I work for this magazine, one that I helped found ... A long while ago, it was, nearly a quarter-century back. I'm the features editor now, with a capable assistant, Surya, who does all the work. I lend my presence, and a virtual blue pencil. My boss, co-founder and managing editor, Murali Srinivasan, lets me continue in my job because of our long history. We went to school together, started up this magazine together, branched out into TV together, and things fell apart soon after.

That was a couple of years ago.

No, it wasn't. It was more like five years ago. The booze makes me lie.

No, no, I lie and blame the booze for it. Most alkies do.

Anyway, there's a farewell this afternoon. It's Rajesh Ahuja's last day with us. Srini and myself apart, he's been here the longest: he's had over twenty years with us, and is getting on for sixty. He's an accountant, and has counted our beans ever since he joined, asking searching questions about extravagance and other dangerous expenditure. His standards haven't changed. Most of our expenditure on the TV channel seems questionable to him, and he's happy now to leave the purse-strings to a young protégè who understands the modern world better.

Rajesh taught me that you can't tell a man by his handshake. His hand is limp and he sweats a lot so his handshake is clammy and leaves you wanting to wash your hands afterwards but he's also one of the most honest people I've ever met, and not just in matters of money. Seeing him go will be more than a twinge.

At four we'll clear the hall and lay out the tables along the sides and the caterers will lay out a finger food buffet on those tables. There'll be a little bar in one corner – early, but old journos can drink any time – that'll keep most of us busy. Srini will make a pedantic little speech and present Mrs and Mr Ahuja a little token of the company's appreciation of Ahuja's services, and after we eat and drink too much we'll all go home, Rajesh never to return.

Except Srini and me. Srini called me earlier today. 'Time

for a little chat,' he said on the intercom. 'After the Ahujas leave.'

'Right,' I said.

The party itself is mostly forgettable, the speeches maudlin, the conversation regrettable, the food safe but stolid, rescued only by the booze, which is good. I arrive on time – just after the bar opens – as do most of the old-timers who've known Rajesh since the old days, but the staff from the TV channel make brief, staggered forays to shake hands with Rajesh and Srini before disappearing again into their lair above.

The stars, hosts, presenters and anchors, arrive one by one, solitary and glamorous, trying to hide their hatred of Rajesh, and their relief that he's leaving for good. They spend a few minutes hovering around Srini, because no one else rates their individual attention, and leave as soon as they can, pointedly avoiding the food, drink, and company as if it's infra dig.

Then comes one R Vishwanathan, Vish to anyone he can't bully, money-grubbing and devious, also, like me, a director of the company, although he exercises his rights more regularly. He smirks and shakes hands, looks pointedly at my glass of Scotch, and asks, 'Enjoying yourself?' He himself holds a glass of orange juice that he will nurse through the evening.

I smile and nod without deigning to reply, noting only that his smirk is brighter than usual, meaning he's been able to kick somebody when they're down. Who, I wonder, as I wander away.

One other little incident sticks in my mind. Two large whiskies – this is Scotch, mind you, miles better than my usual tipple – into the evening, after the stars have left, Rajesh catches me unawares, with a clammy hand on my shoulder. Lurking behind him is a large young man with impressive shoulders. Turns out it's his son, who works for a chain of gyms. While the youngster mashes my small thin hand in his large and powerful – and, like his father's, sweaty – one, Rajesh introduces me to him as 'Bloodhound' Bala, which they used to call me in the days when I was a hotshot investigative reporter.

Actually, it's 'fucking bloodhound', and it was a crooked policeman, an assistant commissioner, who gave me the name when I discovered that he had hushed up the involvement of an industrialist in the murder of a young engineer who had had the temerity to woo his – the industrialist's – daughter. In a single bribe, the cop collected enough cash to see his son through a master's degree in computer science at some obscure American university. Despite my efforts, both the cop and the industrialist got away, but the name he gave me stuck, though people usually dropped the first half when they used it in my presence. The only good from that story came in the form of two friendships: one new, with Gaurav Seth, the officer who succeeded the crooked one; the other renewed, independently, with one Gokul Rao, a cynical, bribe-resisting middle-ranking police official and former college-mate.

The name, like my investigative talent, is history.

So, here I am, after the farewell, making my way towards Srini's room, wading through the debris of the party. It's a long walk. We have a large office, because we got it when office space was relatively cheap. These days the real estate itself is worth a number I'm afraid to calculate, like the distance from here to Alpha Centauri in millimetres.

Sorry about that. It's all that good Scotch making itself felt above the rum, making my mind wander. I'm not noticeably drunker than usual, but these days it takes a hell of a lot to get me really smashed.

Srini. Srini is the quintessential backroom boy. He runs a magazine and a TV channel but all the personal mileage he gets out of it is his name on the masthead of the magazine. Right from the beginning, we'd all go out in the field and he'd hang around in the office pulling strings, arranging loans when we needed them, fixing contacts, building up networks, and all the backup that a good journo needs. That's what he likes, sitting at the back, pulling strings. Unflappable, available, and understated. He's managing director, and he attends every meeting of the board, unlike me.

Srini's room's a bit larger than mine, but shabby, because of the constant stream of visitors: during working hours, it's a rare moment when there aren't a few people waiting to see him. The furniture's a bit worn but there's never enough time to change it. The curtains are worn, too, but Srini hasn't had the time to select new ones and he doesn't trust these fancy interior decorators so he makes do with frayed curtains and furniture that's quite obviously seen better days.

He's sitting at his desk watching his own news channel on a large bright LED TV set on the far wall. The TV is new and gleaming and out of place but it's the one thing that he changes regularly: he insists he can't afford not to have the best.

When I sit across from him, he turns off the TV. 'I'll miss Rajesh,' he says. 'I asked him to stay on for another year or two but he's had enough.'

'He's been unwell,' I tell him. 'Besides his salary and savings, his job got him hypertension and worsened his diabetes. But he did give it his best.'

He takes his spectacles off and puts his elbows on his desk and steeples his fingers so I know that something nasty is on its way. I don't know if he does it consciously, preparing the other party for the bad news, but he does it each time. 'It's been a long time since you gave of your best,' he tells me finally. 'The bloodhound is gone. What's left is an old mushroom.' He coughs delicately. 'A pickled mushroom.'

'Yes,' I tell him. 'But my job is more to manage the features section than to write. Surya does the rest of it very well.'

'Umm, yes, Surya does it very well. He's been doing it very well for the past couple of years, and he wants your job.'

A lurch inside. 'He's not getting it, is he?'

Srini wipes his spectacles, meaning the bad news is due. 'A few hours ago I told him he is.'

'Are you telling me I'm sacked?'

Srini puts his specs back on. 'No,' he says, fiddling with a pen on his blotter. 'No. We wouldn't have been here without you. So we promote you as well.'

'To what?'

'Consulting editor.'

'And what do I do in that job?'

He looks me straight in the eye for the first time that evening. 'You tell me,' he says. 'You're not doing very much now, so you should think in peace until you find what best you can do here.'

It's preparatory to the sack. 'Okay,' I say, giving him the opening he's looking for. 'How long can I take to think?'

More fiddling with the pen. 'How long do you want?'

The anger and bile rise in me. It's a physical thing in the abdomen, a beast rising up through the diaphragm to the chest. I ignore it. 'Six months?' I suggest, thinking that's how long it'll take me to get another job.

'Take three,' he says. Straight in the eye again. 'Have another try at rehab, if you wish. But no more.' He pauses. Swallows. 'You've done a lot for us, but with the competition and high salaries we can't carry you longer than that.'

'How about a golden handshake?'

'How much do you think you've cost us in the last few years?' he replies.

'You tell me.'

He shakes his head. 'No. Let's leave the history aside for now. You asked for six months, which I can't give you. Take three months, that's the most I could get the board to give you … But then, you don't even have to come here. Think at home, if you wish. Check in once a week. That's the best I can do. And the rehab offer holds. We'll pay for it.'

You know where you can stick your best, and the rehab with it, the thing in my belly wants me to scream at him, but I don't. Coward, I tell myself instead. As always. 'Okay,' I tell him, and rise to leave.

As I reach the door, he says, 'Bala, I'm sorry it had to come to this.'

I turn back for a moment. He looks mildly triumphant, smug. The belly-thing continues to call me a coward. 'So am I,' I tell him, and walk out. Back in my room, I take a discreet but hefty slug out of the bottle of Old Monk rum that lives in the bottom drawer. I've got the movements down pat. A quick twist to get the cap off, a quick lift of the arm, a quick warming hit, another quick twist to get the cap back on, and the bottle disappears back into the drawer. A few seconds is all it takes, and the rum's comforting warmth moves down my oesophagus, silencing the belly-beast.

For the time being. Briefly.

What am I going to do? Fiftyish out of shape drunkard with fading – or perhaps faded – professional skills and an expensive, damaging habit. Won't last anywhere.

What am I going to do? This is the belly-beast waking up again, sooner than I expected, demanding. It's insistent.

Live off the missus, at worst. I'm not going to starve, am I?

But she's not going to pay for the booze, says the beast. And what about pride? Will you hang around the house all day, waiting for her permission to spend cab fare to town?

Come to think of it, life's already like that. She tells me not to drive to work and I don't. We can afford two cars now, but she insists we need only one … her decision, again. Actually, I think we can even afford a driver, but again she says no. Oh, she has her reasons for it, of course, all very good and relevant, but the decision, eventually, is hers. Like all the other big ones. A little more of the same, that's all that'll happen.

Talking to the beast is instant exhaustion. It can bring you down to earth instantly from the highest of clouds, the happiest of heavens.

I head wearily for the nearest Metro station, M G Road, with its crowded trains and clouds of BO and tired chatter. Besides the announcements, of course, loud, incomprehensible, and almost continuous. This is the third leg of my exercise for the day. First leg, walk from home to Metro station at Baipanahalli. Second leg, walk from Metro Station M G Road to the office, which is on St Mark's Road. Legs three and four are legs two and one in reverse.

Ten brisk minutes for each leg in the morning, hurrying to get to the office and the day's first shot, and fifteen sloppy unsteady minutes in the evening, in no hurry to get home to recriminations and studied, purposeful ignorance.

I don't know if ignorance is the right word for being ignored. A damaging admission coming from a writer, but I did say my professional skills were fading. It's years since I looked up a dictionary or a thesaurus. But it's not indifference, because then it wouldn't be studied …

In any case, I'm in no hurry to get home to recriminations from my wife and ignorance from our daughter, who seems of late to have become her daughter alone.

This Metro must be the most underworked in the world. Once all lines are complete, I suppose there'll be more people using it, but that's still some years away. Until then, peak hour will be tolerable. At this time of the evening, it's crowded, by

Bangalore standards. Not jam-packed, like the local trains in Mumbai or Chennai, but all seats are full and a few straps occupied. I get into a genteel mob-sandwich hurrying for a door and get pushed inside. In front are youngsters wanting to be cool and first in, and at the back another bunch of youngsters wanting to be cool and unhurried, but determined to get in regardless. In the middle, filling the sandwich, are people like me, who don't mind being pushed around as long as its in approximately the right direction.

Nearby is a man who doesn't wash as often as he should, but I don't feel like moving away. It's a matter of breathing lightly until I get to Baipanahalli station, from where home is a fifteen-minute walk now with the rum still massaging my innards. It takes a little under an hour, doorstep to doorstep, in the evening.

I wish it were longer. Even the polluted air of Bangalore at rush hour and the BO in the Metro are better than the atmosphere at home.

I let myself in with the latchkey to find that Mohini, my wife, isn't back yet, but Pallavi, our daughter, is. Doesn't matter: we all have a key apiece and we each have our own timings for coming and going. Pallavi doesn't emerge from her room when I walk into the house – she must have recognized my step or something – and I head straight to the bathroom for a wash and a change.

When I've showered and changed into the sloppy, comfortable clothes – a dhoti and a T-shirt – I wear at home, I head for the dining room, not to eat but because the bar's there. Pallavi's at the dining table watching TV. When she sees me she picks up her plate and walks off to the sitting room where she can watch the TV at closer range, leaving me free to use the dining table, which I do.

'Good evening,' I tell her, as I pour myself one more. Just

one more, I tell myself, the alcoholic's perpetual excuse. I make it large, and then add just a bit more. This is the day's last, after all.

'Good evening,' she says, eyes still on the TV.

'What's that you're watching?' I ask.

'*Bones*,' she replies. On the screen, a woman with a weird delivery describes a dead man from a bit of what she says is what's left of a bone from his big toe or something. Forensic anthropology and other sciences, mixed with murder in a TV serial that's got Pallavi engrossed. Only I don't know if she's really engrossed or just avoiding me, and I'm too nervous to ask. But the last time we spoke of anything serious she did mention she'd like to do forensic anthropology.

Pallavi's mother arrives before the conversation can continue. Mohini is always well-groomed but a certain stiffness to her posture tells how tired she is, and how badly she wants to get into something comfortable and relax. But the stiffness only increases when she sees the drink in my hand. 'When did you get back?' she asks.

'About twenty minutes ago,' I tell her. 'More or less as usual.'

'You usually wait a little longer before starting on the booze,' she says. She says it 'neutrally' but there's a world of accusation behind it.

'Yes,' I tell her. 'But today's not like every other day.'

'Why not?'

'Essentially, well, I got the sack.'

She lowers her bottom gracefully onto the sofa, placing her elegant briefcase next to her. She has her ammunition now, and, with a tightening of the mouth, fires the opening salvo of the evening. 'I'm not surprised,' she says. 'What are you doing about getting another job?'

'Since I only got to know at half past six, nothing yet.' A

decade ago, when she'd gotten her business going the way she wanted, she told me to quit my job and work on the novel that had been in the back of my mind ever since we'd got married sixteen years back. Now, of course, the belly-beast makes sure I won't write a book.

'You must have seen it coming.' Her eyes are bleak, without hope. Like mine, no doubt.

'No.'

'You must have been blind drunk.'

Behind her Pallavi swallows the last of her dinner and flees to the kitchen. She doesn't like watching these fights. My cellphone rings: it's Srini. 'Switch to our channel,' he tells me.

'Why?' I ask.

'A lifeline for you.' He hangs up.

I walk ten paces and pick up the remote with Mohini watching, still bleak. 'Who was that?' she asks.

'Srini. He wants me to watch the news.'

The prime-time anchors are two slick young women with accents as fake as the red of their lips. They take turns at reading out news items, and you can hear the outrage in the voice of the one speaking now, of the charges laid against one Swami Sarvananda, an up-and-coming young godman – he's barely forty, according to some accounts – whose base is in the foothills of the Western Ghats, set in a picturesque valley near a town called Padubidri.

The charges are serious. First, a female devotee has accused him of attempted rape. The accusation is difficult, if not impossible, to prove. The woman says he groped her thrice over as many days a couple of months ago, and tried to rape her. There's no evidence, but her statement alone is sufficient for at least a short stay in jail for him if she cares to file a report with the police.

He runs a trust that in turn runs the ashram, which

includes a house for himself – it's some family's old house – and a sort of hostel for devotees, and some charitable works in the district, including a small hospital and a home for destitutes. The second charge is that he's been skimming off the top from the trust funds.

Among the people staying in his hostel – that's what they claim, at any rate – is the thirtyish son of a cabinet minister, now wanted for fixing cricket matches: he's been paid off by gamblers who make much more money betting than the cricketers do playing the game. The minister's son, says the report, is inside the ashram, where the police don't go, because the local politicians stop them. That's the third and most dramatic charge, then, harbouring a fugitive or whatever, from which stems a secondary charge that he himself is into match-fixing and betting and money-laundering and stashing cash in a Swiss bank. Then comes the question, the man's guilt implicit in it: can we let someone get away with this?

Like most TV news stories, there's little depth and much repetition, with many opinions, mostly uninformed and long-winded. They figure that outrage sells, so the anchors manufacture it, reporting selectively, using visuals to shock and anger. Anchors acquire larger-than-life personae, which in turn leads to distorted news and opinion. It's inevitable with 24-hour news channels, which need something to fill in the cheap seconds, the ones with no advertisements. I don't like those channels, though one of them pays part of my salary.

When the next story comes on I call Srini. 'I saw the story about the Swami. Is that it?'

'Yes,' he says. 'Get me a good investigative feature on it and you can consider yourself a productive member of our team. That's why I said it's your lifeline.'

'Okay.'

'So go down there, ask around, and answer me a few

questions. One, is the man the usual charlatan, or is there something different about him? Two, does he shelter crooks? Three, is he a sexual predator?'

All these are familiar charges: they've been levelled at practically every godman, and the first two at some godwomen as well. But the public itches for sleaze, especially on godmen, so the story will sell. I don't know whether I should do it, but Srini's in battering-ram mode – which he adopts seldom, to be fair – and I don't have an option. 'Right,' I tell him.

'Make your own deadlines, but don't take too long. Check with the Mangalore office for a cameraman or whatever else you might need.'

'Right,' I repeat.

'Stay off the bottle.' Then, after a pause, a typically Srini-ish instruction. 'Watch the money like it's your own.' Pause. 'Good luck.' He hangs up.

'Jawohl, mein Fuhrer,' I tell the silent phone, and get on with the planning. Padubidri is some thirty-odd kilometres from Mangalore, less from the airport, I think. I call the people who do our travel work: they're used to being called at odd hours.

'Where are you going?' Mohini asks when I hang up.

'Padubidri, near Mangalore,' I tell her. 'Following up that story on TV, about Swami Sarvananda.'

'I thought you were out of that job.'

'Not quite yet,' I tell her. 'Srini says the sacking won't happen if I can come up with something good. Like this story. Which also means I have to lay off the booze for a while.' There's no sign of softening on her face or in her eyes. 'I'd better pack. I'll be away a few days.'

'How many?' she asks.

'No idea. Not more than four or five, in any case.'

'How are you going?'

'Early morning flight to Mangalore, cab from there.'

A few minutes later comes a text message: I'm booked on an early morning flight to Mangalore, and a cab will pick me up there. I make another call, making sure a cab from our regular service will pick me up here at five.

Packing, even at my leisurely pace, with regular breaks for sips of coke fortified with rum, occupies all of fifteen minutes, at the end of which a black suitcase stands by the door, ready to roll. And now there's this deep fear that I'm going to screw this job up as well but also a sense of lightness, of leaving behind some of the baggage as I embark on something new.

Partly because of this lightness I knock on Pallavi's door to tell her I'm going away for a few days. From inside her room comes the shout, 'What's it, Dad?' Mohini's knock sounds different, I guess.

'I'll see you in four or five days,' I tell her. 'Off at five in the morning. Before you wake up.'

'Okay, Dad, see you when you get back,' she says. No 'Have a good trip,' or anything of the kind. She doesn't even open the door. I stare at it for a while, then give up and walk away. Just three years ago, at twelve, she'd hug me tight when I left on even a one-day business trip.

Oh, it's cost me a lot, this demon rum. For all that, I go back to it. I can't help myself. I stayed off for some time last year, some weeks, and during those weeks found mornings relatively easy to get through. Lunch without the rum became tasteless and joyless, and afternoons wakeful and filled with irritation. Evenings brought more irritation, some of it neutralized by a brisk walk. But nights, without exception, were sleepless nightmares. I read, absorbing nothing. I wrote, and, after throwing away everything shoddy, found nothing remaining. I broke one holiday evening, after a yelling match with Mohini. I went to a bar, downed three quick rums, and, returning to apologize, found an iceberg in her place. Damned if you drink and damned if you don't, I thought, and went back to my old habits. They were still new habits, actually, but felt old, if you get what I mean.

I break free of these thoughts and turn my mind to the job at hand, and to what I can do that the others can't: pull old strings. My phone has a long list of contacts, the only thing I back up rigorously, for without it I am nothing. Names of three potentially useful people in Mangalore: Gokul Rao, my cop friend, due to retire soon but still in service; Tauseef Ahmed, son of an old reporter friend, now owner of a cookery website and a restaurant; and Sivakumar Pai, a real estate dealer with fingers in many pies.

Too late to call them now, I decide, and nod off at midnight, the iceberg already snoring gently three feet away.

## Chapter Two

THE ALARM WAKES me at half past four. Abu, my regular cabbie, calls at five to tell me he's at the gates of the apartment block where we live, and I tell the watchman to let his cab in. I wave a sort of farewell to Mohini, who's just got up to go to the loo and is preparing to go back to sleep for an hour. I shut the door quietly as I leave and in another few minutes I'm in the cab heading for the dual carriageway northwest, towards the airport, speeding comfortably along the broad highway except when we encounter clumps of traffic, mostly buses and other cabs all headed for the airport as well.

Bangalore at that time is cool, and I roll down the windows to get a blast of air in the face. It helps with the hangover. Besides, I'm free to, umm, break wind, which is necessary after a night's drinking. One of the smaller penalties, not usually noticeable, but obtrusive, and usually offensive, in public.

There are messages on my phone. First, the cellphone number of the cabbie who'll be at Mangalore's Bajpe airport to take me to Swami Sarvananda's ashram, which is about fifty kilometres away, about an hour and a half given the state of the roads. Second, that they're holding a room for me at a hotel in Mangalore, but I can always take another if it's not all right: apparently it's the quiet season and rooms are available in all the better hotels, but there's nothing near the ashram.

The check-in is brief and the flight itself notably

uneventful, except for the landing, when I think we're going into the trees, which we don't. The disembarkation is quick – my suitcase is small enough to carry on so I don't have to wait for baggage – and there's a driver with my name on a board waiting at the arrivals exit. We descend a staircase – only the escalator going upwards works – to a parking lot where, under a tree, sits a white diesel-engined Swift that will be my transport for the next few days.

Clouds gather in a cool breeze as we get in the car. The driver, one Anil, a stranger to me but a regular with the company, asks whether I want to go to the ashram first or to the hotel. 'What do you think?' I ask.

'Ashram, sir,' he says. 'Sometimes there's a long queue of people waiting to see the Swami. You might have to wait.'

'All right, then,' I tell him. 'The ashram it is.'

We take the road to Mangalore city, turning off to the right fairly soon after we leave the airport. From there on the road to the ashram winds through the foothills of the ghats, across a stream and through forests and fields and cliffs, a relief from the concrete of Bangalore. Half an hour later, we're on the highway north, only to leave it again ten minutes later, onto another winding road and forests, all green and heavy from recent rains. Some twenty minutes and fifteen kilometres on, at a village called Belman, which is a T on the road with a small bus stand and plenty of shops, we get off this road onto a rutted sort of path with only patches of tar, and follow it to a point where the tar disappears and we're running on packed earth. The path here is just wide enough to accommodate two cars, and we slow down for every oncoming car. 'Next year this road will be much better,' Anil tells me. 'Swami has influence.'

'Does he do any good?' I ask.

'Yes, yes,' Anil says, a bit shocked that I could ask such

a question. 'A school, a clinic, a small hospital … all near Belman.'

We come upon the ashram gates beyond a clump of unlikely shops and stalls selling tender coconuts, bottled water, soft drinks and packaged snacks. The ashram is fenced in, and beyond a gate lies a path – beaten earth, again – to an old-style building with eaves and a tiled roof, in front of which is a sort of open hall with many pillars, also with a tiled, peaked roof. In a corner of the compound is a covered garage where two vehicles stand, a battered old Bolero and a relatively new – perhaps two years old – low-end Tata hatchback, besides a couple of small motorcycles. At the gates is a young acolyte in a white dhoti and shirt showing people the way to the hall. As with most such places, you're supposed to leave your footwear outside, and a set of long shelves are provided for the purpose. There's also a tap nearby where you can wash your feet if you wish. I put my shoes on the shelf and walk into the hall.

Missing are the security men. Every VIP surrounds himself with a ring of hard-eyed men in unlikely safari suits with things sticking out of their ears, or cops with fearsome-looking small arms and hissing walkie-talkies. These are conspicuous by their absence. Anyone wanting to harm this Swami can walk right up and shoot him between the eyes.

In a corner, another acolyte in white stands guard over a row of bags and suitcases: I've understood that people come here straight from the bus stand. Further on are rows of mats with people sitting on them, about a third of them girls and women. On a dais at the eastern end sits a lean bearded man in a dhoti and a shirt, the Swami, and flanking him are three men, dressed similarly in white. Facing him is a devotee, and the Swami listens to him, nodding and smiling, completely unhurried. He's remarkably restful, the Swami, no odd gestures, just a smile of deep contentment.

As I watch, the devotee finishes his recital. The Swami nods at him, smiles, and does a namaste, after which the devotee walks off. One of the three men indicates the next person in the line, a young woman, who walks onto the platform to sit facing the Swami, who greets her with another namaste. More unhurried chat, more smiles, a bow from the devotee, and the same unfussy departure. It's taken about three minutes. I look around and count: there are at least fifty people in line ahead of me. I'm going to have to wait at least a couple of hours to see the guy.

This guy is a small-timer. The big ones have thousands of people visiting them every day, and proportionately larger budgets and establishments. The comings and goings of their devotees support acres of shops, even malls, and whole townships, besides regular bus services from nearby cities, and, in one case, even a train service. This guy's generated only these few dozen shops outside his ashram.

Swami Sarvananda seems to go for quality, not quantity, and doesn't seem to have any of the frills – flowers, sycophants, sleight-of-hand, armies of uniformed volunteers to guide visitors around, billboards with his sayings plastered all over them, large florid buildings in which to hold public appearances, and so on. But then this guy is supposed to have some really heavyweight believers, so the numbers should rise very quickly. Unless, of course, he ends up in prison for rape or embezzlement or something.

Another couple of people have arrived and have sat down by me. I tell one of them I have to go to the toilet, and to please hold my place. When he nods agreement, I stand up – that hurts, because it's years since I sat cross-legged on a mat on the floor – and ask an acolyte about toilets. He tells me to go to the 'backside' of the hall, showing me the way. The toilet is basic but clean, and after I relieve myself I decide to take a little break and go look for a place where I can get some booze.

There isn't any nearby. The shops around sell everything but booze. I ask one of the shopkeepers and he tells me I'll have to go all the way back to Belman to find a bar so I return to the hall and my place in the line. The signal strength on my cellphone is quite good so I get online and see what I can dig up about Swami Sarvananda, and find very little, except that he was born in these parts, is a native of a small town some fifteen or so kilometres from Mangalore, and qualified as an engineer from a college in Surathkal, less than thirty kilometres away, twenty from Mangalore. Even his given name is doubtful, as is his age, though he looks fortyish.

There are a couple of trusts in his name, one running a small hospital nearby, another a school, besides maintaining this ashram. Considering the depth of information you get on the internet, this man keeps a very low profile. His name, before his elevation to godhood, was Prakash Shastry. He is the only child of parents who are now dead, and a construction engineer who taught himself programming and became a computer person.

On the dais, he continues in his unhurried way. I notice now that he blinks much less often than most people. The devotee before him bursts into tears, and he lays a comforting hand on the weeping man's shoulder. Despite the lack of hurry, few people spend more than a few minutes with him. I wonder why.

My turn comes at eleven, after nearly three hours of waiting. Two people have spent more than twenty minutes each with him, versus the average of three or four minutes. But as I get onto the platform I understand why people don't take more than three or four minutes: one of the three men with the Swami whispers in my ear in Kannada, 'Please don't take too long.'

And then he's smiling at me, folding his hands in the conventional namaste, gesturing me to sit, which I do. Close up, he looks fresh, despite the hours of sitting and listening, despite the beard, despite the slightly crumpled cotton clothes, thin to the point of emaciation, and with a suggestion of smugness in his manner. 'What brings you here?' he asks in Kannada. 'You come to ask questions, not seek comfort.' That unblinking gaze seems to see all.

'Yes,' I tell him. 'I work for an English-language weekly in Bangalore. My name is Balaram Kamath.' I hand him my card.

'Very well!' he nods, switching to English, looking down at the card. 'Features Editor. You seem to be a big man in your office. What can I do for you?' He speaks with a heavy Kannadiga accent, but slowly, clearly, and fluently.

'Spare me some time. In private. As you say, there are questions.'

'It's very important for you, isn't it?' he asks. 'More than just a story for your magazine.'

'Yes,' I tell him. He's indeed very perceptive. 'Much more.' I'm tempted to tell him it's a lifeline. There's something about his demeanour that invites confidences. You feel safe telling him anything. You know he'll listen without judging, and not speak out of turn.

'Then let me check my schedule.' His smile broadens. 'Probably your lucky day. I don't think there's anything lined up.' He turns to the oldest of the three men with him, who must be about sixty-five. 'Any appointments in the afternoon?'

'No one from outside,' the man replies. 'There are accounts and letters. We need a decision on the palms in the eastern compound. The contractor is waiting.'

'All that can wait some more,' he says. He turns back to me. 'The simplest thing would be for us to eat lunch together.'

He's hesitant. 'Umm, we are all vegetarian and teetotal, and the food is very plain. It might not suit you.'

'I can survive on anything,' I tell him boastfully, wondering why he said teetotal. Anil, the cabbie, couldn't smell my breath from closer up. I'd taken the precaution of asking him when I'd got out of the cab.

'I have lunch after seeing all the visitors, usually around one. Raju will show you to a room where you can wait, or you can go elsewhere and look around and return by about one.'

'I think I'll look around, if you don't mind.'

'Of course.' Another smile, another namaste, and I get the message that I should make way for the next in line. I head out into the sunshine, and find a young man with a backpack arguing with one of the acolytes on guard duty. I can't help overhearing bits of their conversation as I pass, and gather that the youngster is a reporter with the Bangalore bureau of a Delhi-based newsmagazine, come to interview the Swami. The reporter smiles briefly at me, but I have no idea who he is, so I move on to call Anil and tell him to bring the cab to the gates. I get in and ask him to head for town, where I intend to find a place where I can have a drink, or at least buy a bottle of rum.

On the way to Belman, the nearest little town, I start with the calls, to Gokul, Tauseef, and Pai. Gokul picks up at the first ring, saying, in English, 'Where are you, bastard?'

He hasn't changed. 'Looking for booze in Belman,' I tell him.

He can put two and two together faster than most, and he follows the news religiously. 'Going after the Swami?'

'Yes.'

'Last time we met I thought you were too old for a job like that. Like I'm too old to investigate a burglary.'

'You're right … More when we meet?'

'I'm on my way out of town. We're going for a wedding in Mysore, Jayanthi and I. Back the day after tomorrow. We can meet then.'

'Okay. Call me when you're free. Come to the hotel.'

'Okay. And listen …'

'What?'

'Take care, you bastard. If you're in trouble, just hold on.'

Bastard, for him, is an endearment, and has been ever since we first met at college. His father and mine were childhood friends, who kept in touch through occasional letters over the years though his father was in Belgaum and mine in Hassan. He and my elder brother were classmates, though not very close. We first met in Bangalore where I studied commerce and he was already a policeman, driven into a job he didn't like by circumstances. Surprisingly, we took to each other, and like our fathers, we've been in touch ever since, through occasional phone calls and email messages instead of handwritten snail mail. We last met a few years ago, during the bloodhound case, and I was delighted to find that we got along as comfortably as before. 'Okay,' I tell him. 'Thanks.'

Tauseef doesn't respond to my call, and neither does Pai. Either they'll call back or they've given me up, so I give up on them and get back to thinking of booze. I can't find a decent-looking bar back in Belman – the one I do see is dark and smells strongly of sweat and stale fried fish and onions – and so I find a booze shop and buy some rum and a bottle of Coke, and in the shop next door a litre bottle of food-grade plastic that the owner washes out for me. I pour the rum and the coke discreetly into the new bottle so I can sip it in the car. With the air-conditioning on and driving slowly along the green hilly roads and a bag of peanuts to go with the rum, I feel much better than I would sitting in a bar breathing BO, onions, and stale fish.

At half past twelve I ask Anil to turn around. The cellphone signal is still strong, so I get back online to dig up more on the Swami, but there's really very little more. His parents were lower-middle-class folk, neither studied past high school, his only sibling, born nearly nine years before him, lived only a few days, his extended family is scattered and he doesn't seem to keep in touch with them … It's a remarkably simple life, except that some people seem to think he's also an influence-peddler, thief, and would-be rapist.

All of a sudden I feel vastly underprepared. It's years since I did anything like this and I like to dig out as much as I can about whatever I'm due to face. Part of the print tradition, I guess. I've always tended to be a little contemptuous of TV for two reasons: its lack of depth, because visual impact is far more important than any real content, and the tendency, specially among anchors, for personalities to overshadow content or reality. Print, to my mind, is much more balanced, and you absorb material at your own pace, not the anchor's.

Trouble is, the print media have been dumbing themselves down. Competing with TV does that. Glitz sells, as does easy writing – not necessarily correct or precise – and glibness. A sudden wave of depression takes me off balance, and by the time I get my bearings again we're at the ashram gates and it's almost one.

The same acolytes are at the entrances, but when I enter the hall the Swami is speaking to – no, listening to – the last-but-one of his visitors for the day. I walk up to the bits of mat closest to the stage and sit down, anticipating that the Swami will be free in fifteen or twenty minutes.

He makes it faster. Perhaps the last man is in a hurry, or just fed up enough to want to get back to wherever he came from. In any case, he takes just two minutes of the Swami's time before he leaves. The Swami rises slowly – if he's been sitting in that position since half past eight or whatever, his joints must be on fire – and staggers once before regaining his balance. He smiles at me, indicating I should follow, and we enter his quarters in the old house behind the hall.

His living quarters are a surprise. The house is an old tiled building with a verandah enclosing a small courtyard, with rooms off it. To the right, the first door opens to a large sort of sitting room with very little furniture – everyone sits on mats and uses low tables – and thick dark curtains that have been drawn aside now to let in the bright afternoon sunshine. He waves me to one of the mats. 'Give me a few minutes,' he says. 'I need to freshen up.' He disappears into what seems to be a simple bedroom. His friend Raju, leader of the three companions who've come in here with him, asks if I want to go to the toilet, and, when I say I do, leads me along the verandah and on to another room, a bedroom, with a toilet attached.

When I get back to the dining room, he introduces me to the other two assistants. The older of the two, a pale sixtyish plump-cheeked man in white shirt and trousers, is Narsimha something, and the younger man, slimmer, and smiling, is Pratap Rao.

Narsimha looks owlishly at me when I ask him how long he's known the Swami. 'About four years,' he says. 'Just after I retired from government service.' His gaze is mildly unsettling until I realize he's watching not my eyes but my lips. Is he reading them, I wonder, and begin to ask if he's slightly deaf, when Prakash Shastry – I find it hard to think of him as the Swami – returns.

I give up on Narsimha and watch Shastry as he settles down on one of the mats, sitting cross-legged and straight-backed. I notice that he's actually sitting in a yogasana, the siddhasana, which I can recognize because I attended four days of a six-week yoga course a couple of years ago. The others prepare to sit, but wait for me before actually settling down. 'Do you mind if I record this?' I ask as I descend into an ungainly sort of sprawl on a mat facing him.

He nods. 'Go ahead,' he tells me. 'I am recording this, too, you know. I may listen to it some years from now and wonder how I could have said such foolish things.' The smile flashes, and the hint of smugness deepens. 'Or wise things, you never know.'

This is the strangest conversation I've had in years. This man's lifestyle is basic. How do his influential devotees manage to live here? Is their faith strong enough to enable them to suffer this simplicity while they're with him? 'Don't you think you could have a more comfortable place for people to visit you at?'

'This is comfortable enough, thank you,' he says.

'Others might not think so,' I tell him.

'They're welcome to go wherever they find themselves comfortable,' he replies, with an air of finality. 'This is all we can afford … And it's more than I need.'

Time to change the topic. 'Do you practice yoga?' I ask.

In his personal quarters, his smile is dimmer, the air of peace deeper. 'About an hour every morning,' he says. 'A little more in the evening if there's time.'

'Do you have a regular yoga routine?' I ask.

'A rough routine, yes, but it's quite flexible.'

'Does it help you deal with your devotees?'

'Not devotees,' he says, shaking his head. 'I think of them as visitors. The morning's practice prepares me for the day. Otherwise I wouldn't be able to sit still for so many hours at a stretch.'

'Have you been practicing long?' I ask.

The smile flashes again. 'Most of my life. My father started me on it when I was six, and I kept it up throughout school. I gave up for a couple of years in college.'

'Why?' I ask.

'I tried out many things. Drink. Substances … but I gave that up, too, and got back to being conventional.'

'Didn't you get impatient with your father and the yoga when you were a child?'

He laughs. 'Yes. I used to hate him for it. For the first year.'

'Do you also spend time praying?'

'Yes. An hour every morning. But that, too, is flexible, and it's not really prayer because I don't know whom to pray to, what to pray for.' A pause. Then, 'Tell me, what troubles you so much about this story that you're doing?'

I'm taken aback, but recover. 'Nothing's troubling me,' I reply. 'Perhaps you're the one who's troubled. You're the one who's being accused of all kinds of things.'

'You don't have to tell me your troubles,' he says, ignoring my dig, 'as long as you tell yourself.'

'I'll do that, thank you,' I tell him. 'But I came to find out whether there's any truth to the accusations people are making against you.'

'What accusations?' he asks.

'It was all over last night's TV news,' I tell him, 'and probably this morning's, too, but I haven't looked today.'

'I wondered why we had so many reporters here, asking to see me,' he says. 'Now I understand.' A pause. 'We don't have TV here, so I wouldn't know about the charges.'

'A little cut off?' I ask. 'Hiding, perhaps?' I can't help that dig.

'Not at all. We have an internet connection here for those who want to keep in touch. It's just that I don't watch TV, and neither do the people who live here. Visitors, well, if they insist on TV, they can stay in a lodge in Belman … I tend to catch up with the news in the afternoon, on the web, and I didn't see anything yesterday. So, what charges?'

It's best to be blunt. 'Three, mainly. One, that you're taking money improperly from the trust funds in your name. Two, that your ashram shelters known criminals because your influential pals make sure the police don't come here. Three, that you tried to, well, molest a woman some months ago.'

An older lady brings lunch in steaming pots before he can answer. 'Would you like a low table?' he asks.

'That would be nice,' I tell him. 'I haven't tried eating sitting on the floor for decades.'

'I understand.' He turns to the old lady and tells her something in deliberate, clear Kannada. That's how he speaks any language, slowly and clearly.

A low table arrives, and on it the lady places a banana leaf. For the Swami, there's a similar leaf on a mat on the floor. The lady serves rice, sambar, vegetables, papad, buttermilk, a regular if rather bland meal. I dig in with the appetite of someone who's skipped breakfast. 'We'll have to change this system soon,' he says as he starts eating. 'Banana leaves are increasingly hard to find.'

'Would you mind the change?' I ask.

'Not at all. We grow bananas here, so there are a few leaves, but not enough to take care of everyone living here.' He smiles. 'It's often hard to accept change, you know. But everything changes. You grow older, and sometimes that's hard to accept ...

'We will change from banana leaves, perhaps in the next few days ... Those charges that you mentioned. How do you intend to find out if there's any truth to them?'

'The first thing, of course, is to ask you.'

A smile at this. 'Have you come across a single person accused of these things admitting to them to a media person in their very first interview on the subject?'

'No,' I tell him.

'Whether or not I've done these things, I'm going to say I haven't. So why do you ask?'

'The idea is to get your version, not just a denial. Also, from your manner, try to guess your inner reaction to the charges.'

He shakes his head. 'Make what you like of my reactions. And what do you mean, my version?'

'If these are lies, who might be behind them, and why. How you intend to defend yourself. What effect these charges might have on the work you do.'

'I don't have a version of the stealing and influence-peddling. I do take money from the trust from time to time, with the permission of the trustees, and return it as soon as possible.

'For instance, the last time I did that was three weeks ago. I took a little over two lacs, to spend on some improvements here – I have to meet a contractor later today about that. I could have paid for it myself, but that would have involved breaking a fixed deposit that's maturing in a fortnight or so, and losing quite a bit of interest, so … in any case, I instructed the bank manager to transfer the contents of the fixed deposit to the trust when it matures.

'Every time I take something from the trust, it's paid back, as best I can remember.'

I interrupt. 'Every time? Every single time?'

He smiles. 'As best I remember. We should check. We will check. If I've missed any payments, I will make restitution by tomorrow, and if there are legal consequences, I will accept them without wriggling or complaint. In any case, the books of the trust, and my personal accounts, are open to audit. Feel free to send your auditor here to verify that.

'As to the influence-peddling, I have no idea what my

visitors might have done. I'm very careful not to ask them anything of the kind, or even hint at it. You know, like King Henry asking who would rid him of a certain troublesome priest … I haven't done any of that.

'Sanctuary in the ashram, well … You see, we don't vet people here. Anyone who comes is allowed in unless they threaten violence or something else that's disruptive. And I don't know everything that goes on here. We don't have a compound wall, just a barbed wire fence, and people can get past that quite easily. People who know the place can get here across the fields. Someone could get into the compound, sleep in a clearing, use the toilets and baths, and leave without being noticed. People do get past the fence, sometimes, to steal produce. But we can't afford to build a wall now.

'The attempted rape or molestation or whatever. I've been celibate for a decade now. Some women who've visited me here have tried to seduce me, and I've turned them away as gently as I can. But you know, rejection is always painful, and the woman who's accusing me of rape might just be lashing out at me. I don't know.

'I have no idea who might be behind all this. I don't think I have enemies who dislike me enough to take all this trouble to get me in jail. I can't defend myself until I know more … All I know is that I don't have much money for legal fees.

'How will it affect my work? Well, if I end up in prison I won't be able to see visitors, but that's it. The old people who live here, the needy ones, they'll continue here.' He shrugs, and again I sense his smugness.

'Some details on your encounter with this woman might help substantiate what you say. Were there witnesses? When did it happen? And so on.'

'I don't even know who's saying I tried to rape her: I'm just guessing that it could be a woman whom I turned away. So what details can I give you?'

I can't imagine this guy groping someone, but you can never tell. 'The woman's name is Smita Sharma,' I tell him, looking at my notes. 'She says you groped her several times two months ago.'

'You've seen the number of people I meet every day. I don't remember names.'

'I have a photograph.' It's on my phone, which I show him.

He looks at it and nods. 'She's familiar. It's very likely she was here some time ago, I don't remember exactly when. Give me a few moments to try to recall the circumstances.' He closes his eyes for a moment. 'Yes, I remember her. She was here a few months ago, like I said. She spent a few days at the ashram. She was depressed and suicidal … I'm going to have to check with Raju because he was around part of the time she spent with me.'

Raju nods when I pass him the photograph. 'Yes,' he says. 'She was here. She wanted to kill herself.'

'How did she find her way here?' I ask.

'Some friend in Bangalore recommended that she see Swami,' Raju replies. 'She came here and someone took her to Narsimha. Then she stayed at the ashram.

'Like I was saying, she wanted to kill herself but Swami told her not to. For three nights she cried. One night she came to see Swami at one o'clock. She wanted poison. Sarada and Swami and I sat with her.'

'Who's Sarada?' I ask.

'One of the ladies who lives here,' Raju replies.

'What happened on those nights?'

'She was crying loudly,' he replies, 'walking blindly in the corridor of the guest house at the back. Someone brought her here, to see Swami, because it seemed an emergency. I woke him up, and called Sarada.

'She sat here crying, insisting she didn't want to live any

more, and then Swami told Sarada and me to go to sleep, because he could deal with her by himself. She agreed, so we went to our rooms.

'I actually waited a few minutes outside the door ... He's not getting enough sleep. I told you that. Then Narsimha came along, and we discussed it, and we decided that I would come back in half an hour to check, and if she hadn't gone, make her leave Swami alone. But I thought I heard someone walk by less than half an hour after I left, and thought it was her. I went to Swami's room to check, and found that she had really gone.'

I can't help asking him, 'And do you hang around Swami's room after he tells you to leave?'

He senses that I'm needling him. 'One of my responsibilities is to take care of him as well as I can, and as well as he allows me to. I do my best with that. If you think there's something wrong with some of the things I do, I don't care. Shall I continue?'

'Please,' I tell him.

'The same thing happened the next night, and the night after that, except that we had people watching for her after she left, so she wouldn't hurt herself.' He smiles. 'And, of course, Narsimha didn't come and tell me to go back to my room.'

I turn to the Swami then. 'So there were no witnesses for some of the time you spent alone with her on each of those three nights,' I say.

'No, no witnesses,' he responds. 'She wanted it that way.'

'Did you record those meetings?'

'I don't remember immediately,' the Swami replies. 'Let me think for a moment.' A pause. 'On the first of those evenings, I asked Raju and Sarada to leave because she didn't want anyone else to hear what she was going to tell me. After they left, I told her that I was recording the meeting, and she asked me to turn off the recorder. I have that much on record, anyway. The second and third times followed a similar pattern, but I was beginning to think she was … Well, she seemed to be wallowing in self-pity, and needed professional treatment.'

'And what did you do after you turned off the recording?' I ask. 'Did you fear any kind of entrapment?'

'I don't fear entrapment,' he replies, 'but I want to avoid it. Hence the recording equipment. I want to make sure we're safe.

'Despite everything, she seemed really depressed … she showed all the signs. She had dark circles under the eyes, she didn't seem to have slept well in a long time, her hair wasn't combed or anything, she was dressed, well, shabbily, with no thought of appearance … I thought she was genuinely suicidal, and sat with her and listened to what she had to say, and sent her off telling her she should meet a psychiatrist.' He smiles. 'I think roughly the same thing happened on all those nights, and then she went away. I called a doctor from the clinic who told her the same thing. I hope she went to a psychiatrist after that.'

'What did she say to you when she was alone with you?'

He shakes his head. 'I'm not going to discuss that with you.'

'Why not, now that she's accusing you of rape?'

'Well, I promised her at the beginning that I would keep it all to myself. Of course, if the investigation goes further, I will answer questions about the charge, to the police or to a judge. Until I do that, she can withdraw her complaint and get out of this without any mudslinging.'

'Is that a threat? Are you saying you'll sling mud if she doesn't withdraw her complaint?'

'No threats.' A smile. 'I'm just saying that if I have to defend myself in court, I might have to tell the open court what she told me. In the absence of recordings and witnesses, I might not be able to substantiate that, of course, but it could still hurt her.'

'In that case, how do you expect to prove anything?'

'There were details that she told me … details that might be verifiable. But all that can wait. Like I said, I will not say anything about that now.'

'That's no defence.'

'Do I need to defend myself against these statements?'

'Not legally, but your reputation could take a beating.'

'My reputation doesn't matter. If people stop visiting the ashram, so be it. If people stop donating money, well, we'll do without.' He pauses. 'It looks like there's no evidence of what really happened. It's too late now for any forensic medical examination. So, given the legal system here, in a court, it will come down to my word against hers. The only thing in my favour is the recording of her asking me not to record what she was telling me.'

Most journos develop, over the years, a sense for when someone's lying. Of course, there are plenty of people – an increasing number, these days – who can lie without signalling it strongly. This man doesn't show any sign of lying. Either he's very good at it, or he's telling the truth. I assume he's being straight. 'Essentially, yes,' I tell him. ' And the judge is likely to take her word for it. That's the system.'

'I know,' he says. 'So I could go to prison for that.'

'Yes.'

'So be it, then.'

'Do you think the legal system will deliver justice?'

'Since I don't know what you mean by justice, I can't tell you. The legal system does what it does. Whether that's justice or not is in our minds.' He smiles. 'As is the notion of justice itself.'

'Isn't it important that someone who attempts rape be caught and punished?'

'You tell me.'

'Don't you have an opinion on it?'

'Not really. As far as I know, this particular attempt at rape didn't happen. You're free to assume what you like, but I know I didn't do it, and that's all there is to it.'

'What if you end up in prison?'

'The Americans have a wonderful phrase for it, you know.' He smiles. 'Guess?'

I shake my head. 'This is too serious for games.'

'Shit happens!' The smile again. 'Look, I told you earlier, I'm prepared for the consequences. They don't matter.'

'You don't have to have tried to rape her, you know. There's this legal definition of what constitutes rape. Groping her or something is enough to put you inside for a long time. Have you done that? Even touched her?'

'As far as I can remember, I haven't touched – except maybe accidentally – a woman for some time now barring a few that have wept on my shoulder. There's no question of groping someone. I just don't do it.'

On further questioning, he sticks to his story on the embezzlement charge as well. 'I earned some money fairly young,' he tells me. 'I used to write software, and I got lucky. So I came back here and thought I'd spend some time thinking about things. A real estate agent told me about this place – there was this old house and eight acres of farmland by a small stream – and when I saw it I liked it, so I bought it. We did just enough repairs to make the house habitable, and I moved in here with some relatives who were finding it difficult to live by themselves. Raju, an old friend, came along.

'After some time the visitors began to flow in. People came and talked to me and it seems they went away comforted.

Some of them wanted to give us something in return, so Raju started a trust, to which I transferred most of my money. We didn't have much here by way of medical facilities, so the trust started a clinic, and then a school … Now there's a small hospital, and more people here, and a block where visitors can stay – you, too, if you wish, but you must know that we don't approve of people drinking here – and a garden for vegetables and so on. It's a small community.

'It just happened, more or less. Now, as you say, there might be visitors who have influence with the government, with the police. I don't know, but I ask them for nothing, and I offer them nothing more than I've offered you. If they offer services I think illegal or unethical or dishonest, I turn them down.

'I don't travel, and I live simply. I eat simple food, some of it grown here, I wear simple cotton clothes, and sleep on a mat on the floor. The only people who sleep on proper beds here are the ones with painful knees, because they find it hard to get off the floor.

'Look around. This is how we live here. Let me put it this way: this is all we can afford. Really. People who find it insufficient, well, they're free to go elsewhere.' That hint of smugness has disappeared.

By the time we're done with lunch – which lasts quite a long time because the Swami eats very slowly – I'm also done with the questions about the accusations, at least for the time being. It's been like talking to a stone wall but there seems to be some substance to his denials of swindling, for his lifestyle is very simple. Unless, of course, he's been smart enough to stash the proceeds where they aren't so visible. I switch to something else. 'Why did you pick this name Sarvananda Swami?' I ask.

'I never use the title "Swami",' he replies. 'Ask whoever

calls me that why they do it. Sarvananda, well, that's the name my mother wanted to give me. All joys. She was nearly forty when I was born, and both my parents were overjoyed. Father wanted to call me Prakash, and he used that name when my birth was being registered. Mother refused to use that name: she called me Sarva, and I think it was accurate, for her. I was her entire world … My name, legally, is Prakash Shastry.'

'How would you like me to address you?'

'It's up to you,' he says. He smiles. 'What you call me isn't going to change your attitude to me. Most of my friends at college used to call me Prakash. You, too, are free to call me that. Or Shastry, or whatever you like.'

'I noticed that you don't bless your devotees,' I tell him.

'Please. I've already told you, I don't call them devotees. They're visitors. Understand, we're all equals. I'm no one to bless them, or anyone else. They have my good wishes, for whatever that's worth. Nothing more.'

'But they tell you things, and they fall at your feet.'

'Some do. Look, some of them find relief in talking to me. Some of them find it in just being around me, but I'm not doing anything. I'm not giving them any advice, or selling them anything. I just listen without judging.

'Look at yourself, for instance. You say you've come to ask questions, you work for a well-known magazine that belongs to a group that also has a TV news channel, you're middle-aged and you hold a senior position. But you smell faintly of alcohol and something you've used to cover it – I have a very strong sense of smell, you know – so you've probably had a drink in the morning, you're on a job that's too small for your position, there's something weighing very heavily on your mind, but you're serious about this story, so it means a lot to you. '

I nod. Nothing new here except that bit about his nose.

'So I followed my instincts and when you asked for some time, I agreed. That's all that's happened. You also have my promise that whatever you tell me in confidence is safe with me, except anything related to a crime, which I might pass on to the police. You're not a devotee, not an enemy, but just another person. Like me.

'You don't have to tell me anything. The important thing is to tell yourself. Important to you, not to me.' He smiles, and the smug air is back. 'Very few people do that, you know.'

'Umm, yes.' I find this embarrassing, which is terrible since I have to ask him awkward questions, so I change the subject. 'You said you've been celibate for some years now.'

'Yes.'

'How about before that?'

'Do you mean, have I had sex? Yes, I have.' He laughs. 'Have I had enough? No, I haven't. Will I have more? I don't know. At present I don't intend to, that's all.'

'Why not?'

'Think of it as an experiment. There are no moral reasons for it. Nor is it because I think that sex weakens the soul or anything of the kind.'

'Do you think about sex?' I ask.

He laughs deeply at that. 'Of course. It's somewhere in the back of my mind quite a lot of the time …' He laughs again. 'And at the front of my mind most of the rest of the time. Isn't it the same with you?'

'Yes, it is,' I admit. 'Even at this age.'

'Well, there you are, then.'

'Were you married, ermm, before you became celibate?'

He laughs again, with a hint of mockery. 'No, never. I never had that privilege.'

'Privilege?'

The laughter vanishes, and his gaze sharpens. 'You find

marriage a burden, not a privilege … Let me ask, do you consider your wife beautiful?'

'Yes,' I tell him. 'Very. And not just me. Everyone who knows her does.' And indeed she is. In the beginning, I used to wonder what she saw in me.

The belly-beast rears its head without warning, in fighting trim. These days I wonder whether she still sees whatever it was she saw in me. No. And, god help me, I fear even more that she sees it in someone else. Specially after I started to drink. No. After I became a drunk.

I shouldn't have started on this. It's downhill all the way.

Those unblinking eyes of his seem to be reading my every thought, and with an effort I look straight back.

He tells me, 'You're an alcoholic about to be sacked. You're here to save your job. You're not hopeful, which means your family doesn't support you. Your work has been affected only in the last few years. It's something to do with your company's TV channel, perhaps.' This seems a bit spooky but I know shrinks who are good at interpreting non-verbal cues and can do this sort of thing quite a lot of the time.

He blinks. 'Your burden is not your marriage. It's shame. No amount of drinking is going take away your shame.'

Up comes the beast. What the hell does this smug bastard know of my life? It's none of his business. I'm not the one going to jail for groping a woman …

He seems to see all that, too, and backs off. 'Okay,' he says. 'This is difficult for you. Go ahead with your questions.'

We turn to something that's been bugging me all along. 'What did you say to the other reporters?'

'Nothing. I had them sent away.'

'Why?'

'They came, spoke to the people who guide visitors around, said they were reporters wanting to talk to me. The guides asked me, and I asked them to tell them to wait in line, like the other visitors. They sent away those who weren't willing to wait, just as they send away anyone who isn't willing to wait in line.' He smiles. 'You're the only one who sat in the verandah and waited. You didn't even try to jump the queue.' The smile widens. 'And then, you were willing to come back after a couple of hours, and not intrude on the other visitors, and so I thought I'd speak to you.' The smile disappears. 'But I think one journalist is enough.'

'Why?'

'I don't need to repeat myself.'

'What about when people ask you for solutions to their problems?'

He grins. 'I rarely tell them anything. I just listen. Most of the time they figure out what to do. I have nothing to do with that, but they don't believe it.'

And so we return to his personal history. 'What got you into this retreat?' I ask. 'Most others would have gone into business, or bought a house and continued in a job, or something.'

'The usual,' he says. 'Discontent.'

'With what?'

He laughs. 'An old lady put me onto it. My friend's 85-year-old grandmother, whose mind had begun to slip. She wouldn't stay put anywhere. She lived with all her children in turn, and a pattern emerged. When she moved in with one of her children, she'd be okay for a few days. Then she'd start thinking they were trying to kill her, or stealing her money, things like that, and she'd want to go elsewhere. This went on until one day she broke her hip and had to stay with her eldest son, and until she died, she kept accusing him of trying to kill her.

'She had dementia, and she was paranoid. The suspicion

was clearly unfounded. Her discontent was with herself, really, not with her children. That was when I began to ask this question seriously: is my discontent with myself, and not with anything outside me? So I got to thinking about it, and all kinds of other thoughts began to follow.'

'Like what?'

'Like, well … The most important thing in my life seemed to be to get around things about myself that I couldn't stand.' He grins. 'Some of it is funny now. You know, my feet cost me a lot. They're flat, you see, so there were a few things I couldn't do. I couldn't run very well, for instance, or play games like football. I hated that … I hated myself for being flat-footed. I don't know if I wanted to play football, but I would have liked the glory of being a good footballer.

'We skirt around some simple bits of our life. You say you've come here to get my version of the charges. That's only a very small part of it. You've got a lot of other things riding on this, like I've told you.

'You tell me I'm accused of hiding the son of some minister in my ashram. What you'd really like to find is a secret, something illegal or immoral that the minister and I are trying to sweep under the carpet, so that you can get back your reputation as an investigative journalist. I can tell you straight away that I have no such secrets.

'Nothing is what it seems to be. Not even your own reason for being here. You might consider that when you do your research on this story.' He smiles again, transparently. 'Or when you think about your marriage, or your job, or whatever you're doing.'

'I certainly will,' I tell him. 'Any more tips?' A little sarcasm, maybe.

'Just one. An angry man's anger is reasonable to himself. A vindictive man's need for vengeance, a greedy man's greed, a jealous man's jealousy, a selfish man's selfishness, all are reasonable to the man himself. Be careful how you defend yourself.' He raises his hands in a namaste. 'You're not ready for more advice right now.' That takes care of the sarcasm, I guess. Then, 'I must move on to other matters now. Stay here as long as you wish. There are rooms in the block behind this house. Simple but sufficient. But people rise early here, and their movements and prayers and rituals might disturb you.'

There are more questions to be asked, but I need a break because I'm not sure I can handle the beast. 'Will you be able to spare some more time for me? Say tomorrow?'

'Time, yes, but I'm not so sure when. Let me check.' He rises effortlessly from the mat and goes looking for Raju. They're back in a minute, Raju looking a little harassed. 'Lunch tomorrow as well?' he asks. 'About the same time?'

'Thanks,' I tell him. 'I'll go to my hotel room in Mangalore. I would have stayed here if you'd told me to come at six in the morning.'

'I understand,' he says. 'Get here at about one tomorrow. If there are many more visitors than I expect, you might have to wait a little.'

'That's all right,' I tell him.

'Raju will show you out,' he says with another namaste, and I find myself being led out to the front door, through the hall, and all the way to the gates.

'Please don't take up too much of his time,' Raju tells me at the gate. 'He doesn't get enough rest as it is.'

'I'll try,' I tell him, 'I'll try to finish with him by the time he finishes eating so he can have a snooze straight after lunch.'

'Please do that,' Raju says, and waves me off.

Something about Raju's protectiveness irritates me. He and the others who hang around the Swami are protecting their own interests, not the Swami. In that sense, Prakash is more or less like any other godman. He's an investment for them, even if not a financial one. There's a whole ecosystem floating around him, and a political subsystem. The question of whether he's got anything godly going for him matters much less than the power structure that's been built up around him.

What matters, to me, is whether he had anything to do with those things that have come up around him. From what he says, it seems he hasn't, which means he's a pawn. Like it or not, he's a pawn.

I must take this up with the man when I get a chance.

I tell Anil to take me to the hotel, which is at the outskirts of town, one of a low-priced no-frills chain, with comfortable rooms but no fawning bellboys and so on. It's getting on for four when I check in and settle down in the room – I've picked up some rum on the way, enough to see me through the rest of the day, and the night – and I send Anil away with instructions to return at eleven next morning. As he's leaving, I remember one of my old habits: getting cabbies to talk. 'Do you watch TV?' I ask. 'News programmes? And read newspapers?'

'Yes,' he says. 'When I'm waiting I read newspapers. At home, if I have the time, I watch the news … if my wife isn't watching a movie. But mostly Kannada.' He grins. 'I can't read English very fast.'

'Do me a favour, then,' I tell him. 'Watch out for news about the Swami, on TV, in the papers, and even gossip. Your fellow taxi-drivers get some business out of the Swami, don't they? Tell me about it when you pick me up in the morning. Whichever language you like.'

'Of course,' he says. I think he's happy he's found something with which to while away his hours of waiting for me.

When Shafiq, who runs the Mangalore office, calls to find out how matters are, and whether I need anything, I tell him everything's fine, that I'll call him if I need something. He tells me he's been ordered to get people on standby in case we need to get a TV crew there in a hurry. You know how it is, he says, and I tell him I do, and that I'm going to spend the rest of the day on the internet, or writing up my notes for the story.

I pour myself a rum and coke and some soda – coke by itself is too sweet – and sip it while I make my notes from the recording I've made. It's a long time since I transcribed anything, and just the act of doing it takes me back to decades ago, when the magazine was new and everyone did whatever needed to be done. I'm no longer very fast at it, but some skills return quickly when you practice them, and in fifteen minutes I'm at my laptop, typing reasonably quickly, even if nowhere near the speeds I could do fifteen years ago in the days when they called me the bloodhound … Now I know why. You can't drink and be a bloodhound at the same time. Dammit!

It's when I start reading the transcript, though, that the trouble begins. The man is denying everything, as expected, but the man himself is a complete surprise. His simplicity, scepticism, and uncommon sense stand out. He's the first godman I've come across who doesn't believe blindly in god, so it would be a mistake to call him that. But there is about him an air of acceptance – he insists that he will take the consequences – or even of wisdom, though I'd hesitate to call it that in someone a decade younger than I am.

More to the point, he let me know that he had figured out at least three uncomfortable bits of my past – the drinking, the marriage, and the trouble at work – but didn't insist on talking about those matters. But what did he mean by saying that my burden is shame? Even thinking about it brings the beast back to life so I reach for the bottle and pour myself another, telling myself I'll be careful when I speak to him tomorrow.

## Chapter Three

One advantage of being known to be a drunkard is that I don't have to present myself at the Mangalore office in the morning. Shafiq, a teetotaller, is happy to arrange matters on the phone, asks no questions, and offers only minimal assistance considering that I'm the big shot from HO, as they call the Bangalore office. But then, they know I'm on the way down, if not out.

Fine by me. I want time to think. Anil is due at eleven, more than early enough to get me to the ashram by one. So, after a leisurely breakfast at the restaurant downstairs, I consider having the day's first rum and coke, then decide against it. I'll be back by three or four, and I'll make up for my abstinence then. I'll try not to smell of booze at the ashram today.

The room overlooks the highway – a flyover a few hundred metres away covers the horizon from this vantage point – and plenty of green that Bangalore used to have but is now disappearing. I sit for a while looking at the view and then get out my notes once again but my mind keeps coming back to the bit about shame. How could he have said something as stupid as that? And what did he mean by saying it's got to do with the TV channel?

I never wanted to work with the TV channel. I didn't want to be an anchor, or anything. They invited me thrice for comments on political scandals, and I didn't do very well, and made it clear I wasn't cut out for it, so they didn't ask me again. Nothing shameful in that: it was all open and clear. Only Mohini had a few cutting things to say, but by then she had cutting things to say about almost anything I did.

And what did he mean by that bit about nothing being what it seems to be, followed by that dig about my not being ready for more advice. I don't even know if it was a dig because his smile when he said it seemed genuine, and so did his offer to let me stay on the premises.

So what did he mean, I wasn't ready for more? Was he just pulling my leg? Or was he just spooking me with some mentalist stuff? I'm not sure but another chat or two with the man should take care of that, and then I'd go back to the office and expose him.

I've got some material for the story but no real backbone – that will come today, I hope – and I put it all away ten minutes before Anil is due. Over the years I've found it best to leave these things simmering in the back of my mind until something usable emerges. I'm restless knowing I don't have a tot of rum available but decide to live with it for the time being. I can – I will, in fact – pick up some after lunch with Prakash.

Anil gives me a recap of some Kannada headlines as we leave town and reach the highway south. 'The local papers say that someone is trying to hurt the Swami,' he tells me, 'but the Kannada channels all say that he might be … a criminal. We don't know.'

'And the gossip? You must have talked to some of your fellow cab drivers.'

'Yes. They're not interested in these things. For them it's more traffic, because all of a sudden there are more people coming to find out.'

When I get to the ashram at ten to one, Prakash still has about a dozen visitors to meet, and won't be free for at least another half hour. As I sit down to wait, Raju gets off the platform and leans by me. 'You can wait inside if you wish,' he says. 'Have some coffee or something like that.'

I don't want coffee so I shake my head. 'Can I listen to the conversation the Swami is having with that visitor up there?'

'Let me ask,' Raju tells me, and goes back up on stage, whispering what seems to be my question in Prakash's ear in the next gap between visitors. Prakash shakes his head, and Raju comes back to me. 'He says it's not fair. People tell him things in confidence, and your presence there could be an intrusion.'

'Okay,' I tell him. 'Can you ask him to record the conversation and give me the bits that aren't confidential?'

'He knew you would ask that,' Raju tells me. 'That, too, is not possible. For him, everything is confidential unless the visitor says otherwise. He will have to ask the visitor, and that might mean some discussion, and it's too late today.'

'Some other day, then,' I tell him.

'Yes. I'll keep it in mind. Tomorrow, perhaps.'

'All right.'

Today's visitors are voluble and it's nearly two when the last one leaves and Prakash rises to leave for lunch, but he's still as untroubled as ever. I follow him into the same room where we'd eaten yesterday, and wash up and get ready for lunch. As before, an old lady brings in the food. Minutes after we get down to eat, however, there's the sound of vehicles drawing up outside, and the mutter of soft conversation. Moments later, four policemen, from their insignias an inspector, a sub-inspector, and two constables, walk into the room.

They've left their shoes outside and the inspector, when he addresses Prakash, speaks softly and perhaps a little deferentially, in Kannada. 'The magistrate has issued a warrant for your arrest,' he says. 'The charge is attempted rape. It's a non-bailable warrant, so you'll have to come with us.'

Almost by reflex I take out my camera and switch the recording to video mode. This is going to be an exclusive. Always the media man, I tell myself cynically.

The possibility of a spell in prison doesn't make a dent in Prakash's calm demeanour. 'Will you let me finish my lunch?' he asks.

The inspector thinks a few seconds. 'All right,' he says.

'Sit down if you wish,' Prakash tells him. 'I'm not going anywhere. Eat if you're hungry. I'll take about twenty minutes.'

'We'll wait outside,' the inspector tells him a little shamefacedly. 'I know you're not going anywhere.'

The cops leave us to eat, and Prakash continues as if nothing has happened. 'Do you have a lawyer?' I ask.

'No,' he tells me. A smile. 'You have the only video recording of the police telling me they're taking me in. Congratulations.'

I ignore that. 'Shall I get you one? I'm sure the office will be able to fix up someone in Mangalore.'

'I don't have the money to waste on lawyers,' he says flatly.

'Let me see if we can work out some sort of a deal with the office.'

'No,' he says firmly. 'No deals. I told you when we first met that I'm willing to take the consequences.'

'All right,' I tell him, sticking my neck out. 'No deal. I'll pay for the lawyer. My pocket, not the office, and no strings. You don't even have to talk to me.' That's going to be difficult, and I don't know how Mohini will take it, and I haven't quite figured out the hold this man is beginning to have on me. All I know at the moment is that I can't just stand by and let him go to jail.

He smiles, shaking his head, and, perhaps, sensing my fear and doubt. 'I'm sure there are other visitors willing to pay, but I'm not going to accept any of that. They have better things to spend their money on, and so do you. The trust money is for the hospital and the school. My personal money is for those who live here. So, no lawyers.'

'How about your friend, the minister?' I ask.

'How about him?'

'Ask him to intervene.'

He shakes his head slowly. 'The minister's not my friend, he's a visitor. Like the others.' A pause. Then, with a smile, and a little flash of worldly wisdom, 'He never gives anyone anything without a string attached. Sometimes a dangerous string. That's what got me here in the first place. So I'm not going to ask him for help, or accept any from him if he offers it.'

'That inspector was quite respectful,' I tell him. 'Perhaps you yourself have some influence.'

'It doesn't matter. I'm quite happy to follow the system, no matter what.' This is with a finality that tells me he doesn't want to talk any more.

Some hours later, after a ride in a police SUV to the magistrate in Mangalore and an hour's sweaty wait in the shade of trees outside the court, the magistrate reads the FIR and the warrant and remands Prakash to judicial custody – prison, with the same status as someone under trial – for ten days while the police look for evidence in the case against him. The magistrate doesn't offer Prakash a chance to present his side of the case, and, Prakash being who he is, doesn't even try. A cameraman from the channel has arrived and is recording the proceedings.

'We could have tried to get you out of here,' I tell Prakash as we wait for the next step, with the video camera turned on us. Worry for him overrides my distaste for being on camera. 'We should have got a good lawyer right away.'

'I'm sure they'll feed me in prison,' he says, smiling a little. 'And I don't think they're going to beat me up, either. You saw: they were quite considerate when they arrested me.'

'That's not the point.'

'What is the point, then?' he asks.

'If you're innocent and you're outside you can try to find out who's doing this, and why, and see if you can get the charges dropped.'

'Why would I want to do that?' he asks. 'This is a good time to see how the system works.'

'Well, I can tell you it's loaded against you.'

'Fine,' he says. 'I'll take my chances.' He smiles broadly. 'We've been through this before.'

There's no time for any further conversation because the police now come to drag him off to the van which is his ride to the district prison nearby. I pull out my accreditation card and get a moment with the sub-inspector. 'Can I visit him there?' I ask.

The policeman nods. 'Yes. Follow the procedure.'

Then he, along with Prakash, disappear into the van and I call Anil, who has followed us to the prison, to head back to the hotel. My phone rings as we pull out of the prison compound. It's Srini, who knows about the magistrate's decision. 'You've got some exclusive footage,' he tells me. 'Have you had a chance to talk to the man?'

'Yes,' I tell him. 'You saw the transcripts.' I've emailed them to him.

'I did. Nothing definite. You have to dig some more.'

'I intend to.'

'We've found the woman who filed the complaint. She's here, in the city somewhere. I'm sending someone to talk to her but that won't be exclusive. I'll send you the transcripts and anything else we get.'

'Okay,' I tell him. 'My gut feel is that the guy is straight. Someone's using him.'

'Not good enough. You have to get some specifics: who's using him, and to what end. Also, if anyone's working against him, and why.'

'I intend to find out over the next few days.'

'Make sure the story's safe,' he says, meaning I must make sure there's enough smoke to indicate a possible fire. Preferably a serious one.

'I'll do what I can,' I tell him. The urge to see that Prakash is safe is surprisingly strong.

'That might not be enough, Bala. If this works out …'

'I know,' I tell him. 'It's my job on the line.'

'Don't forget that.'

'I won't. Srini, there's something you must do if you want to help things along.'

'What?'

'Call the state's prison chief and tell him to arrange access to Prakash for me. The regular procedure is tiresome. I'm sure he can speed it up.'

'I'll take care of it. Do you want a lawyer? We can get one if your friend Prakash is willing to make a deal.'

'He refused a deal with us. He says he'll accept whatever the system does. He can't afford a lawyer and won't take favours from anyone.'

'What about his pal, the minister?'

'Nothing doing. I've recorded it all. I'll send you the recording as soon as I can, and you send me the transcript straight away.' I don't fancy another evening transcribing.

'Done,' he says. 'Bala, good luck. Don't react when he talks about you.'

Srini's read the transcripts, then. 'Yes,' I tell him, 'I'll watch it.'

Back in the hotel I realize it's early evening and my hands are trembling from not having had a drink all day, so I go out for supplies and spend an hour catching up. I place the recordings on our office server so Srini can transcribe them and then try to catch up with Mohini and Pallavi. Mohini's still at work, busy with a meeting, and Pallavi's busy with her homework, or maybe those are just excuses. The familiar sense of unease engulfs me. The strange thing is that I'm as uncomfortable at home as I am away, so the discomfort probably has nothing to do with them.

Our channel has my cellphone clip of Prakash being arrested, highlighting the bit where the arresting officer agrees to wait for him to finish his lunch. Does the Swami exert undue influence, asks the anchor with the lipstick and the accent, or is it one of his political patrons. At the end, of course, is the usual message: watch this space for more.

The competition have been equally active with apparently far more material, but less real content. Prime-time news on every channel now covers the basics of Prakash's arrest. The theme of the coverage is outrage, most of it centred on the woman's complaint, with one of the channels carrying an interview with the Chair of the National Council for Women saying that exemplary punishment must be meted out to public figures who take advantage of women. The three most-viewed national news channels mention Prakash, none of them favourably. All of them say that they haven't been able to reach Prakash in prison to get his views.

All channels report the Swami's financial misdeeds, the occasional transfer of money from the trust's accounts to his personal accounts. None mentions that the money has been paid back in every case but the last. All slide nervously around the accusation of sheltering fugitives, saying, essentially, that there's no smoke without fire. All include interviews of police officials, visitors, and rationalists, all of whom are against all spiritual leaders and particularly those who use their following to make money and generate influence.

Print media coverage, sadly, is as poor, if not as elaborate. Thinking about it, I wish I were doing a good long feature for a weekly ... Working on features for a weekly, that's what I'd like to do.

Srini calls at nine to say that the transcripts are in my mailbox, and that I'll be allowed to see Prakash any time during working hours, for as long as I like, but I won't be allowed to give him anything – there'll be a double layer of mesh between us when we chat – and there might be a warder watching as we talk. None of that is going to be a problem, I tell Srini, and we hang up on a neutral, if not positive, note.

I'm curious about how Prakash will bear up in jail. I'm sure he'll have no trouble dealing with the clothes and the food, and perhaps even the sleeping arrangements. But his living quarters are almost antiseptically clean – his simplicity helps with that – and prison will be dirty, especially the toilets. I wonder how he'll deal with that, and hope he won't fall ill.

At this point I'm mildly surprised to find I'm worrying about him, though he's a stranger who has said nasty things to me, and could be a criminal with clout enough to get his way out of the jam. He might be going through with all this just to make himself look good ... as he himself said, nothing is what it looks like.

Next morning I'm free again until about ten – the jail is in the heart of Mangalore, about ten minutes from the hotel by cab, and I'll be allowed to meet him only by ten – so I dawdle over breakfast and get to the jail at five past, only to find the parking lot full and the entrance crawling with armed policemen, none of whom is willing to tell me what's going on. I discover, eventually, from one of the chauffeurs, that the state finance minister, Prakash's friend or follower, is visiting him, and the vehicles contain the man's entourage, which, the chauffeur tells me, includes a leading high court lawyer from Bangalore. 'He'll be out tomorrow,' the chauffeur concludes, in chaste Kannada.

'Why do you say that?' I ask.

'That's what lawyers are for,' he says.

I don't tell him that I'll be disappointed if Prakash agrees to take on the lawyer but move on and find a prison warder who tells me that it's unlikely I'll be able to get to see Prakash today. 'Why?' I ask.

'Minister,' replies the warder. 'Lawyer. Special meal for Swami.'

Even as we speak, the minister emerges from the door, surrounded by armed policemen, climbs into a large car parked right in the centre of the lot, and takes off, preceded by an SUV with lights and sirens. 'The minister has left,' the warder says, 'but the lawyer hasn't.' He pauses a moment. 'Maybe another lawyer will see him in the afternoon.'

He's right. When I check with the prison officials they tell me that Prakash is with a lawyer and won't be free for some time, that I can keep checking from time to time but they can't say when he'll be available. 'What about tomorrow?' I ask.

'You'll have to check,' he says. 'When they hold this long a meeting with the lawyer they are usually planning a bail application, which the lawyer can submit today. If he gets it, he will be released tomorrow, and you'll have to see him after that.' He smiles. 'That's outside our jurisdiction.'

'Thanks,' I tell him and leave.

There's nothing to do but hang around another day, and I decide to try the ashram instead of lounging around the hotel. Wanting to avoid a recurrence of yesterday's shakes, I stop for supplies on the way, and three large tots on the go brings me up to the daily average. I take out my phone to call Srini and find that the battery's dead because I forgot to charge it. Anil gets me to the ashram by noon, and when we get there it bears a deserted look. The stalls by the gate have disappeared, the shops are mostly closed, and the large hall is empty. I take a last draught from a coke bottle filled with rum and coke, walk straight in to the main door, and by it find a bellpush that I press.

The owlish assistant opens the door and gestures me in. He leads me to the room where Prakash and I had lunch, and asks me to sit. 'I'm sorry, I forgot your name,' I tell him.

'Narsimha,' he tells me, a little miffed. 'Narsimha Shetty. I was with Swami when you came to the ashram the first time.' He looks intently at me all the time we're speaking. He sniffs disapprovingly. 'Your memory might not be so bad if you drink less.'

The door opens and a younger man joins us before I can respond. 'I'm Hassan,' he says. 'Raju asked us to help you.'

'Where's Raju?' I ask.

'At the jail,' Hassan tells me. 'Waiting to see Swami.'

'What about bail?'

Narsimha answers this one. 'I don't know,' he tells me. 'Swami didn't want bail.'

'What's Raju doing there?'

'Raju arranged a lawyer.'

'What for, if not bail?'

'He didn't tell me. Raju will tell you when he comes back.'

'When do you expect him?'

'He'll come when he has finished his work or when the working day is over. The jail closes at five, so he should be back by six.'

'Will you give me his cellphone number?'

'He told me not to give it to anyone. You can meet him at the jail and get it from him ... Swami said you can come here any time. You can stay here as our guest. Will you have lunch with us? It should be ready in half an hour.'

Without the leaven of Prakash's company, the bland lunch they serve here has no appeal, but on a whim – thinking of the uninspiring food he must be eating in jail, perhaps – I tell Narsimha I haven't eaten yet and would like to eat at the ashram. 'But only if we all eat together.'

There's a pop from somewhere nearby, like a small firecracker, followed by a loud, rough hum. Narsimha begins to respond even though I can't hear him clearly, pausing only when Hassan puts a hand on his arm. He continues when Hassan takes his hand off, which he does only when the hum diminishes to a low throb. 'That's not possible,' he says, smiling. 'Three people serve us while we eat. When we have finished, one of us serves those three people. That's the system here. Everyone who lives here takes turns at it.'

This is exactly the kind of detail I want to know about the ashram. 'What about the Swami himself?'

'He is usually busy during the day, but he also serves at the night's meal, and washes his clothes himself when he has time.'

'Washes his clothes?'

'Yes.' Another smile. 'That noise you hear is our washing machine. We have to run it four or five times a day. The power supply is very poor. Sometimes, in the day, the voltage is too low for the machine, so we run it at night, but it's still not enough. So sometimes we have to wash our clothes the traditional way. We all take turns at it, except some of the older ones who have arthritis or are too weak to do it.'

'Doesn't the noise disturb you, specially at night?'

Hassan replies. 'I sleep in the extension, in the new section at the back of this house, where it's not so loud.'

'Isn't it awkward, living in separate buildings?' I ask.

'We get used to it,' Narsimha replies. 'This has come about over the years. We all lived very simply, but now there are more people, more visitors, more resources … We can't afford to demolish the house and rebuild, so the ashram just grows as we need it to.'

I can see that. Lots of old houses have grown exactly the same way. I nod and change tacks. 'Your setup here seems to be a commune of sorts.'

'It is a commune.' The smile again. 'But we are not communists.'

'How did it come up?' I ask.

'Swami got some money and bought this place. He told some of his relatives – his parents were gone by then – that he was shifting here, and that they could live with him. That was all. They came with him. Everyone does what they can. Everyone eats well, lives well. There are people to take care of anyone who falls ill.'

'Where does the money for all this come from?'

'Interest. Swami invested his earnings in fixed deposits with government banks and in a limited portfolio of shares. There is enough coming in from that to take care of the ashram as it is now. He created a trust for the income to be paid to, so there are tax benefits. There is enough for now.'

'And afterwards?'

He smiles. 'I don't know. We'll try our best to keep this going.'

'And you? What's your stake in this?'

A smile again, a fleeting one this time, followed by a flash of worry. 'Nothing. I have my own property, part of which I donated to the trust when I came here. If necessary, I can always go back to my hometown.'

'How about the rest of you?'

'Four old people here, three women and one man … I don't know how they will manage. Everyone else will … they might not be well off, but they will have the necessities. Visitors who know us might help … I don't know.' He turns to Hassan. 'Go make sure that lunch is ready on time.'

As Hassan disappears, the anger flares up. How could Swami abandon these people? But then, again, maybe he didn't. He's not wasting the trust's money on lawyers.

'Can I have a few minutes with you?' I ask Narsimha. 'I'd like to know how the ashram runs.'

'We can sit in my room,' Narsimha says. He leads me down a corridor to the extension where he stays. His room is small and bare, with a desk and a chair in one corner, a bedroll in the other, and an armchair by the desk. On the desk is a hibernating laptop, and beside it a printout of a few pages. Above the desk are a couple of two-pin plug points, one vacant. Above the points is a little shelf on which are a few books, mostly about Vivekananda. At one corner lies a small dropper of the kind used to measure ink or medicines, a tube with a small bulb at one end, holding a couple of teaspoonfuls of fluid.

Almost as soon as Narsimha closes the door there's a knock on it. He opens it, and a youngster asks him if he could come along for a minute. Narsimha turns to me and says, 'Excuse me for a few minutes.'

'Sure,' I tell him. 'Before you go, may I charge my phone there?' I point at the plug point. 'Also, may I check my mail on your computer?'

'Go ahead,' he says, and leaves me to his devices.

I get my cellphone charging and sit at the desk. The computer comes on immediately and I discover it doesn't run Windows, which I've been using all along. Instead, it uses

Linux, and a browser I haven't used before. I soon get the hang of it, though, and in the process get a look at his browsing history: some of the latest are searches for Ayurvedic cures for irritable bowel syndrome, and how to prepare them, and so on. The printouts on the desk seem to be from those pages.

I ignore all that and check my mail, find nothing of note, and am rising from the desk when Narsimha returns with Hassan. He looks at his watch. 'I'm sorry,' he says, 'we should have lunch now. The others are waiting. Hassan will take you along, and I'll follow.'

Hassan shows me to a toilet before leading me to where we're going to eat. On the way he explains, 'Narsimha is slightly deaf. He tries to hide it, but we all know.'

'Don't worry about it,' I tell him. 'I'll pretend I don't know.'

This time we eat in a larger hall, the mess hall, so to speak, sitting on mats on the floor. Narsimha doesn't offer me the small table that Prakash did, or introduce me to the others, but I smile at them and at the people serving us, and, as I rise after a rather quick meal, offer to serve them. This brings forth gentle laughter from some of them, and Narsimha explains: 'Guests are not allowed to do that. If you want to serve us, move in.'

'Not yet,' I tell him.

His cellphone, a cheap Samsung, rings, and when he sees the caller ID he picks it up immediately. 'Anything new?' he asks. There's a long silence during which the person at the other end – Raju, I presume – issues instructions loudly, and then, 'He's here.' More instructions follow, and he says, 'All right,' and hangs up.

'Raju will meet Swami at two. Swami doesn't want bail. He wants a lawyer to look at the terms of the trust. They will discuss that in the afternoon, and also the lawyer will prepare

Swami's will. You can meet Swami at the jail tomorrow. He will refuse to meet anyone else. You can meet Raju here afterwards if you wish. He has asked me to give you his cellphone number so that you can fix up a time with him if you want to meet him. Call him tonight, between seven and nine.'

I can't find my cellphone but Narsimha remembers it's in his room, from where Hassan fetches it. I take Raju's number. I'm curious about the nature of the trust and what it controls and who the trustees are, but Raju will be a better source of information on that. Sitting here I get a sense of how Prakash ran the trust – he denied that he ran it, but his presence made it possible, and I'm reasonably sure his inner peace was the lubricant for all the little bits of friction that so many people living together must generate. It'll be interesting to see how the place runs minus that lubricant, but it's too early to say anything about that. People still haven't understood that Prakash might not be back. At all.

Wondering what to do, I call Srini, who asks where I've got. 'Nowhere,' I tell him. 'I haven't been able to meet him today.'

'Why not?'

'He was busy with a VIP, and then a lawyer.'

'I understand he doesn't want bail.'

'Yes.'

'Why the lawyer then?'

'Something to do with the trust that runs his ashram. He also wanted to make a will.'

'Is there a lot of property?'

'No. Some of the people living with him in the ashram have nowhere else to go. He's making provision for them, I think.'

'You sound like you believe him. Bala, don't get involved.

Remember the first thing about reporting. Look but don't touch.'

'Right.'

'You think he's straight?'

'Seems to be. He refused a deal with us, refused a deal with the VIP.'

'That must be Krishnappa Gowda. Finance minister. His roots are near Udipi, not far from the ashram.'

'Look, can you get some background on how Gowda met the Swami?'

'I'll do better than that. If Gowda was at the prison this morning, he'll be in his hometown now. I'll try to get you an appointment. Call you in five minutes.'

Srini knows lots of people in high places. So do I. So did I, actually, but the booze put paid to that. I don't bother to keep up. Srini does. Well, good for him.

He calls back in three minutes. 'Got him. You've got fifteen minutes with him at his house near Udipi. Five p.m. Be prepared to wait. Gowda doesn't like to keep people waiting but this is his hometown and everyone will want to see him. I'll text you the address right now.'

'Right,' I tell him.

'One more thing. The deputy superintendent who runs that part of the district, one KV Gowda, is his first cousin. That might be why the cops don't enter the ashram.'

'I'll ask the minister about his cousin, thanks.'

There doesn't seem to be any point hanging around the ashram after that conversation so I get Anil to take me back to the hotel. I give him Gowda's address and ask him if he knows the place. He grins. 'Every cab driver knows it,' he says.

'How come?' I ask.

Anil laughs. 'He had a cab company, then became real estate dealer with the help of underworld contacts. Then he learnt some manners and got into politics.' He shakes his head. 'He buys votes. Otherwise no one would vote for him.'

'I'm supposed to meet him at five.'

'I'll pick you up at the hotel at three forty-five,' he says. 'We'll get there a little early.'

Despite my apparent inaction – most of my time here has been spent waiting for one thing or another – I've actually been more productive here than I've been in years. This story is drawing me in. It's drawing me in so strongly that even the combined burden of Mohini's hostility and Pallavi's indifference seems to be easing a little. Strangely enough, I find myself wishing it didn't. I sit around wishing I could sort out all the trouble between us and go back to the old life, and then, in a flash of insight, understand that there's no going back.

There *is* no going back. Not at work, not at home.

Trying to get back to the way things used to be is impossible. No wonder there's a sense of hopelessness to life.

But there's something else, too. Do I really want to go back?

Good question. I don't know. Not yet, anyway.

My phone rings: it's Gokul, back from the wedding. 'I'm in town,' he announces. 'Should be free by about half past six. I'll introduce you to some toddy after that.'

'I've got to meet someone soon, and I'm done for the day. I'll call you when the meeting's over.'

By the time I've worked my way through all my questions and reread the notes and had another drink it's twenty to four, so I go downstairs so we can get moving as soon as Anil gets in, which he does on time. We draw up outside Gowda's ancestral home, which is now surrounded by an eight-foot-high wall topped with an electrified fence. The gates are large, black, and ominous, lying wide open, the guardhouse just inside manned by four armed policemen in khaki uniforms.

This guy takes his security seriously. These men bristle with weapons, black high-tech looking things that make you breathe lightly around them. He more than makes up for Prakash's lack of such trappings. But then he's a minister, and you can't be a minister unless you take yourself very seriously.

When the car stops, one of the policemen emerges to take my name and my ID. He goes to the guardhouse and makes a call on an intercom, returning to tell Anil to drive in slowly and stop in the porch of the big white house past a formal flower garden. Another armed policeman at the foot of the steps takes a minute to recheck my ID and tick my name off a list before signalling me on. I assume he'll tell Anil where to park and move into the verandah where Purshottam Rao, Gowda's secretary, waits.

Rao is an old acquaintance, though not a friend. He is self-effacing and scarily efficient, teetotal and very organized, and we have detested each other since we first met nearly twenty years ago. He smiles and holds out his hand as I climb the steps towards him. 'Long time no see,' he says.

'Yes,' I tell him. 'You're looking well.'

'So are you,' he says. 'Older. Distinguished.'

He's always been adept at flattery. He's expert at getting you off your guard and stabbing you in the back. 'You look just the same,' I tell him. 'Not bad, since it's eight years since we met.'

He nods modestly. 'I asked the boss not to keep you waiting,' he tells me. 'I think he's free right now. Let me check.'

As he heads inwards, though, another man emerges from the front door, a stocky balding man carrying a briefcase and speaking on a cellphone. Rao stops, holding up a hand for the stocky man to stop as well. He turns to me. 'Meet Sadashiv Uchil, chief of security.' Sadashiv Uchil mutters softly into his phone, disconnects, puts it in his shirt pocket, and inspects me briefly out of hooded eyes. It's a policeman's quick inspection, judgment withheld. He holds out a stubby hand, four chunky fingers and a broad thumb sticking out of a palm like a bit of plank, hard and confident. His face is round and should be jolly, but he seems full of menace instead. He doesn't bother to smile, just nods, takes back his hand, and continues on his way to the porch where he hands the briefcase to an assistant before retrieving his cellphone and putting it to his ear.

'A retired policeman?' I ask Rao just before he turns away.

'Yes. He used to be a superintendent. Up through the ranks, the hard way.'

'Those are the best,' I say.

'Yes. Sada is the best of those. I don't think anyone could get past him.'

I think on it while Rao goes into the house. Every big politician has at least one Sadashiv around, to direct and control frighteners, manage bags of cash and crates of booze for discreet distribution before elections. And, of course, to knock off whistleblowers and other inconveniences. They float easily from one side of the law to the other, equally at ease everywhere because they are in fact beyond the law. They operate in the shadows, trading information and services, experts at false identities and trails witnesses, impossible to pin down in a court

Rao emerges to tell me that Gowda is indeed free, though I'm fifteen minutes early. There are others waiting, Rao tells me, so if I can finish quickly – in the fifteen minutes Gowda wants to give me – everything will go smoothly and I will be out ahead of schedule. Implying, of course, that it's Rao's good management that's done the trick. 'Sure,' I tell him. 'There might be some details I want from you later, though.'

'Call me any time, ask questions, record the answers, no problem,' Rao says, leading me into the big man's room.

It's clear immediately that this isn't going to be a private meeting. Gowda sits at a desk in a large hall, with about fifteen people, men and women, all sitting in tube-frame chairs at the far side. Across the desk from Gowda are four chairs. Rao takes one. I take another. Gowda offers a smile and a brief handshake, just three limp fingers. 'Srini said you wanted to talk to me,' he says. I'll only get to see his public face here, which means he's going to avoid tough questions. I'd like a look at his private face, but that'll have to wait for another day.

'This is about Swami Sarvananda,' I tell him.

He breaks into a laugh, shaking his head. 'The Swami. The Swami likes to stay in jail. He told me it's like a holiday.'

'Didn't you try to persuade him to get out this morning?' I ask.

'Yes. I offered to get a lawyer, to get him out on bail by tomorrow. I told him I'll take care of everything, he only has to sign the petition. He refused. His principles don't allow it.'

'How did you first meet him?'

'See, when he shifted here I came to know of him. I know everybody here, and people tell me everything. When he bought that place I got to know. After some months, people began to tell me that the Swami is very helpful. People go to him with problems and he solves them. No publicity, no donations, nothing.

'So one day I also went.' He smiles. 'I am also like you, I have problems. He told me something useful, some advice, and I don't like taking something without giving something. So I went again. I gave him something. He didn't want it. So I told him, take the money, do some good with it. He wanted to use it for his clinic. I said okay, and told him that if he wants more he can always call Purshottam. No problem. I went there a few more times, then some of my people went to see him, they also found him useful. You've met him, no?'

'Yes,' I reply.

'Very peaceful man. I also felt the peace. I also like to see him. So I visit him once in a while, and so do some of my people. That is all. But he is doing good work, good clinic, he should not be in jail. I thought I would get him out.' He shakes his head. 'Nothing doing.' He shrugs. 'What can I do?'

'What about these accusations about your son?'

His guard comes up instantly. He's an okay liar, but not the best I've seen. 'I have seen the TV reports. I have seen the police complaint. There is no proof. I won't respond to all these things. No need. If the investigating agencies find some proof then we have to do something. Otherwise why should I bother?'

'There is evidence. Phone records. His presence in hotels with bookies and players …'

'How is that proof of my son's involvement in match-fixing? He is a cricket fan. Yes, he meets players. Is that a crime? Bookies also go to matches and he sees them there, what can he do if his friends introduce them? You want him to be rude? To say, you are a bookie so I won't shake hands with you or watch cricket with you? But do you have records of money? Of bank deposits? Of assets, benami assets? There is nothing.'

'Your son …' I begin.

He cuts me off. 'My son is thirty years old. If he does something, don't blame me for it, or the Swami. Don't interrogate me. My son is a free adult. Find him. Ask him whatever you want. Why should I interfere?'

'People say he's hiding in the ashram, and you won't let the police go there.'

'How can that be? Police arrested the Swami himself. If

they can go to the ashram and arrest him, how can you say they can't arrest my son? How can you say I stopped the police? Or Swami stopped the police?'

'The deputy superintendent in charge of the area is a cousin of yours. Did you get him posted here?'

'My cousin is a regular policeman. His transfers are an administrative matter for the police department, which is under the home ministry. I am the finance minister. Why don't you ask the home minister why he transferred my cousin here?'

'Your cousin could have told your son to leave before letting the police in.'

'See, you have to decide whether you are looking for faults or facts. You will find whatever you are looking for in politics. If you are looking for faults you will find them. Please look at the facts. I have not interfered with the police in any way.'

'This is a grey area,' I tell him. 'Someone who works for you might have done it. Somebody who thinks you need his help.'

'See, I can't be responsible for something that some wellwisher somewhere might have done. I have not told anyone to treat anyone in my family differently.'

This is the standard defence: an over-enthusiastic underling. 'All right,' I tell him. 'Do you remember your meetings with the Swami?'

'Yes, yes. He was very peaceful.' He scratches his head. 'He told me to be patient and open-handed, that everything would be all right, that I would win the election. That happened, you know. Then I began to think he is something special. Some of my people also began to visit him, they all found him special. So now I visit him regularly. I don't think he has done anything wrong, but you know these people, they have enemies everywhere.'

'Enemies? Like who?'

'How can I name them? Ask him. Ask the police.'

'Do you contribute regularly to the ashram?'

'I give to the trust. Sometimes I give cash, sometimes I give a cheque. It depends. Nothing directly to the Swami. He told me not to. Everything to the trust.'

'So you've seen the ashram grow?'

'Yes. In the old days you could spend time with the Swami. One, two hours, without problem. Only ten or fifteen people would come to see him every day. Then it increased, and now I think hundreds come to see him. His name is spreading. Last time I went people had come from Kerala to see him. I helped him. He had to get permits, and NOCs for the clinic and other buildings he was putting up. I got him all that because I know he is a good man.'

'That's why people are accusing your son of hiding in the ashram, then.'

He laughs again. 'See, my son is an adult. I don't monitor him. I don't know where he is. If you find him, please ask him to call me, okay? If he is in trouble I might be able to help.'

'What about your security chief, Sadashiv?' I ask. 'How come you have a personal security chief besides the people the government gives you?'

'See, I am also in business. Today I am a minister, tomorrow I might be out of the Cabinet but I will still be in business, and like any successful businessman I have competition, and some enemies. So I thought, why should I make the taxpayer pay for my security? Right? Not fair, no, because in politics I have no enemies. Only in business. So Sadashiv will be with me always, after the next election, whether I win or lose, whether my party wins or loses.' He smiles and rises. The interview is over. 'If you want more details, talk to Purshottam.' He, like Prakash, does a namaste and Purshottam leads me out into the verandah.

'You were always very negative, Bala,' Purshottam tells me when we're past the front door. 'You could have done so much if you didn't find fault. Even now we can do something. We can have a good future working together. You just have be careful what you say, what you write.'

'I am very careful,' I tell him, 'more careful than you think.'

His smile is knowing. 'Really? But I heard you don't write much these days.'

'Right. There are other things to be done.'

'Of course,' he says. The cab pulls into the porch with Anil at the wheel. Purshottam holds out his hand and I take it. 'Call me if you want anything,' he says before turning his back to me.

It's easy for the minister to say he doesn't know where his son is. The system works on untraceable prepaid cellphones. It's no big deal getting a prepaid SIM card using forged or false identity papers. People can keep in touch using these cellphones and never be traced.

What with the difficulties of gathering evidence, the vagaries of the courts, the appeals process, and the reluctance of investigating agencies, a political VIP can, even if caught red-handed, expect to remain free for more years than he expects to live. A sense of the futility of what we do comes back to me.

One item in ten of the news stories we do is about VIP misdeeds. Of these, one in ten is acted upon. Of these, one in ten results in a lower-court conviction. Of these, one in ten results in a higher-court conviction. Only one case in a thousand results in an effective conviction. In other words, if you're a VIP, the chances are you'll get away with it. Your only problem is likely to be other VIPs competing for the same profits.

If I get someplace with this investigation, what then?

I give up, for the time being.

## Chapter Four

MOMENTS AFTER I'M back in the room, just as I'm pouring one, Srini calls. 'Did you see Gowda?' he asks.

'Yes,' I tell him. 'He denied everything. But he did say in passing that he encouraged the growth of the ashram.'

'How so?'

'By being there, spending time with our man. All his hangers-on began to do the same, and the Swami soon had more visitors than he wanted.'

'More or less what you expected. Did you ask Gowda about his cousin, the policeman?'

'I did. He told me to ask the home minister, who controls the police department in which his cousin works. But he didn't seem worried about anything.'

'He never is. He's prepared. Besides, he's got money, he's got muscle, he's got lawyers, he's got voter backing in his constituency. Nobody's going to touch him. All we really have is a brief glimpse of his dark side. But let's not lose focus. This is the Swami's story, and you stick to it.'

'Okay.'

'Listen, you sound better. Take as long as you like with this one, okay? As long as you don't let someone beat us to it.'

'Okay. One more thing.'

'What?'

'What's on Gowda's mind now?'

'Could be lots of things. He's on several committees. He controls lots of handouts.'

'Well, find out what's biggest on his mind.'

'I can do that. Tomorrow. By lunchtime. Tell me if you want to meet him again.'

'Thanks.'

'What are you going to do now?'

'Chase up some old contacts. Try to find a new lead.'

'Okay.'

I call Gokul, who's free, and tell him where I am. 'I'll pick you up in fifteen minutes,' he tells me.

While waiting for him I call Mohini. I've been speaking to her every day now, and to Pallavi, but none of these chats have gone past a minute and a half. There seems nothing to say, except that we're all fine, which we aren't, and that I'm not sure yet when I'll be back. This time, though, it's a little different. For one, Srini has called up to tell Mohini that I'm likely to be here for some more days, that he can't say when I'll be done because the Swami is in prison, and so on: he's done it apologetically, taking the responsibility for my being away, but Mohini seems to have understood it to mean that I'm working again, and I sense what might be the beginning of a thaw. For another, I can hear party noises in the background, loud music and laughter. 'What's going on?' I ask Mohini.

'Some of Pallavi's friends have come over,' she tells me. 'They're having fun, and I thought I'd put up with the noise. How's the story going?'

'It's a good story,' I tell her. 'Like in the old days.' In the old days when I really chased after stories, that is.

'Good,' she says. 'I hope you're drinking less.'

After a moment's reflection, I say, 'A little, yes. But that might not mean anything.'

'Hope for the best,' she says.

Despite the tinge of regret that Pallavi never invites her friends over when I'm in town, this is the longest and warmest – the least icy, at least – conversation we've had in weeks, if not longer. Perhaps it's the separation that's doing it. But the fact remains that I've been focussed on the story for the last few days, and that's something different.

And then the strangest thing of all rises in my mind, a fugitive thought as I finish my drink: it's because of Prakash. The Swami I'm supposed to investigate.

The hotel phone rings: it's Gokul, from the lobby. He looks much the same as he did three years ago, when we last met: short and lean and wiry, with greying hair cut short, with long sideburns and a drooping moustache, watchful eyes, and an air of menace, like a hoodlum. He grabs me by the arm. 'What have you been up to,' he rasps. 'You look like shit, bastard.'

'Let's find a place where we can talk,' I tell him.

His personal vehicle is an old Jeep that's beat-up on the outside and in the best of condition inside. He takes me a couple of spectacular winding kilometres on the highway to Sholapur, then drives off the road, coming to a halt outside an old tiled house with a bit of tarpaulin tied across its open front. Past the tarpaulin, in a verandah, are a couple of long plywood coffee tables with mismatched plastic chairs set about them. One of the tables is occupied by a fat man with a moustache with a bottle of a milky fluid in front of him, and a small plate of what looks like chicken curry.

A bare-chested middle-aged man in a lungi appears from the front door, smiling at Gokul. 'Robert,' Gokul says in Kannada, 'this is my old friend Bala. Take care of him.' He turns to me, switching to English. 'Robert's got the best toddy in town, if you can take the ambience. And he's got fish and chicken and pork to go with it, if you like.'

A cellphone rings: Gokul digs it out of his pants pocket, looks at the caller ID, and rejects the call. The phone rings again. 'Just a moment,' he says, and replies. He speaks angrily, loudly, saying that he's with a friend from Bangalore and can't be disturbed for the rest of the night except in an emergency. There's a squawk from the phone, he tells the caller to call in the morning, and hangs up. 'Something from work. I have to yell sometimes to get my message across.'

The toddy is sweet and unfermented: it tastes a bit like sweetened buttermilk, but with a slight edge. When we've emptied our first glasses, he turns on me. 'What's happened to you?' he asks, forgetting to add the routine 'bastard'.

'Been drinking too much.'

'Stupid bugger,' he says. 'Stop it.'

'I can't,' I reply. 'I really can't.'

'Go to a doctor, then.'

'I'll do that one of these days.'

He glares at me. 'Make sure you do. Maybe I'll call Mohini one of these days. Get her after you.'

The belly-beast surges up. What business is it of his anyway? But then the concern in his face shines through, and the beast subsides. 'Don't do that,' I tell him. 'Don't even think of it.'

He sits up. 'Trouble?' he asks.

'Yes,' I reply. A pause. Then, before I can help it, the truth I've been avoiding. 'It might be terminal.'

'And Pallavi?'

I evade, unable to bear the possibility that I'll lose her irretrievably. 'I don't know.'

'Well, it happens. Tell me anytime if there's anything I can do to help.'

'I will.'

'I always wondered why you married her. What were you trying to prove?'

Gokul's presence seems to have triggered something. Perhaps it's the safety I feel with him. Answers emerge, faint, each less bearable than the last, and I turn them ruthlessly away. 'Later,' I tell him. 'After I finish with this story.'

'End of lecture, then … What is it about this story?'

I tell him. I tell him everything, from the chat with Srini right down to my meeting with Gowda and my need to get behind the minister's private face. He's smiling as I finish. 'What's so funny?' I ask.

'Gowda's got a mistress here,' he tells me. 'He's been married more than thirty years now, to this woman from Kundapur, and he has two children by her. He can't stand her, but can't get rid of her because a divorce would torpedo his political career and getting her knocked off would be too much of a scandal. So he shows up at functions with her, for the photographers, and for fun he keeps a mistress.'

'How do you know all this?' I ask.

'Don't ask. It's more than your job is worth to know. I work for the CB-CID, you know, and we have informers all over the place.'

'So who's this mistress?'

'She changes every couple of years or so. He's getting old but he needs to keep up the image, so he gets a younger woman regularly. In fact, the present one has been on for a year, and will probably last another … the point is, over the years he's got used to seeing a woman every time he visits the Mangalore area. He bought a house in someone else's name, an anonymous kind of place, and he used to meet his women there. Until his wife found out a few months ago.'

'And then?'

'It seems that his wife confronted him with it. Told him to be more careful seeing other women, because if she could find out, so could others, and that would give her a bad name. He told her that he would take care of her name, and his affairs were none of her business. Hit her.' Gokul grins, real delight in his eyes. 'According to what I heard, she hit him back. Once. Knocked him down, he hit his head on the floor. Maybe he was drunk. He couldn't complain that a woman had knocked him down so he spread the story that he slipped and fell … Anyway, he's developed a new system since. For the time being, at least.

'His secretary, that's your old pal Purshottam Rao, and his security chief, one Sadashiv Uchil, take care of it. Uchil and Rao check into a hotel in separate rooms whenever Gowda comes here, Uchil alone and Rao with his wife. The woman visits Rao's wife in the evening. Gowda comes along to visit Uchil later. Gowda and the woman spend a couple of hours in Uchil's room while Uchil and the Raos hang around in Rao's room, and then they go their separate ways.

'Officially, Gowda is in a private meeting with his security chief, and the Raos are entertaining a lady friend of Mrs Rao's.'

'Which hotel?'

It's one of the more expensive hotels in town, a boutique hotel, strangely named the Goldfish. Uchil has friends there, Gokul explains, so they can be discreet. Gowda enters the lift in the basement carpark, taking the lift there to the appropriate floor, while his mistress enters through the lobby with Mrs Rao.

'He's probably there right now,' Gokul says. 'He sees the woman every day he's near Mangalore. If we get to the hotel by about eleven we should be able to catch him in the carpark on his way out. The woman will leave half an hour later because Gowda thinks his time is more important than hers. Mrs Rao will show her out through the lobby, and a cab – hired by Uchil through one of his intermediaries – will take her home. Which, incidentally, is a flat paid for by one of Gowda's business associates.'

'You seem to have a thing for Gowda.'

'No,' he tells me. 'Gowda's too big. I can't touch him. I'm after Uchil.'

'Why?'

'Uchil's a bad man … You know, plenty of cops are corrupt. You pay for postings, and earn back five times what you paid in the couple of years your posting lasts. You learn to turn away from some things. But Uchil pushes the envelope. He was a sadist and a hoodlum in uniform, and he continues to be just that after he retired.'

'Tell me about him.'

'Don't tangle with him. Some businessman threatened him a few years back. The man's body washed up on the banks of the river ten days back. Mind you, this wasn't a businessman in the business sense of the word: he had a middle-sized gang behind him. The story was that Sadashiv killed the man himself. He knows all about how the police investigate murders, so he left no clues. That's the kind of guy he is.'

'Okay. And what about his relationship with Gowda?' I ask.

'He's been Gowda's hatchet man in every election the man has won. Every single election.'

'Hatchet man?'

Gokul smiles. 'Misleading term. The logistics of winning an election are very complex. Some of that activity is visible, very visible, the stuff with speeches and rallies and so on. But there's usually even more activity that's hidden, and it's built around money and, well, buying voters or intimidating them.'

'I know that.'

'You might not know the specifics. These guys started with spending crores of rupees twenty-five years ago, and now it's hundreds of crores. Some of that goes directly to voters. Gowda's constituency has several hundred thousand voters, of whom he's paying cash to maybe a sixth, mostly poor people. That's close to fifty thousand people. The last elections, he paid them a couple of thousand rupees each. That's ten crore rupees right there. That itself is a huge exercise. You have to deliver that much money, in packets, to the right people, over an area of a hundred square kilometres, over a week or less.

'Then there's the army of volunteers, party members who do the campaigning, going house to house, distributing pamphlets and so on. They might claim to be volunteers but they're largely paid volunteers. They get uniforms and gifts, besides rolls of tax-free cash. Thousands of shiny new cellphones, thousands of bottles of booze, TV sets, tablets, laptops, all kinds of things. Then there are the frighteners for individual booths, to make sure that people vote the way they're supposed to, there are election officials to be bought off, and so on. Then there are promises to be kept: promises of jobs, paying for marriages, school or college fees, all bribes of other kinds.

'Just paying this out costs him several crores because it's got to be done in cash and discreetly, and he has to pay off the policemen who are supposed to stop all this from happening. And so on.

'The thing is, when you're dealing with this much cash in the system, you can't deal with it with the usual delivery systems. You have to go to the gangs, because otherwise they'll just loot you. So you let the gangs handle your money – or at least leave it alone – and then you owe the gangs so if you win the elections you can't touch the gangs who worked for you. Since the gangs work for everyone in much the same way, all the big ones are safe.

'Elections are big business and organized crime, and most of the action is underground. What you see is only the dull bits, the shouting and the speeches and so on. The real action happens elsewhere, safely out of sight.

'That's where Uchil comes in. He's very good at dealing with gangs, essentially because he's a super gangster himself. He made his name by killing another mobster in Udipi, one Janardhan Hegde, some twenty years ago. He hacked off the man's arms and legs and let him bleed to death. It was quite spectacular. Then he arrested most of the senior members of the gang.

'That got him commendations from the police and a chance to set up his own gang to run the place, and that's what he's been doing ever since. He left operations to others while he was with the police, but when he retired he's taken over control, and with Gowda's protection, he does what he likes. He gets a percentage of every bit of business in the district.

'Gowda takes his share of all that. But I'm beginning to think lately there's been a sort of twist. Gowda owes Uchil too much, and is beginning to feel it. It might be Uchil calling the shots now, which is quite scary. I think your Swami is too small a fish for Gowda and Uchil to chase, but we'll poke Gowda anyway.'

'So what do you suggest? I just wait, let Gowda and Uchil see me in the hotel so they know that I know? And then a telephone call to the woman or something, just to drive home the point?'

'Exactly. You don't have to say a word. He won't be able to touch you for some time because you just interviewed him a couple of days back.'

The toddy isn't much of a drink: it has very little alcohol, but I find that it goes down very well with a stiffener of rum, which Gokul has brought along. By the time Robert is ready to close the place for the night, around half past ten, I have a nice little buzz going. Gokul, who has to drive, has been holding back on the rum, and while he doesn't have a buzz on, is quite happy.

We reach the hotel in fifteen minutes despite the driving rain: this is a small town, and no place is too far from any other, in pleasant contrast to Bangalore. It's just ten to eleven when we enter the parking lot, and Gokul's bare statement that he's with the police overcomes the watchman's reluctance to let us in.

We have to wait well over half an hour before a door in a dark corner opens and an obvious bruiser emerges, followed by Gowda and then Uchil. Gokul and I step out of the jeep as they pass by, and the bruiser turns to look at us, hand going to his beltline behind him. Uchil steps forward and pats him on the arm, and he relaxes. 'Gokul,' Uchil says. His eyes flick over me and back to Gokul. 'What are you doing here?'

Gokul smiles pleasantly enough. 'I just wanted to see the minister,' he says. 'Maybe I can get another promotion in the few years of service I have left.'

'This is not the time and place,' Uchil says neutrally, the neutrality more of a threat than a growl would have been.

'All right, then,' Gokul says. 'My friend Bala, the reporter, and I wanted to tell the minister that we hope you had a pleasant evening with Ms Ganapati.'

'Who is Ms Ganapati?' Gowda asks. 'I came for a business meeting with Sada. Private.'

'As you wish,' I tell him. 'Perhaps we can talk tomorrow, then. I'll call you.'

'Yes. Speak to Purshottam.'

They're gone, and we climb back into Gokul's jeep. 'I hope this won't have repercussions for you,' I tell him.

'I'm a cop, and I know enough about him to prevent him from doing me any harm,' Gokul tells me. 'But you, you've got nothing. That's why I came along, to make sure he knows that if he touches you he might have me to contend with.' He grins. 'And if he touches me he might have the press to contend with.'

'We'll see about that.'

'Yes,' Gokul says. 'Back to the hotel?'

'Please.'

'Bala, I won't tell you how to do your job. But something about this assignment of yours strikes me as very fishy. I can't put my finger on it but you should. You're dealing with some very dangerous people, and whoever sent you here should have covered you better.'

'I've done this a hundred times before, Gokul,' I tell him.

'You've been out of it for some years,' he replies. 'The world has changed. It's richer and more corrupt and more violent. Don't take it lightly.'

In the hotel's parking lot I promise to think about it, and to drop in at his house next day to say hello to his wife, Jayanthi, and, back in the room, drop effortlessly off to sleep. I come awake disturbed, an hour later, wondering about whether my meeting with Prakash will go through or not. After a more or less sleepless night and a chaser to keep off the hangover I call a warder whose cellphone number Srini has got me. The man's on duty, and will be on until five or so. No one's come to see Prakash today, and I can see him any time after ten, he tells me, so I arrange for Anil to pick me up at the hotel at ten.

I leave him in the parking lot outside and for the first time in my life enter a jail complex. The walls around are high – twelve feet high, topped with a barbed-wire fence – with a huge arched door big enough to take a fully loaded truck, with a judas gate set off-centre. The walls are whitewashed and clean, and gleam in the bright sunshine, and the inside is surprisingly spacious, with an old, battered barracks to one side and a relatively new and more spacious barracks further on.

Prakash is in the new centre, and a warder leads me to a

hall where there are cages where you can speak to a prisoner through a mesh. Another prisoner is meeting his lawyer in another cage further on, but it's otherwise empty when a warder leads Prakash into his half of the cage. A couple of warders watch, but there's little supervision, perhaps because neither Prakash nor the other man has been convicted.

Prakash turns and thanks the warder as he enters the cage. The warder smiles and moves off to a corner from where he can keep an eye on us. Prakash greets me with the same smile and namaste as he did in the ashram, to which I respond with a 'Good morning.' From what I can see of him he's exactly the same here as he was there, but I can't help asking, 'How are you?'

'How do I look?' he asks, his smile widening.

'Fine.'

'Well, I *am* fine. I slept well, had a light breakfast, did my yoga on a blanket, and now I have all the time in the world for you. You should be happy, you know. I wouldn't have been able to spend this time with you at my place. Not with all the work to be done there.'

'What about bail?' I ask.

'I'm having a holiday here,' he says. 'I cleaned the toilets this morning, and I have to wash my own clothes, but otherwise I've got nothing to do.'

'But you can't get out of here. You have no privacy. Lots of restrictions.'

'You're right, of course. I didn't say I'm free. All I said was, I can spend time with you – or another visitor – that I wouldn't be able to do back at the ashram on a normal day. But then, that's all I want to do. For now, at least.'

'Maybe I'm not making myself clear. In your other life you chose do to what you did. You chose to run that ashram, to offer shelter to old people, spend time with your visitors, and so on. Here you don't have that choice.'

'What you say is very clear,' he tells me, grinning. 'What you're saying is that outside of jail, I do what I want to, even if doing that prevents me from doing some of the other things I might want to do. Here, I've got to do what I'm told to do, eat what I'm given to eat, wear what I'm given to wear, sleep when and where I'm told to, and so on.

And all I'm saying is this: if you don't know why you choose whatever it is that you do, your choice doesn't mean anything.'

'And why would that be?' I ask.

'Actually, you don't even know whether you're making your choices or you only think you're making them. If you are indeed making those choices, then mostly you don't know why. '

'What do you mean, we don't know whether we make those choices?'

'The real question is, do you know who you are?'

'I don't.'

'If you don't know who you are, how can you know whether it's really you making those choices?'

'I believe I am.'

'Belief is dangerous. I know of people – magicians – who can get you to pick the card they want from a pack without your knowing of it. They can even get you to tell them the reasons why you picked the card you did … doesn't that tell you something?'

He's playing with me, tossing me these little tidbits about what magicians can do, and I find the irritation rising. 'Who else could be making those choices then? Some magician inside my head?' There's a little bite to the question because he seems smug and argumentative.

He laughs out loud. 'Why do you get angry at these things?' Then, quietly, 'There is someone else inside your head, not a magician, and you know it. If you want to get serious, well … All those times you've wanted not to drink or not to quarrel and you've ended up doing what you didn't want … There used to be an old Pink Floyd song that you're old enough to remember. It went something like this, "There's someone in my head but it's not me …" I think it was called "The Lunatic".'

'Those are just two sides of me. Two of my many parts …'

'You have to look at the nasty corners of your own mind if you want me to talk about this.'

'Okay.'

'The last couple of times I drew your attention to these corners you warned me off. About the alcohol. About the shame. Remember?'

Of course I remember. The belly-beast comes awake with a speed that leaves me breathless, my mind frozen. 'Isn't it like that with everyone?' I ask, buying time.

He knows, and, shaking his head, gives me a wry look. 'What others do is their business, not yours,' he says. His brow lightens in another luminous smile. 'Don't evade on the grounds that everyone does it.' The smile fades. 'You've got yourself in a fix now. Walking away from this is going to be unpleasant. You're not sure whether facing your fears will be even more unpleasant. Better the devil you know than the devil you don't.'

'What do you mean?' I ask.

'You know what I mean. You can keep doing what you've been doing all along, or let it go and suffer – or enjoy – the consequences.'

The belly-beast is in full cry. Nonsense, it says, he's leading you to ruin. There'll be nothing left of you if … For the first time, like a worm poking its cautious way out of its hole, comes a question in response to the beast: If what? I ignore it and say, 'I've got nothing to hide, nothing to be ashamed of. What the hell do you mean when you say I'm ashamed?'

'I can see the shame in you,' he says. 'I can't tell you what you're ashamed of.'

'Nonsense!' I can't help reacting angrily.

'Don't argue,' he says quietly. 'I've had plenty of practice reading expressions in recent years. All those visitors.' He pauses. 'I wasn't talking down to you when I said your burden is shame. I have my own burden to carry.'

My impression of smugness is gone now. Perhaps it was all in my mind. I'm reading feelings that don't exist. 'I don't know about it,' I tell him. 'I really don't know.'

'That's better than denying it outright,' he says, 'so we'll move on if you wish.'

'We're here to talk about you,' I tell him. 'Let's leave me aside for the time being.'

'So what do you want to know?'

'How are you spending your time in jail?'

'Like I said, I'm on holiday,' he replies. 'For the first time in many years I don't have to think about food or clothing, I have time to meditate and follow a good yoga routine and sleep enough.' He grins. 'The company's not too bad either. Interesting, to say the least. I'm learning to play cards, and am not unhappy at the thought of spending more time here.'

'Do you get any privileges here? Anything that the ordinary prisoner doesn't?'

'I've asked for none. My only complaint is that there are too many mosquitoes and therefore a risk of malaria or filaria or dengue. For everyone, including the warders.'

'And what about the charges? What about the investigation? Since there are some political personalities involved, do you think the investigation will be fair?'

'I don't know. I know what I've been charged with. I have

no idea what questions the police are asking other people, and I'll be able to tell you if the investigation is fair only when they tell me what they've found.'

'Do you think anyone might manipulate the investigation?'

'Look, I have enough trouble finding out what's in my own mind. I'm not going to waste time speculating on what others might be thinking or doing.'

'You're not helping out at all, are you?' I ask.

'Am I supposed to help you?' he asks. 'Tell me what you want me to do, and I'll do it if I can.'

'It's not me you're supposed to be helping,' I tell him, 'it's yourself. You say you're innocent of all the charges. Don't you want to prove your innocence? To get out of here?'

'I know I'm innocent,' he tells me. 'It's up to whoever it is to prove that I'm guilty. If the law happens to be that I have to prove myself innocent, I don't know how to do it.'

'That's what lawyers are for. To tell you what to do.'

'But they're expensive. I can't afford them.'

'In that case you'll have to stay here … unless you let someone else pay them.'

'I've already said I'm not ready to let someone else pay, and that I don't mind being in jail.'

I lose my cool. 'What're you playing at?' I ask him fiercely, without raising my voice. 'Don't you understand the stakes here? Do you really want to spend a few years in a prison for a crime you probably didn't commit?'

'Nothing, yes, and no.'

'Then why are you not doing anything about getting out of here?'

'You're missing the whole point,' he tells me. 'You're too caught up in what you think is my suffering to think straight. I'm grateful, of course, that you care for me enough to do that. Also that you believe I'm innocent of those charges.

But you should look elsewhere as well. Perhaps to your own flanks.' He smiles. 'Be a good bloodhound, Bala. Question everything.'

A warder turns up. It seems someone has come to see Prakash, a VIP. He smiles at me, and firmly tells me that my time is up. On the way out of the visiting area, I bump into the VIP: it's Sadashiv Uchil. He gives me a nod and smiles with his lips as he moves past, his cellphone at his ear as usual. The prison complex, full as it is of policemen and criminals and lawyers, seems to be his natural environment, and he moves as if he owns it. He seems completely unaffected by last night's encounter.

Why would Gowda send his security chief and hatchet man to prison to see Prakash? To deliver a threat? I can't think of any other reason for Uchil to be here.

The cab is outside, locked, with Anil nowhere in sight. I call his cellphone and he tells me he's gone for a cup of tea, and will be back in five minutes. I tell him to take me back to the hotel, stopping at a liquor shop on the way to buy a bottle of Old Monk and a litre of coke. I eat lunch at the restaurant, then make my way up to the room, switch off my cellphone, and get to work on the Old Monk.

# Chapter Five

THE RUM BOTTLE stands nearly empty on the bedside table when I come awake at six. It appears I forsook glass and coke towards the end of the evening's revels, of which I remember only the first half, and the first five triple pegs I poured. The rest I infer from the level of booze in the bottle and the size and texture of my headache.

Turning on the cellphone in this condition calls for extraordinary courage, but I do it: the screen shows no fewer than a dozen missed calls, the callers including Srini, Purshottam Rao, Raju, Mohini, Shafiq, and a couple of numbers I don't know. It's too early to start calling back, so I lie back, hoping to slide back to sleep.

The phone rings again almost immediately, cutting off all hope of more sleep. At the other end is a familiar voice that I can't place. 'This is Narsimha Shetty,' the man explains in response to my mumbled greeting. 'From the ashram. Swami's assistant, Raju's colleague.'

I have a vague memory of a middle-aged white-clad man staring owlishly at my mouth from behind large reading glasses. 'Yes,' I tell him, 'I remember you.'

'There is bad news,' he tells me.

'What?'

'My colleague, Raju … Raju passed away.'

That wakes me up properly. Raju, Prakash's quiet assistant.

I can't help thinking of Sadashiv Uchil and hired killers, but I ask, 'What happened to him?'

'We don't know,' he says. 'I don't want to tell you more on the phone. The doctor wants to talk to me. The police are coming.'

'All right,' I tell him. 'I'll be there in an hour and a half.'

Anil is free, and when I go down to the hotel lobby twenty minutes later I see his car in the parking lot outside. I tell him to make it as quick as he can, and he speeds up. On the way I tell him about the death in the ashram: he hasn't heard of it yet. 'Ask your fellow-drivers what they know about it,' I tell him, 'and what they hear about it. Pick up all the gossip you can.' We make good time on the highway to the ashram and we're past the gates a quarter-hour earlier than I'd promised.

The place is swarming with policemen, most in uniform, a few in plain clothes, some plainclothesmen carrying objects in plastic: evidence. Not a policewoman in sight, I notice. Shetty sees me as I enter the hall and comes scurrying up. 'The police are looking for evidence,' he tells me. 'They will be interrogating all of us over the next couple of days.'

'All of you?'

'About forty of us. Everyone who was on the premises last night.'

'Have they questioned you?'

'No. They will start soon.'

'Can you tell me what happened?'

'At four-thirty, a junior volunteer, Laxman, was passing by Raju's room. He heard sounds ... sounds of vomiting and pain. He stopped and called Raju. There was no answer for a while. He broke the bolt on top of the door and went in. Raju was on the floor, in a pool of vomit. He was conscious but ...'

'But what?'

'He seemed to be talking nonsense. Maybe he was in pain. He thought Swami was calling him for something.'

'And then what?'

'Laxman sat with Raju for a while, tried to calm him down. When Raju kept insisting that Swami was calling him, Laxman shouted for help. Someone heard him and came and called me. We called the doctor in Belman but he was attending to another patient. By the time he came Raju was gone ...'

'Didn't the doctor know how he died?'

'The doctor is not highly qualified ... he is only MBBS. Retired government doctor. He was not willing to sign the death certificate.'

'So now what?'

'So he called the police. Now it is a police case and the body will go to Mangalore Wenlock Hospital for post mortem and forensic examination.'

'Do you know who's going to do the autopsy?'

'I think it will be one Dr Balakrishna Hegde. Chief pathologist.'

Sadashiv Uchil with the hooded eyes and broad fingers lurks in my thoughts, delivering handfuls of cash to poisoners and briefcases of it to pathologists to certify a murder as a natural death. Inevitably, there follows the question: will Prakash be next?

But first, more details. 'Could I see Laxman?' I ask.

'Of course,' Shetty says. 'Please wait.'

Some ten minutes later, he leads a thirtyish-looking bearded man to me. 'Laxman,' he tells me. 'He'll go when the police call him.'

'I'll make it quick,' I tell both of them, and Shetty leaves.

Laxman is anxious and shaken and seems to be feeling some intense guilt. He has little to add to what Narsimha told me, but under repeated questioning tells me of a similar incident a week earlier. 'I found him talking ... not nonsense, but not sensibly. He seemed drunk but his breath was not smelling, and he was walking straight and I know he doesn't drink so I didn't know what to do. After a while he vomited a lot and then he seemed to become all right, except for a headache. He had a bad headache. So when I saw him today I thought it was the same thing, that he might be better after the vomiting. Maybe a more serious case of the same thing. I was telling him that he must see a doctor later in the day when he stopped listening.

'He was unconscious. Since this was not the first time I was not so worried ...' The reason for the guilt becomes clear. 'Maybe I should have called the doctor earlier. Or put him in a car and taken him to a hospital. He might have been alive if I had thought of doing that.'

I console him as best I can but a moment later a constable hauls him away. Moments later, the senior police officer on the scene, an inspector, arrives. When I give him my card, he looks me carefully up and down before telling me that he will have no comments until the forensic examination is done and the lab results available. 'I don't know what you have heard from here but please be careful what stories you write.' He doesn't seem to think much of the Fourth Estate, clearly. There seems no point in hanging around, and the possibility of Prakash being done in next weighs on my mind, so I decide to head for the prison to talk to him.

In the cab on the way to the prison I call Srini and tell him about Raju. 'I want to meet this guy Hegde,' I tell him. 'Tomorrow morning, if you can fix it, if he does the autopsy this evening.'

'I can fix it,' he says. 'I know the hospital's director.' No surprises there. Srini knows everyone.

'I also want transcripts of all the interrogations relating to Raju's death.'

'That, too,' he replies, 'but not as soon as they're made. You could get them a day or two late. Let me see what I can do. What are you up to?'

'I'm going to see the Swami,' I reply.

'Afraid he might be next?' Srini asks.

'Exactly. Unless he was behind it.'

'If he dies in prison it'll just confirm there's someone powerful at work behind the scenes,' Srini tells me. 'That'll take it up to a different level. I don't think that's going to happen, but you stay there to follow up if it does.'

'I hope it doesn't,' I tell him, 'but there's at least one minister involved.'

'Yes. We'll see.'

The prison system continues to work as usual, despite any deaths among people close to prisoners. Visiting hours remain unchanged, and, on enquiry, one of the warders reveals that Prakash has still not applied for bail. And, since the system functions normally, I get an appointment with him for ten in the morning.

When Anil picks me up he seems to be bursting with news. 'What's it?' I ask him as I get into the car.

'There are some drivers here who work for Sadashiv Uchil. You must have heard of him.'

'Of course. I've even met him.'

'Very dangerous man,' he says. 'He can kill you without feeling.'

'Yes. I've heard the same.'

'If I ask too many questions, one of his drivers might tell him, and then I'll be in trouble.'

'Right,' I tell him. 'No matter what, stay out of trouble.'

'Yes,' he says, looking at me in the rear view mirror. 'You shouldn't misunderstand.'

'I won't.'

'But I have a friend who used to be among his drivers, and I heard something.'

'What?'

'The lady who complained about Swamiji, that Smita Sharma.'

'What about her?'

'She used to be Gowda's keep.' I remember some of the photos of Smita Sharma. Well-endowed, even lush, attractive but no sex symbol. 'Uchil used to take messages between them. He arranged their meetings.'

'Does your friend have specifics? Dates, times, places?'

'He says he does.'

'Can he tell me direct?'

'No. He's afraid. If Uchil gets to know.'

'The company will provide guards.'

Anil shakes his head. 'Guards are no use. Who'll guard his parents? His brothers and sisters? Their children? Family is a big thing.'

'Right,' I tell him. 'Tell me whatever's safe, then, and no more.'

'Yes, That's what I'm doing. If Smita Sharma was Gowda's keep, did he ask her to file the police complaint?'

'Not an easy question, but I'll try to get the answer,' I tell him.

At the prison, Prakash looks much the same as he did the last time we met, minus his smile, a little distracted, and less at peace. 'Condolences,' I tell him.

'Thank you,' he replies.

'A most unlikely death,' I tell him.

'Yes. But let's wait for the autopsy reports and body fluid analysis before we say anything more.'

'Can you think of anyone who might want him dead?'

'No, I can't ... but that doesn't mean no one wanted him dead. Like I said, let's leave this until we get the reports.'

'Sadashiv Uchil visited you. He's your pal Gowda's hatchet man. Do you think he had anything to do with Raju's death?'

'I have no idea. All I can tell you is that Uchil came here on behalf of his boss to try to persuade me to try to get out of here.' He pauses. 'What he promised me was this: he'd be happy to arrange for a lawyer to get me out of here on bail. He'd be happy to arrange for me to get out of India when I get out on bail – meaning a false passport and visas and money for me to live happily ever after … somewhere safe. He'd also be happy to arrange for a large sum to be paid to the trust so that my dependents can live happily ever after.'

'What did you tell him?'

'That I don't believe in fairy tales. That I won't be beholden to him or anyone else.'

'Did he threaten you when you refused?'

'No. He just heard me out, asked me just once to reconsider, and went away. But then, his presence by itself is a threat, no?'

'Would killing Raju constitute a separate threat?'

'I don't know. I'm not going to think about it that way until I know more about what happened to Raju.'

'What if you're next?'

'If I'm next, I'm next. So what?'

I'm stumped. 'Are you suicidal or something?' I ask.

'Not at all. It's just that death will come when it comes … After that, I don't know. If there's no afterlife, there's nothing to worry about. If there is, we don't know anything about it, so there's no point in worrying about it anyway.'

He seems to be straight about it, and it ties up with the absence of security at his ashram. 'Okay,' I tell him. 'I heard you haven't applied for bail.'

He nods. 'That's right. My presence at the ashram tomorrow won't help anyone there.'

'Tomorrow? Not today?'

'Yes. Even if I apply today, and the magistrate grants me bail, they probably won't let me out before tomorrow afternoon or so. A lawyer told me that's how the paperwork moves. Unless there's an emergency or a VIP behind the scenes.'

'So you've got a lawyer?'

He shakes his head, and a flash of the old luminous smile shows. 'One of my fellow-inmates is a lawyer. He told me.' He shakes his head. 'He told me that people will say I had Raju murdered to prevent him from leaking secrets.' Another rueful smile. 'Also that I got myself in jail to make it look like someone else got him killed. There'll be all kinds of rumours.'

'We'll have to ignore them. It's all the more important for you to get a lawyer.'

'No lawyers. If I go to jail, so be it.'

'How will the people at the ashram manage without you?'

'I have no idea, but they'll have to manage.' He smiles. 'They'll find they can, if they have to. The ones who might find it difficult are the old ones, the helpless ones. The ones who have cots to sleep in because they can't sleep on the floor. I think everyone else there will be able to fend for themselves.'

'So you're giving it up?'

'The ashram? I don't know. Even before they brought me here I'd begun to ask whether it was time for me to leave the ashram.' For a moment he's serious. 'You know, I'm learning a lot from coming here. I'm learning to let go.'

'Let go?'

'Of the ashram. Of ideas on how my life should be. Of things. Of people. Mostly I'm learning that letting go is in the mind.'

'How so?'

'You're not really letting go of anything. You're letting go of your pictures of things or people or whatever. Of your picture of yourself.'

'That's beyond me.'

'All right,' he says. He smiles. 'I think you'll get it, by and by. Keep it somewhere in the back of your mind and one day you'll get it.'

'So what do you plan to do now?'

'Plan?' he asks. 'What do I plan for? I'm going to be here until they let me out, that's all. I just hope they do that in time for me to attend Raju's last rites, which should be held in about ten days from now.'

'I thought the rituals were meaningless.'

'I never said that. Rituals might mean something to those who perform them. Since the gods to whom they're addressed don't exist, they don't care. Whoever's dead is dead, and they don't care, either. That leaves the living.'

'Why do you want to attend Raju's last rites, then?'

He looks at me strangely. 'For my own peace. Isn't it obvious?'

'Do you want to postpone this chat?' I ask. 'If you'd prefer to be by yourself for some time ...'

'No, nothing like that,' he replies. 'I don't mind talking to you.'

'You were talking about rituals, and their meaning to survivors.'

'Yes ... you know, for some years before I came to prison I used to listen to a few hundred people a day. About one in ten of those spoke of some guilt that they carried about someone dead. A parent, a spouse, a child, a pet, sometimes ... rituals might be one way to ease the guilt.'

'Do you feel any guilt about Raju?'

'Yes. I should have listened to him more ... I should have taken better care of him.'

'Be more specific?'

'No. It's meaningless to anyone who didn't know our relationship well. And anyone who knows about our relationship would automatically know the nature of my guilt.'

'How do you get rid of that guilt?'

'You don't … I don't think you can look at guilt by itself. Guilt comes from somewhere deeper, from the same source as many of your other feelings. Guilt is just one more way for you to fool yourself into thinking you matter.'

I find I can't hold back a reaction. 'That's a truly horrible thing to say.'

'Don't ask me questions if you want politically correct answers.' He speaks evenly, without a hint of a snap, and looks me steadily in the eye. 'What I said about guilt applies to me, too, you know.'

'Okay,' I tell him. 'I apologize for what I said.'

'If you really meant it there's no need to apologize. You don't ever have to apologize to me for being honest. Even if that honesty involves being rude to me.'

'Fine. In that case, just explain what you said about guilt being one more way to fool yourself.'

'It's very simple. Guilt is what you feel when you think you're responsible for something bad happening. How do you know you're responsible for anything at all? We went through this yesterday, remember? Do you really decide what you're going to do, or do you only think you're deciding it? We don't know. We have no idea how to find out, either. I think we're fooling ourselves.'

'Then why do you feel guilty?'

'Obviously because I haven't learnt my lesson yet.'

'Are we heading for one central point in all this?' I ask.

'You tell me,' he says. 'You're the one asking the leading questions.'

'Then let me change topics. Do you think there's life after death, and all that stuff from the Hindu scriptures?'

'Let me put it this way: I'd be surprised if there is,' he replies.

'There are stories of people remembering bits of previous lives, and of verifying some of those details afterwards.'

'There are. Doesn't mean they're true ... Not one instance of claimed reincarnation has been verified by anything like a rigorous test.'

'So you don't believe in reincarnation?'

'I don't really know. Look, if you ask me, do I hope to meet Raju in an afterlife and apologize to him and so on, yes, I do wish it. If you ask me if I think that'll happen, no I don't. I'd be very surprised if it did.'

'The scriptures are full of death and what follows it.'

'They are. That's probably just because most of us spend a lot of time thinking about death – or avoiding thinking of it – after we reach middle age.'

'Do you think about it?'

'Yes.'

'And what do you think about it?'

'It's like a wall that you'll never see the other side of. Anything people say about what's after death, including everything in any scripture, is just so much speculation. Streams of milk and honey, virgins for the just, an unending stream of pleasures ... eternal fires, unending torture ... no, I don't think any of that is true.

'Let me ask you this: can you imagine the universe without yourself? I can't. No matter how I try, I can't. So, are you the universe?'

'No point asking me these questions now,' I tell him. 'I've got work to do. Find out what happened to Raju. How you came to be stuck here. And so on.'

He shakes his head. 'This is what I want to talk about. If you don't want to discuss these things, well, find someone else to question.' His smile robs his words of offence. 'Bala, let me put a little time bomb in your mind. Consider this: whatever will be will be.'

'You've got to be kidding,' I tell him. 'Have you given up, or what?'

'I'm not kidding,' he replies. 'And since I'm not in a fight of any kind, there's no question of giving up.'

'Why don't you give me a straight answer for a change? You have some reason for wanting to be in here, and you won't admit it. Do you think you're safer in prison than outside?'

'Come to think of it, yes, I'm probably safer in here than outside,' he says. 'Out in the ashram, anyone with a pistol could finish me off. Not here. But why do you find it so hard to believe that I'm just going along with the system?'

'I can't believe any sane person would be unwilling even to try to get out on bail, that's why, and I don't think you're insane.'

He smiles. 'Okay, I'll tell you why I'm not trying. I'm just testing an idea. If I'm due to get out of prison I'll get out, regardless of whether I try. And if I'm due to be stuck inside, I'll be stuck, no matter what I try.'

'I made a mistake. You must be nuts. How will you get out if you don't try?'

'If someone influential enough wants me out badly enough they'll pull enough strings to take care of it, I guess. Have the charges dropped, or whatever. And, if I'm due to stay here, even if I get bail there's no one stopping people from filing fresh charges. So … let's find out.'

'So all that stuff about not being able to pay for lawyers was so much bullshit, right?' I ask.

'Oh, no. It applies, all right. You see, you wanted reasons

and I've found money is usually the best reason for doing or not doing something.'

The warder – the same one that stopped the meeting yesterday – turns up yet again, shamefaced. 'The inspector wants to ask you some questions,' he tells Prakash. 'About the death in the ashram. Your friend.'

Prakash shrugs. 'We can catch up later if you wish,' he tells me.

Of course I wish! 'Tomorrow,' I tell him. 'We should be able to get some time tomorrow without being interrupted.'

'Yes,' he says. 'I hope you'll find yourself pleasanter tomorrow.' He smiles. 'You seem to be able to get in and out of here at will.'

'Yes,' I tell him. 'My boss has plenty of friends, and if that doesn't work, my father-in-law has plenty of money.' I don't mention that my father-in-law and I barely manage to be polite to each other.

'Your father-in-law?' he asks.

'Yes. One Chandramohan Venkatesh.'

He nods. 'I've heard of him. CV. Businessman. Umm, not the most honest, perhaps.'

I laugh. 'Exactly.'

'Lucky you,' he says, and moves off behind the warder.

## Chapter Six

In the cab back to the hotel I call Srini. 'Anything about the transcripts?' I ask. 'The transcripts of the interrogation of people at the ashram after Raju's death?'

'It's like this,' he tells me. 'I spoke to a forensic type who knows the guy who's going to do the autopsy. The first doctor at the scene, the retired government doctor, was right. There was something fishy there. Dilated pupils, violent vomiting, perhaps some diarrhoea and so on, some symptoms of poisoning. All informal, of course, so we can't use this information. But you can assume that it was a murder.'

'It'll take another few days to know what poison it was and how it was administered, right? Any way to speed it up?'

'The labs take their own time,' he replies. 'A few days. Maybe a week. Where have you got with the Swami?'

'Gut feel is still that he's straight. Raju's murder muddies the water some more. There are already people saying that the Swami had him murdered for fear that he would let cats out of an awkward bag.'

'You don't seem to think so.'

'I don't. We're back at the same question: who benefits. The big thing here is not the Swami but the minister who backed him. Gowda. Who benefits from his discomfiture?'

Srini laughs. 'I can't help you there,' he replies. 'Practically the entire opposition. About a third of the legislators in his own party. His wife, who I believe is estranged. The only loser – besides your pal – is the man's son, who seems to have been fixing cricket matches.'

'That's what? A few hundred people?'

'Yes. All of them – all the legislators, anyway – have the means to generate a false complaint that'll get the Swami in jail. Most of them are twisted enough to be willing to do it. So your list of suspects includes half the state's legislature, and half-a-dozen or so businessmen looking for leverage out of them. Also at least a dozen legislators in Gowda's own party, and perhaps another Cabinet minister or two as well. Umm, Bala, if I had to speculate I'd think you're next on the hit list, not your pal the Swami. You're the one asking awkward questions.'

'Gowda's security chief was at the prison yesterday. The Swami told me he tried to persuade our man to apply for bail.'

'Why didn't your pal agree?' asks Srini.

'We were interrupted just when he began to answer that question,' I reply. 'Someone wanted to interrogate him on Raju's murder. He never got to tell me the whole story. I'll ask him tomorrow.'

'Okay, Bala, so keep going. I'll make sure you get the autopsy results and all the forensic stuff as soon as possible. You'll also get to see the pathologist … Why do you want to see him, anyway?'

'Most of these guys with experience autopsying murder victims get a feel for the death, a hunch, something they might not care to put down in a report. I want to ask him, in confidence, if he got something of the kind.'

'You don't know the man,' he says. 'I hope he'll open up.'

'No harm trying.'

'Right … go ahead, then.' A pause. 'Bala, this is a big one, okay. You might feel you're spinning your wheels, but just stay there. I'm behind you all the way.'

'Will do, Srini. It's my lifeline, right?'

In the hotel I check on the competition, as usual. The murder is hot news: Raju's death has freshened up the outrage, and the story isn't a story, it's a series of questions, the second-biggest of which being, who killed Raju. The biggest question, asked as a kind of afterthought, after putting together selected strings of events, is, did Prakash kill Raju? And the answer, everywhere, is quite possibly.

The reason emerges only towards the end of the coverage of the murder. Raju was the chief trustee. Leaked information reveals that the Swami took money from the trust. Raju would have been the best source of information on how much the Swami took and why. That information would be damaging, and the Swami organized Raju's killing to contain the damage. While the story isn't convincing, it's plausible, and Prakash is doing himself no good keeping quiet about it.

Now comes the hard bit. In the interests of justice to Prakash, I must ask him to speak to other journos. Help the competition, as it were, and torpedo my exclusive. I fear I'm getting too close to the man ... The next time we meet, I'll ask him, casually, to talk to others, but that's it.

Having decided that, I call Mohini and Pallavi. After a minute and a half of desultory conversation I give up. I don't think they care very much, and when I think hard enough I think I understand why. All of a sudden it strikes me that I'm worrying a lot more about Prakash than about my own family ... Maybe they're just giving back whatever they think they get from me.

That's a lowering thought, I tell myself, and reach for the remains of last night's bottle. But the drink doesn't feel as it usually does, so I pour half of it down the sink. Then, feeling restless, I go down for a walk. Out on the street the heat and dust and the diesel fumes and the traffic make walking unpleasant. For a moment I consider asking the receptionist about quiet roads nearby, but change my mind and find a booze shop instead where I buy enough Old Monk to last me a few days, and a couple of two-litre bottles of Coke and soda.

The walk back to the hotel carrying all this leaves me pleasantly tired and I get going on my notes before pouring myself another drink, wondering why I didn't like it just an hour earlier.

It seems to be worthwhile transcribing the recordings of these chats with Prakash myself. It's not just the words, it's also what he puts into them, and allowing someone else to do the transcription or just doing it without thinking about it is a good way to lose that, so with a sigh I get down to doing it.

I have to get to the bottom of this!

I need a drink!

Getting to the bottom of it wins. I get back to the conversation I'd transcribed earlier, and, sure enough, there are no notes, just the words. So I listen to the recording all over again, and find bits that I need to play over.

My listening is interrupted by a call on the house phone. When I pick it up, a strange voice asks, 'Mr Balaram Kamath?'

'Yes,' I reply. 'Who's this?'

'My name is Rahul, and I work for *India This Week*. You must have heard of it.'

It's a relatively new Delhi-based weekly that's available online as well. 'I have,' I tell him.

'You saw me at the ashram yesterday, sir. You were on your way out.'

'Were you speaking to one of the guides at the ashram?' I ask, remembering the young man who smiled at me as I walked past.

'Yes, that was me.'

'Very well. So you're with the competition. What can I do for you?'

'My editor, Kamal Srivastava, asked me to get in touch with you.'

'What is this about?' I ask. I've met Kamal a couple of times – the media universe is small – but know little about him except that he has a temper.

'I don't know. Well, Kamal asked me to meet you, call him, and ask you to speak to him. So when can I come and see you? Can I come now?'

'If it won't take long, sure.'

A minute later the doorbell rings and I open the door to admit Rahul. He shakes my hand, then gives me a card that says, Rahul Gupta, Staff Writer. 'Okay, Rahul, get on with it,' I tell him.

He makes a call on his cellphone, and says into it, 'Yes, Kamal, I'm with him. Speak to him directly.' He hands me the phone and, as I take it, slips out of the room, closing the door behind him.

'Bala?' asks Kamal. 'We met year before last at a Press Club function in Bangalore, remember?'

'Sure,' I tell him. 'What's this about?'

'Rahul tells me you're the only press person the Swami speaks to.'

'Yes,' I reply, 'but that's accidental. In any case, I don't think I'll be able to persuade the Swami to speak to Rahul.'

'Of course not,' Kamal says. 'This isn't about Rahul at all.'

'Well, what's it about, then?'

'I'd have liked to bring this up face-to-face,' he says, 'but I don't think that'll be possible in the next few weeks, unless you think you can fly to Delhi for a day for lunch or something. Our expense, of course.'

'You're right. It's not possible in the next few weeks. But what is this you'd like to bring up across a table?'

'Bala, you used to be a hardcore print man. I've heard you

don't fit well with TV. Also, umm, that you're not very happy in your present position.'

'Who told you that?' I ask. It's common knowledge that I'm on the booze, and that I prefer print media, and it's only natural to infer that I'm not happy in my position from the fact that I'm not happy, period. Even so, I'm curious.

'The word's out,' he tells me. 'I've heard from several people here. None of your colleagues, though. In any case, I thought I'd check with you.'

'Okay. So?'

'Any time you want a change, speak to me first. That's all.'

'Can you be a bit more specific?'

'Of course. We need someone to jack up presence in the south. You might do it.'

'I have some other … problems.'

'I heard. We can work out how to deal with them. But I must warn you of a few things, because we're still new and growing.'

'What?'

'First, the money's not good. Not yet, anyway, but we hope it'll get better soon. Second, you might be better placed in Chennai. Third, we'll start with a year's contract.'

He's cutting his losses, just in case the booze gets the better of me, paying for a year at most. I'm not keen on shifting to a new place, anyway, and if this story works out I'll be back among the living with Srini. As for the money, I have an expensive habit to pay for. 'I'll keep this in mind,' I tell him.

'If you give me your cellphone number, I'll send you my number right away. Feel free to call me at any time.' He laughs. 'Even in the middle of the night, if the need arises. My people sometimes do.'

I feel transplanted in time to the early years, when Srini and I worked round the clock, and bedtime was rarely before three in the morning. Then I come back to earth with a jerk. 'Right,' I tell him. 'I'll call you when the occasion arises.'

'Sure.' He hangs up.

I open the door to find Rahul waiting in the corridor. 'Kamal told me to get myself out of earshot after giving you the phone,' he tells me, smiling, 'so I thought I'd wait out here.'

'No problem,' I tell him. 'How's work?'

'We're still learning,' he tells me. 'It's the best place for someone just starting off.'

'Are you? Just starting out, I mean.'

'Yes. I took a degree in history, and then did a diploma at the Indian Institute of Mass Communication, and then Kamal offered me this job and I took it. It's a bit crazy right now … We don't have many people, so whoever is available does whatever needs to be done … Once we're organized it'll be different, I suppose.'

'Yes.'

'Thanks …' Then he asks the question that he's been wanting to all along. 'How did you manage to get the Swami to talk to you, anyway?'

I grin at him. 'Easily. I just waited in line, and, when my turn came, told him what I wanted. He agreed. He told me that everyone else tried to jump the queue, that he spoke to me only because I waited.'

He looks at me a little suspiciously. 'I thought you knew that minister who's been his patron. Krishnappa Gowda.'

'Of course not. I did meet Gowda, but only after meeting the Swami.'

'Okay. I'll remember how you did this.'

'Sure … Will you have a drink with me?'

He smiles, and shakes his head. 'Thanks, but no. I don't drink.'

I look at his neat haircut, his fashionable jeans and army-style shirt, and feel like a dinosaur. Back when I was his age, reporters were hard-drinking, battered, underpaid types. This present crop look like yuppies. This boy Rahul could as well be an accountant or something, though he's dressed too informally to be a marketing man.

After he leaves, I get back to the notes, and the questions. Why, for instance, did Prakash bring up the bit about Mohini's looks when the subject of marriage came up? Why did he back off? Why, when I asked him sarcastically if he had any more tips for me, did he reply I wasn't ready?

Most of all, why was he focussed on me rather than on getting out of his fix?

Or am I reading it all wrong? Was he just leading me by the nose?

Or does he do this to everyone? Perhaps that's what he does. When he's with someone he seems to think there's no one else in the world but them … which means he's a bloody good listener.

For the rest of this story I will do the transcripts myself, and I will get them right.

Srini calls as I'm starting on my notes. 'Dr Hegde will meet you at nine tomorrow at his house.' He gives me the address. 'He lives close to the hospital, in Pandeshwar, and you should have no trouble finding the place. Take his cellphone number in any case. And keep me informed.'

'All right,' I tell him. 'I'll talk to you after I speak to him. And get me those lab results as soon as they're ready. The body fluids are in the labs in Bangalore anyway, and I'm sure you know people there.'

'I do. I'll get them, don't worry … You sound a little like you used to, Bala. Keep it up.'

'Right,' I tell him. 'I will.'

I call Mohini, and she sounds happy. Turns out she's been spending time getting close to Pallavi ... From what she says, Pallavi seems to have drifted from Mohini, too, retreating into an electronic world of social media, and Mohini's trying to close the distance. More like cutting me out of Pallavi's life, says the belly-beast, and I take a tot of rum to cool off before returning to the notes.

I start at the beginning, with the first meeting with Prakash, going back to what he saw in me. The shame ... that doesn't sound true, though the rest does. The bit about my unhappiness in my marriage, for instance, the drinking, and the trouble at work: he was spot on about all those. None of that bothers me, but the shame rankles, and I have no idea why. Behind is the ghost of a thought: is he right?

I move on then to how he learnt that his discontent came from himself, how nothing is what it seems to be, that I'm not ready yet for more ...

The discontent that came from himself: Does Prakash have a belly-beast that he turned upon?

Nothing is what it seems to be. For the first time, I ask myself this question: does the belly-beast lie?

It seems not to. Its words seem to come from deep within myself.

With a shake of the head I return to my notes. Spending time on the belly-beast will get the story no further forward

So I go back to the basics once again, the question I asked Srini. Who gains from Prakash's discomfiture? Not Gowda the minister, as far as I can make out. His son, if indeed the young man is involved in match-fixing, has lost a refuge. Gowda himself has possibly lost a few votes amongst Prakash's supporters, and quite possibly, more than that.

He might have sent Sadashiv Uchil around to threaten Prakash, he might have arranged Raju's murder, all for the purpose of keeping Prakash quiet. But he wouldn't have started the investigation because he himself stands to lose too much.

So who gains from Gowda's loss?

Srini's answer is too facile. Yes, there are plenty of people who'd like to see him go down, but very few of those would be willing to launch such a specific but sidelong attack on him.

So, once again: who gains?

Then a thought enters my mind: is Srini holding back? A niggling suspicion: he knows a lot more than he's letting on.

Now the trouble emerges: I don't know the stakes. It comes as a deluge, the knowledge of what I've lost for those years on the bottle. Five, even three, years ago, I'd have known. Now I'm ignorant. Time to get back to work, regardless of whether the lifeline works or not.

It's a few hours' work, most of it trawling the internet for information, and it leaves me a little short on sleep and temper. I get to bed a little after two and go to sleep the moment my head hits the pillow, coming awake to my alarm at half past seven. I ask Anil to pick me up at half past eight – he says it's only fifteen minutes to Dr Hegde's house, but I'm not sure of the way so I budget an extra fifteen minutes for the hunting – and cram down a quick breakfast before going down to meet him.

As it turns out, Anil knows the apartment block where Dr Hegde lives, so we get there early. I look at my watch and decide to risk it anyway, and knock on the doctor's door at ten to nine. He opens it himself, a tall, scholarly man in his late fifties, with an overgrown beard and spectacles that keep sliding down his nose. His wife, it turns out, has left – she works at a bank an hour away – and his maid is making sure he eats his breakfast.

He invites me in. We sit at a large dark messy dining table

and the maid brings me a cup of coffee unasked. 'You wanted to ask me about the autopsy on Raju,' he says, sipping his.

'Yes,' I tell him.

'He was poisoned,' Hegde tells me. 'I don't know what the poison was – we should know when the lab sends us the results on the viscera and the body fluids – but he took it voluntarily perhaps without knowing that he was taking poison. There's no sign of force or anything of the kind.'

'The real question is, what didn't you put in the report?'

'Umm … good question. Why should I tell you?'

'No reason at all, to tell you the truth.'

He smiles. 'I appreciate your honesty,' he says. 'So I'll tell you something I haven't put in the report, something I've speculated about. The dead man was poisoned, and I think he could have been poisoned anything like twelve to twenty-four hours before he died … He was very fit for his age. He ate sensibly, exercised, took care of himself, and almost any poison would have taken some time to kill him. He might have thought that the nausea and other discomfort he suffered came from the stress of his boss being arrested, of him being stuck with the responsibility of running the ashram.

'The combination of symptoms doesn't fit with the commonest poisons used for suicide – pesticides. I have a hunch about what it could be. We'll know from the analysis.'

'What?'

'Datura. It contains a peculiar combination of deadly alkaloids. Famous because Gandhiji, as a boy, stole some money to buy cigarettes, and after smoking them felt so guilty that he tried to kill himself by eating a few datura seeds. He didn't die, of course, just slept a lot. I suspect, again, that he picked the wrong seeds. Datura would probably have made him throw up … but I don't know for sure.

'I'll say this, off the record, to any policeman who asks,'

he adds. 'To help the investigation along, not as proof that will stand up in court. And, if you quote me, I'll deny I said anything of the kind. Are we clear?'

'Of course,' I tell him. 'A twelve-hour span means that he could have been poisoned any time in the daylight hours of the day before he died. That makes the investigation harder, doesn't it?'

'Yes. Not my problem, thankfully.' A quick smile. 'Not yours, either, unless I've got your occupation wrong.'

I smile and nod. 'What else did you get from the autopsy?'

'Nothing. The death was not natural. He probably died of poisoning. No injuries, nothing. Of course, it could well have been suicide as well.'

'Thanks, doctor,' I tell him, rising. 'May I come back to you for clarifications?'

'On the autopsy itself, yes. On other matters, well, I don't know what I can clarify.'

Back in the cab, I tell Anil I want to go back to the prison. I'm actually looking forward to meeting Prakash, to try to understand his weirdness.

Two warders, both familiar, let me in without fuss to the same large hall where prisoners meet visitors. A third leads Prakash into the hall, then retreats to stand guard at the door. He looks rested and fresh. 'How was yesterday's interrogation?' I ask.

'They have a very simple technique,' he replies. 'Different people ask you the same questions over and over again, in a different sequence each time, until they find a small discrepancy somewhere, and a sense that you're evading or lying. Then they hammer on that point until they get you to break down.'

'Did they keep you long?'

'Not really. I must say that some of them have a good sense of when you're lying.'

'Really? Did you lie?'

He laughs. 'I did. The third time they asked me something I lied. When they brought it up again I told them they'd already asked me, they had their notes, and they shouldn't waste their time repeating their questions.'

'What did they say?'

'They told me they didn't need my advice to do their business. You know, I've come across more accomplished liars here in the last few days than in all the years before that. Among the prisoners, the police, and lawyers ... I really don't know if this technique would work on a regular criminal, someone who's learnt to lie properly, without showing any signs.'

'You don't seem particularly worried about it.'

'I'm not. You see, we lie all the time. I lie less than I used to, but that's no standard.'

'Bullshit,' I tell him.

He smiles. 'Being rude and honest again? What have I said that's bullshit?'

'About us lying all the time,' I tell him. 'I'm sorry, but that's really how I feel.'

'That's all right. I'm not going to force my opinion on you. But do think about your own lies.'

'I'm going to ignore that for now,' I tell him, irritated.

'As you wish. Like I told you before, your lies are not my problem.'

'You seem to have got over Raju's death.'

'There's no question of getting over it. The grief comes and goes. I don't interfere with it. When I do feel pleasure in a moment when I don't remember Raju, I don't pretend not to feel it just because he's gone.'

'I wanted to ask where you got your ideas from.'

'What ideas?'

'All this stuff you've been talking about: lies, death, grief, relationships, whatever.'

'My father used to read the Gita every morning, and he kept talking about the Vedas and so on. Reading these books got me started on thinking.'

'So you're a Hindu, then.'

'I don't know … Tell me what a Hindu is, and I'll tell you if I'm one.'

'You must have some idea what a Hindu is.'

'I have an opinion on it. It might be very different from anyone else's opinion, though.'

'Well?'

'As I understand it, a Hindu is someone whom the British found wasn't a Muslim or a Buddhist or anyone else they could classify. You could be a tree-worshipper with no idea of Sanskrit or the Vedas or anything of the kind and still be classified a Hindu.'

'So what's a Hindu, really, in your opinion?'

'Someone who asks questions without restriction.'

'Doesn't everyone question?'

'Yes, but others refrain from questioning some things. A Hindu, on the other hand, can, and often does, ask anything. No question is taboo. Actually, Buddhists do the same thing.'

'But the answers are already in the scriptures, aren't they?'

'What do you mean by the scriptures?'

'The Vedas. The Upanishads. The Mahabharata. The Ramayana. The various Puranas.'

'People have been asking these questions for ages. Some of them think they've found answers, so they write them down. This being in the old days, they do it in Sanskrit, in verse, because Sanskrit is flexible, and verse is easy to remember. But, you see, the answers are limited by their context, so when someone else asks the same questions he's got to get at his own answers.'

'Trying to make sense of the answers in our scriptures in these times is like driving while looking in the rear-view mirror. You'll crash. So what we need to do is figure out the questions. But then we don't have to figure out questions that those people asked long ago, do we? All we need to do is ask our own questions. That's all I'm saying: keep asking those questions. That's one way to get rid of sacred cows.'

'In essence, you're rejecting the wisdom of the old people.'

He laughs. 'Of course not,' he says. 'I wouldn't reject wisdom, no matter where it comes from.

It's just that I've found little wisdom in our scriptures. There are a few sublime things in the Gita, but there's also much that's unacceptable. And there are some questions to which there are no answers.'

'Unacceptable? For instance?'

'In the Gita, Krishna says things about the caste system and the position of women that are completely indefensible. There are other bits that seem straight out of a fantasy, like Krishna saying that he revealed some truths to the Sun.'

'And the questions?'

'An example. In the *Kathopanishad*, Nachiketas waits for Death for three days, and gets three gifts, the last of which is ultimate knowledge. This ultimate knowledge is supposed to take you beyond worldly considerations. The question then is, why does he come back?'

'If you leave out all that, there's very little left. But then, in the fragments that are left are some very wise bits, about detachment, and so on, but they're all useless when it comes to sharing wisdom.'

'What do you mean?'

'There's no easy way to wisdom. You have to ask the questions, and work out the answers for yourself. Some of them you have to work out the hard way, and there are some you might never get answers to, no matter how long you ask.'

'Aren't you supposed to have a guru to guide you along?'

He pauses a moment to think. 'There's a catch to this guru thing. In the advaita tradition, a guru must be learned in the Vedas and the tradition, the sampradaya. Besides, he must have realized the oneness of Brahman in everything.

'How does a student decide who is fit to be a guru? Go by a guru's version of his worth? By his reputation? I don't know. There's this book, Sankaracharya's *Vivekachudamani*, that tells you how to get a guru. He has to have some qualities: he has to be of good repute, and so on.

'The strange thing is, you can't have a woman for a guru. Sankara says right in the beginning of his book that you're doubly blessed if you're born a man! I personally thought my mother much wiser than my father in some ways … that really got me thinking.

'At first I tried to make excuses for Sankara. That was how it was in his day, the women were drudges and the brahmins were the only ones free to pursue their spiritual interests and so on. Then it struck me that there's no point in trying to explain someone else's answers: it's simpler instead to try to find the answers yourself. Besides, there was no evidence that the old ways worked.

'Then I reread the Mahabharata and found that the women in the story had much more commonsense. Look at Kunti, for instance. She had four gifted sons – six, if you count Madri's two that she brought up – but her life, and theirs, was mostly miserable. So when she had to bless her great-grandson, what did she wish him? Not courage, not brains, not talent, but luck!

'See, there are these stories about the guru-shishya relationship. Would you like to hear the one that taught me the most?'

'Of course,' I tell him, curious.

'It's set in the time of the emperor Raghu – you know, Rama's great-grandfather, the one after whom the Raghuvamsha was named – when a guru called Varatentu had a shishya called Kautsa.

'Kautsa stayed with his guru in his ashram for many years, and the guru taught him everything he thought he could. Then he told the shishya, there's nothing more I can do for you. Go home and set up on your own.

'Kautsa asked Varatentu what he would like by way of dakshina. The guru, being pleased with his shishya's service, replied that the service Kautsa had rendered him all these years was sufficient.

'But Kautsa insisted. The more the guru denied wanting any dakshina, the more the shishya insisted that he take something.

'The guru lost his cool and asked for fourteen crore varahas, gold coins, one crore for every one of the fourteen shastras he taught Kautsa.

'I think the guru asked for so much expecting the shishya to fall at his feet and beg to be let off from paying this mind-boggling sum as dakshina. Instead, Kautsa set off in search of a king capable of giving him the money. He went straight to the court of the most powerful ruler of the time, Raghu.

'When he got to the palace, though, he was taken aback. The palace was bare. Raghu, who made it a practice to wash the feet of visiting brahmins when they entered his palace, was there, waiting with water in an earthen pot to perform the ritual. Not the silver or gold pot that he used customarily.

'It turned out that he had just performed the Viswajit yagna, which involved giving away his possessions to deserving brahmins, and had nothing left. The richest emperor of the day was broke.

'Raghu washed Kautsa's feet and invited him in to a simple meal, and at the end of it, asked, "What can I do for you?"

'Kautsa looked around at the bare halls of the palace and said, "Nothing, Sire. Just meeting you is sufficient good fortune for a poor brahmin like me."

'Raghu didn't accept this. "You have come here from far away to take care of some need," he insisted, "and I will not have it said that a brahmin left Raghu's palace with a need unfulfilled."

'And so Kautsa explained to the emperor that he wanted fourteen crore gold coins as dakshina for his guru. The emperor asked for a few days' time, and prepared to make war on Kubera, the god of wealth.

'When they came awake next morning, the palace compound was covered in gold coins. Kubera, fearing Raghu's might, had delivered even before Raghu set out. "All this is yours," Raghu told Kautsa waving his hand around.

'Kautsa counted out fourteen crore gold coins, and discovered there was plenty left over. He arranged for transport – fourteen crore gold coins would have weighed fourteen hundred tons at ten grams to a coin – and a train of elephants and camels and horses and donkeys left the palace for Varatentu's hermitage in the forest.

'The story doesn't say what Varatentu did with all that gold. Poor man. But Kautsa returned and distributed the excess gold from the palace compound among the populace.

'To my mind, Varatentu was incompetent. He couldn't teach his disciple how to tell when he himself sincerely didn't want something. Besides, he lost his cool under pressure.

'Kautsa was an unfit student. All those years of study taught him nothing. He couldn't admit that his master was being sincere when he said he wanted nothing. The ritual of dakshina was more important to him than the true desire of his teacher. And when the guru asked for something he couldn't possibly deliver without divine help, instead of doing the honest thing and apologizing for insisting on a dakshina, he caused Raghu and Kubera – and his guru, mind you – a whole lot of unnecessary trouble.

'As for Raghu, he didn't bother to look at whether Kautsa's requirement made sense or not. He didn't bother to check with Varatentu about why he wanted this outrageous sum of fourteen crore gold coins. He was prepared to make war with someone not remotely connected with Kautsa just to make sure that his own reputation for generosity didn't suffer. Like he ran a protection racket.

'The only person in the tale who seems to have any sense is Kubera, who gave up the gold without a fight, knowing that if he fought he'd end up losing both the fight and the gold.'

'I know the story,' I tell him, 'but I never thought about it one way or another. It didn't seem worth the effort.'

He laughs. 'It's probably not. But then it started me on all these questions … I resorted to arithmetic and probability to get an idea of things. One in thousands, the scriptures say, actually seeks the truth. One in thousands of those gets it. So that's down to one in several millions. When you look at the numbers, it seems that there can't be more than a few dozen or so people amongst the billion-and-a-quarter population of this country who are fit to be gurus, so it's highly improbable you or I will ever come across one. For all practical purposes, you're on your own.' He smiles. 'Actually, I think the old gurus were just playing safe. If one of them took on a prince as a student and the prince failed to learn anything, they could just talk of the percentages and get away with it.

'About then two things struck me about some schools of Hinduism. One is very sensible, the notion that we're all fundamentally alone. The other, well, it's myopic at best, and not restricted to Hinduism. It's the notion that mankind is the last step of evolution. It seems silly, because we understand so little of nature. Mankind might be wiped out, like the dinosaurs, and be replaced by better – or fitter – beings. So why all this about saving mankind?'

I don't want to go into all that, so I say so, and change the topic. 'What was that you said about prayer? About discovering what you really want?'

He looks at me keenly for a moment. 'Since you insist on changing the topic … When I was younger I used to have these fantasies about beating up people who I thought made me feel small. I started praying for bad things to happen to these people, and then I discovered that I didn't really want those bad things to happen to anyone … Their suffering wouldn't make me grow, would it?

'So then I started thinking about what I was praying for. I found, when I prayed for money, that I didn't really want money I didn't earn, that I didn't deserve in some way. I thought it was cheating, you know, getting money by praying for it.

'Then I started praying for peace. Then I wondered what exactly I meant by peace, and found I didn't know. I still don't know what inner peace is.

'Now I just pray to, well, to try to understand what I really want, what I really am. That's all.'

'Do you tell people these things?'

'If they ask, yes. It's no secret.' He smiles. 'No one ever asks.'

'That bit about gurus … you could get into serious trouble for that. There are enough people around who believe that everything in the Mahabharata really happened. There are hardcore Hindutva people around who'd be willing to lynch you for these views.'

'I know. So what? I'm only asking questions. If you want to explain why I've got the wrong idea about the people in the Kautsa story, do tell.'

'If they get physical, well, I won't try to do the same to them.'

'How can you be sure?'

He shakes his head, smiling. 'I'm not. I won't be until someone tries to beat me up.'

'Then why do you think you won't respond in kind if someone gets violent with you?'

'I know about pain, Bala.' He pauses. 'I've felt sufficient physical pain to know what it is to have a bone or two broken. I also know enough about humiliation to understand what it is to be helpless in the face of violence.'

'How come?'

'The physical pain? I've had a couple of falls, and I got hit by a car once. I spent some time in a hospital after that, doing physiotherapy and so on. As for the other thing, I learnt quite a bit about it when I was young. Boys can be cruel, especially in groups.' Then a wry smile. 'This is where we get to the real questions about the nature of knowledge. I know about pain … it's not the pain itself I feared. I used to fear doing something undignified when it gets bad. Like wetting my pants, or breaking down and howling, something like that. Letting someone else see how weak I really am. Then I understood that it's not something I can help. If I end up dependent on others to wipe my bottom for me, well, so be it. It's like being ashamed of flat feet.'

'But what does that have to do with knowing pain?'

'Fearing it isn't going to help when it does come.'

'You take precautions.'

'Why does the fear remain when I've taken precautions?'

'Doesn't matter,' I tell him. 'You'll cope.'

He smiles. 'I know. But the difficult bit is the thought underlying the fear. It's not the pain that you fear, it's the exposure … that was how it was for me, anyway.'

'I haven't thought about it as you have.'

'It's quite difficult, because the fear of pain is mixed up with the pain itself. You have to accept the pain to separate the two, and that's very difficult. The fear won't go away if you reason with it, or try to blot it out.'

'Why are you so unsure?'

'Because I can't help feeling that reason is also only a tool ... You know that saying, that if you've only got a hammer the world looks like a nail. This is why I sometimes go back to books like the Gita. Large parts of it attack reason, and some of them seem profound.'

'You said that before, about bits of the Gita being profound. What bits?'

'The idea that we have to get past our notions of good and bad, pleasure and pain.

Also, it attacks the idea that what you choose makes a difference. Choose what you like, it says, but what's going to happen will happen. You know, whatever will be will be.'

'That's the old free will thing, isn't it? We talked of it yesterday. One of those things that you can't prove either way.'

'Yes. The funny thing is that it's roughly where you get when you keep asking yourself this simple question: so what?'

'You spend time wondering about all kinds of abstract things, things you can't prove either way, which seems profitless. Why do you mind wondering who might have killed Raju, or who might have wanted to?'

'I don't mind it, but my mind goes in directions I can't control.'

'Indulge me, then,' I tell him. 'Spend some time on Raju.'

'Okay.'

'I met the doctor who did the autopsy on him,' I tell him. 'Raju died of poisoning.'

'Okay.'

'There's no suicide note. The doctor says that Raju had the poison voluntarily: there's no sign that he was forced to take it. That still leaves it open.'

'Accident, murder, or suicide, then. That's not much help.'

'He didn't seem suicidal, and he'd lined up quite a few meetings for the next day, with the lawyer and a few others. You're unlikely to have datura by accident in lethal quantities. If it's not suicide, and not accidental, then … who? Why?'

'I don't know. I don't think he had enemies, not enemies who hated him enough to kill him. If there was no one who wanted to kill him, perhaps someone wanted to get at me by killing him … The process started before I got here.' He smiles. 'And now, since we know that the process could have started before I was arrested, it could have been me, you know.'

'Do you know they're already trying to pin it on you?'

'Who?'

'The news channels. Whoever's behind the complaints that got you here.'

'I don't know about that. I've kept away from the news after I got here. It's quite peaceful without it.'

'You should keep up. Just to know what's happening in your case.'

He smiles. 'You think I'm innocent?'

'Until proven guilty, yes.'

He shakes his head. 'I'm flattered by your concern, but you should really keep an open mind.'

'Yes, I keep an open mind,' I tell him. 'But when I get something that doesn't fit, I try to take it apart and find out why.'

'Ah! The bloodhound.'

'That's an exaggeration, but yes, that's how I work.'

He smiles. 'If you were a bloodhound with yourself, you'd

probably be a different person. Enough of all this about poisons and death. Let's talk about you for a change.'

'Me?' I ask.

'Yes, you.'

'But why?'

'Why not?'

'Because we're here for you.'

'No. You're here for you. You're here because you want to resurrect your career and you hope to do it through me or whatever I'm supposed to have done.' When I'm silent for a moment, he continues, 'No?'

'Of course.'

'You're in trouble then,' he says.

'How so?'

'You used to be single-minded in your pursuit,' he tells me, 'but you've lost that.'

'How do you know?'

'I know, all right. You should find out … If you were half as focused on yourself as you used to be on your investigative stories, you'd be a lot wiser.' He pauses, smiling. 'Though perhaps no happier.'

'How so?'

'You find yourself drinking too much, and distant from your wife and daughter. Your parents are gone, your siblings far away, your friends are drifting away, and now your job is at risk. You might be better employed looking into these matters than my scandals.'

The belly-beast surges up. 'First, what makes you think all this about me? Second, what makes you think I'm not looking into my personal life?'

He looks me in the eye. 'Don't evade, Bala. It doesn't become you.' He pauses. 'I rarely offer advice, but let me make an exception. That wasn't you speaking.'

'What do you mean?'

'Something in you boils over from time to time. You can't hide it.'

The belly-beast is roaring now. 'What the hell are you talking about?' I ask.

'You know, Bala, you know exactly what I'm talking about.'

'I'm not sure I do.'

'Fine. Let me leave you something to think about, then. Some of the things you hold true about yourself are lies. Don't trust yourself, either.' He rises.

'Wait,' I tell him. 'You can't just walk off like that?'

'No?' he asks, and does just that, leaving the warder to escort me out of the hall.

Back in the hotel I go straight to my room. I need a drink now, worse than I've needed one before on this trip. I have a quick one and pour myself another to drink slowly but the second goes down very fast and then I'm on my third but cooling off. Srini calls at one to ask what's happening. 'He refused to talk to me.'

'Who?' Srini asks.

'The Swami. Who else?'

'Have you spoken to any of his devotees? The ones he calls visitors?'

'No.'

'Why not?'

The frustration surfaces. 'Look, Srini, this isn't a TV show where you talk to fifty people and get a lot of opinions and air time, okay? I'm trying to find out whether this guy is a thief or not, and none of his devotees or visitors or whatever is going to say that he might be one. So I'll talk to them last, when I've got everything else, not before.'

'So where have you got with the everything else?'

'Your three original questions. On the embezzlement, we'll

have to have an accountant go through his books, which are with the police, and being examined by their accountants, and which he never hid. On the attempted molestation, he says no, the woman says yes, and he goes to jail, but in the absence of any evidence he probably won't be convicted. On whether he's a godman, he himself says very clearly that he's not, despite anything anyone else says. That's your three questions answered.

'The murder. It could have been anyone, even our man himself, because the poison might have been administered before he was arrested, and there's some evidence that the killer tried it out a few days earlier, misjudged the dosage, and had to do it again. We've no idea who did it. If he didn't do it, it could have been someone with a grudge against the victim, or someone trying to get our man in trouble. There's nothing yet that points to anyone having a grudge against the victim. No big money deals, no land, no sex, no cheating, nothing.

'So, if the Swami's not a bad guy, who's trying to get him in trouble? We don't know, but I'm beginning to suspect it's someone who dislikes his minister pal. Remember, I asked you to find out about Gowda's pet projects?'

'Yes. I've got them. A factory near his constituency. Some people are being displaced. He says they're not getting the compensation they deserve. Fairly big money there.

'Then there's a road coming up. Land acquisition issues. Part of it goes through a sanctuary.

'Otherwise it's the usual stuff. Finance ministry stuff. Nothing outstanding.'

'Anything about his businesses?'

'He says he leaves them to his associates, who are all family, while he's minister. No interference.'

'He's got this shady retired policeman called Sadashiv Uchil doing his security for him. Uchil looks more like a goon than most goons. I saw him go in and out of prison, talking to the Swami. Why's he involved? Why does the Swami want to stay in prison when there are plenty of people willing – no, wanting – to get him out of there on bail? I asked him why he refused the minister's help, and he said that it came with strings attached, and he didn't like that. What could those strings be?'

'Bala, that's for you to figure. I can only give you the data and the contacts I have. But now that your Swami won't speak to you, don't you think it's time you got back here? You can follow the political bits better from here.'

I don't want to tell him that Prakash's refusal to speak to me is conditional. 'Not yet,' I tell him. 'I need to speak to others at the ashram. The Swami's third-in-command, now that the second is dead. Also, we should have the reports from the forensic people in a couple of days. I'll return after that.'

'Okay. But do remember that the story has an expiry date, and that our budgets aren't limitless.'

The heat is on. Srini's changed his tune, from take your time to hurry up. He does that from time to time, depending on what he thinks the other guy needs. Well, I can deal with that. 'Sure,' I tell him. 'But the Swami is still the source for most of our stuff, and I think I can persuade him to open up again.'

'Fine. Go ahead. Keep me in the loop.'

'And find out what you can about Sadashiv Uchil. Retired superintendent, came up through the ranks, roots in this area.'

'Okay. I'll call you tomorrow.'

Outside, it's raining heavily, as it does in these parts at this time of the year. The winds from the sea blow sheets of water at the windows, and in the dark I have no idea what time it is, but my stomach and my watch tell me it's nearing lunchtime.

My third drink is gone. I pour myself another, swallow it quickly, and head down to the restaurant for lunch. In the lift, thinking of my flight from the prison, I stumble into what seems a genuine question: what is so unbearable about life that I have to use a drink to turn away from it?

It persists through lunch, which is at a quiet corner table, and, in view of the booze I've already had, without alcoholic relief. The end of lunch a half hour later brings no relief but instead, a call, from Srini. 'The police have been interrogating people at the ashram. With what they have, they suspect everyone who's been in and around the ashram for a few days before Raju died. They could even suspect you, if the poison's right … they're only saying it's unlikely to have been the usual pesticide thing because Raju would probably have known from the taste.'

'Can you get me transcripts?'

'No. They don't have transcripts, but they have statements in Kannada, which you can read. I've arranged for you to get copies. Talk to the investigating officer, one Inspector Girish Kavoor. He's at Belman police station, and he'll give you whatever you want. He owes someone who owes me … But be careful when you take favours from cops.'

'You don't have to tell me,' I tell him. 'A senior cop gave me that nickname, remember?' Pause. 'Anything on Sadashiv Uchil?'

'He's been accused of all kinds of things during his career, taking bribes, threatening and coaching witnesses, protecting hoodlum pals, harassing enemies of his mentors, interfering with election campaigns, the works. Nothing, but nothing, stuck, so he's got major clout. He came up through the ranks, you know.'

'Yes. Gowda's secretary is my old pal Purshottam Rao.'

'Ah!' Srini says. He knows, but it must have slipped his mind. 'What did he say?'

'The usual slimy stuff. I just ignored him.'

'Sensible … for a change.'

'Yes.' Then I remember Gowda's mistress. Srini should have known about the mistress, if not the specifics of the hotel and so on. 'Why didn't you tell me Gowda's had a string of women?'

'He has? I didn't know.'

'Your sources are drying up, then,' I tell him, with more than a touch of enjoyment.

He senses it, and laughs. 'I take your point. Keep at it. Well, you should be getting on with the inspector. Here's his cellphone number.'

Inspector Kavoor, when I speak to him a few minutes later, is in Mangalore, but will be available, with copies of the transcripts, at his office by five in the evening. Knowing the habits of policemen, I tell him I'll check with him when I'm leaving the hotel. He laughs. 'Don't worry,' he says. 'I expect to be back by four, and I won't be later than five in any case.'

After a brief nap, with a mild headache coming on, with the sole genuine question of the last few years still hammering away at my mind, I leave for Kavoor's office. He's a tall man, a little older than myself, thin to the point of being scrawny, with a large Adam's apple that bobs as he speaks. He doesn't keep me waiting long, just hands over an inch-thick stack of photocopies. 'Any ideas who might have done it?' I ask.

He shakes his head. 'I have nothing at all. Nothing. I am just following procedure, waiting for the results from the lab. Then we might find something to follow.'

I don't see any point in pushing him so I stand up. 'May I come back to you if I have any questions about what's in the statement?'

'Yes,' he says. 'Call me first.'

I can't help liking the man. He's straight and to the point and he doesn't waste time. I shake hands with him and leave for the hotel, and all the way chew on another question I have to answer soon: how do I get to see Prakash tomorrow?

## Chapter Seven

NEXT MORNING AT the prison it turns out Prakash is quite willing to talk. He looks rested and peaceful, and when the warders lead him to his side of the wire mesh he smiles his usual wide smile. 'Did you consider what I told you yesterday?' he begins.

'Yes.'

'And?'

I tell it to him straight. 'Thinking about why my life is falling apart isn't going to help with getting this story straight, and if I don't get this story straight I'm out of a job, which is worse trouble than anything I am in now, and at my age I won't be able to start all over again. So looking at why my life is falling apart will have to wait.'

'Ah! The usual reason. Philosophy earns you nothing.'

'Yes.'

'I won't try to persuade you otherwise,' he says.

'Why ever not?' I ask, taken by surprise.

'I wish I could get a cup of tea,' he says, surprising me even more.

'Let me ask the warder …' I begin.

He cuts me off. 'It doesn't matter. It really doesn't … You asked why I don't try to persuade you otherwise. Well, it's because I know something you don't, and it's something I haven't told anyone else.'

'Why not?'

He grins. 'Because they didn't ask.' The grin fades. 'Now that you ask, I find I'm uncomfortable talking about it, which is why I thought of tea. An old habit that I gave up years ago.'

'So are you going to tell me?'

'Yes. Nothing shameful about it. It's just hard to describe, that's all.'

'Okay. Take your time.'

'It's not a matter of time. I've been thinking about it for more than ten years and a few minutes is unlikely to make a difference ... unless there's a Eureka moment.' He shakes his head and smiles. 'No. No Eureka. So we'll fumble along?'

'Fine by me.'

'I have these spells of quiet,' he says haltingly. This is the first time I've seen him this tentative, and I listen carefully. 'It's hard to describe. It's a feeling of relief, of freedom.' He pauses. 'That's not correct. There's no emotion to it that I can describe. The word that comes closest is lightness. Nothing matters. A long time ago in the US, I saw a sticker that said, "Everything was beautiful and nothing hurt." That's what it's like, except that ... no, I have no words for it.'

'Quiet?'

'Well, like there's no voice inside your head telling you what to do or what to feel ...'

'Just dropped off to sleep, perhaps.'

'No. I was aware of what was happening. There didn't seem to be anything to do about it, though. I was just lying in bed watching. I was thinking, but not in the usual way. No pressure. Just clean thought.'

'What do you mean, clean thought?'

'Two things. First, when we select our premises for any logical process, we do it out of fear. Or out of want. If you look at the world without fear and want, you end up seeing everything very differently. A different set of premises, without the need for action.

'Second, we spend a lot of energy avoiding things we don't like, memories that make us uncomfortable for one reason or another. In that state, there's no such avoidance.'

'All this just lying in bed?'

'Yes ... the first time it happened I was getting over a flu and one night I just slipped into this state and stayed there until my roommate yelled at me and I snapped out of it.'

'And after that?'

'It's happened several times ... no patterns that I can see.'

'Did you try to get back into that state?'

'Of course! That's all I've been doing since. I even tried heroin a couple of times. There was this guy I knew who said the heroin high was beautiful. I told him I didn't want to inject things into myself. He said I could try it without mainlining: he said to take a pinch of the good stuff and rub it on my gums. It would go straight into my bloodstream from there and things would happen.'

'Well, did they?'

'Yes, but nothing as good. With that I gave up the idea of trying out chemicals. Then I went to a psychiatrist, a shrink. I had a couple of sessions with him and discovered that he'd learnt something about diseases of the mind but nothing about well-being. All he wanted to do was to get me functioning in society without too many problems. He wanted me well-adjusted, whatever that means.

'I don't think he even knew what I was talking about because he thought I had some kind of a disorder and wanted me to go through some expensive tests to find out if there was something wrong with my brain. They have this thing called *Diagnostic and Statistical Manual of Mental Disorders* that's a kind of protocol through which you put a person who's, well, not normal. The idea is that you go through this protocol and at the end of it you know what ails the patient. It's not as mechanical as that but it works with a large proportion of people who go to psychiatrists.'

He grins. 'He told me it was probably a dissociative state, but then he got a little confused because my symptoms weren't consistent with anything in the book so he wanted to write a paper about a new disease and I didn't want to help him with that. I think he was a little disappointed I didn't want to cooperate with him in making minor medical history.' He grins again. 'If a real mystic turned up at a mental hospital they'd probably think he was out of his mind. They'd put him through all kinds of tests and conclude he was insane.'

'And then?'

'I went to a psychologist, a clinical psychologist. This one asked me about my childhood and about all kinds of things I wanted, and told me to take notes when I was in that state. I told her I just couldn't control what happened, and she told me to try, and then I gave up.'

'Back to work?'

'I never stopped working. But I took to religion instead. Advaita.'

'Why advaita?'

'Two reasons. First, it acknowledges that we are fundamentally alone, which I've told you. In that dissociative state, that I call a state of grace, you see that there might not be an "out there". It might all be in your head. I thought I was one with the universe. Not different from. Advaita. Still alone, but complete. And so I went straight to Sankaracharya, the founder of advaita, who I discovered probably had no more an idea of how to get to that state than I did, though he did feel a little of that quiet from time to time.'

'Why?'

'There are some bits in his writing that make me think so. About infinity and so on.'

'But what about all the things you didn't like? About castes, and women?'

'Context. When he got into that state, he just assumed that his prayers or meditation caused it ... If B happens after A, you think B happens because of A. Sankara made that mistake.' He grins. 'If I made the same mistake I'd recommend you get a fever and look out for the state when you're recovering.' He pauses. 'Then he made a bigger mistake. Since he'd followed one scriptural instruction and had it work, he assumed that everything in the scriptures – about castes and the treatment of women and so on – was true. You remember what I said about questions and answers and context? This is an example. Buddha was one of the few who figured out that those conditions might not cause the state.'

'Why do you think so?'

'He said you should question everything, including what he himself said,' Prakash says, 'which means he wasn't hung up on rules, and knew you had to find your own way, though others could support you.'

'So do you think there's something worth following in the scriptures?'

'Worth following? There's very little in the Hindu scriptures worth following. But when you put aside the nonsense there are some striking notions in them. For example, there are references to a witness in us. Something that watches the world go by without judging, without the need to correct anything. That comes closest to describing this state I find myself in. And then there are sections, in the Gita, for instance, about going beyond good and bad, beyond rules and so on. But in the same scriptures there's talk of rituals and the hierarchy of gods and so on, which I can't really swallow.

'So the question is, how do you decide if something's worth following? How do you decide what parts of the scriptures work and which don't?

'I didn't have an answer. So I read the scriptures, understood what I could of them, and bumped into another messy area. We call it free will, and you and I have spoken of it before. As I understand from some parts of our scriptures, we have none. Other parts seem to hint that we do. Mostly they say we have limited free will, but don't say anything about the nature of the limits. I personally think we don't have any.'

'Why is that?'

'First, you don't get to choose your parents, the personality you're born with, and most of the events of the first few years of your life. From there on, you're a prisoner of your character. You're making decisions based on values you've been fed, and not of your own free will.

'Second, every particle in the universe follows a set of laws. There's some unpredictability built into those laws, but that's part of the universe itself. So your body is just a set of particles following those laws.

'None of this is proof. There are arguments against this, that laws that apply to elementary particles aren't the ones that apply to large aggregates of particles, but few of those arguments are based on logic. Mostly they seem a defence of the position that there is free will. It's a kind of cornerstone of science, that you have free will, and people defend it when there's nothing to defend.'

'That's very abstract, especially the bit about the laws of the universe,' I tell him.

He nods. 'It is. You see, in that state – that I call the state of grace, just a label – of quiet, I found something else. The little twinge of anxiety that accompanies us always, the little edge of discomfort that never really leaves you, that was gone.

Completely gone. I was what I was then, and I was free. A decision taken in that condition would be an expression of free will.

'So the most important thing for me is the sense of freedom that comes with the quiet. You don't have to do a thing, but if ever you wish to do something you can do it. After going through something like that, everyday life, everyday being, is prison.' He pauses, waves his hand around. 'A prison like this one is nothing to the prison of the mind.'

'Now you're talking like one of those people who explain the scriptures. The fellows who talk of the glory of the Supreme Being and the immanent effulgent eternal self and all that.'

He laughs. 'Yes. They use a lot of adjectives, and they fumble for words, and end up saying things that mean nothing to the rest of us.'

'Do they mean anything to those who say them?'

'You'll have to ask them. But I don't think so.'

'Why not?'

'If you feel that state of grace, you don't want anything. You don't feel the need to help people, or improve the world, or even your own life, or anything. You can shut up without pain. So all those godmen and godwomen, they're fooling themselves or they're fooling you.'

'Does it happen often to you, this state?'

'Not often enough,' he says. 'I wish I could be like that always. But it just comes and goes, and I haven't been able to figure out a pattern … one more reason why I don't think of myself as better than anyone else. I need guidance, too, like anyone else.'

'So where do you go from here?' I ask.

'I don't know. The only useful thing I found was in some of what Buddha said. Help others to help yourself.'

'How was that helpful? I thought you didn't need to help anyone.'

'That's only when you're in that state of grace. Otherwise, when you give, you feel the pinch. Giving away small amounts, insignificant parts of your income, to charities or beggars is easy, and it gives you some satisfaction. Giving more than that, of your time or your money or your heart, shows you what you really fear. I think that's why Buddha said you should do it: to understand and get over your own fears.'

'Fears?'

'Fears. I discovered that my own fears centred around what people would think of me if, for example, I went broke, rather than going broke itself. It was always what people would think of me if I screwed up rather than screwing up itself.

Being foolish, stupid, abject, poor, homeless, and so on are less important than what people will think of me. I haven't got over it, which is why I hang on to the property.'

'What property?'

'The land, the ashram. It's in my name. I'd only willed it to the trust. After I was sent here – to prison – I got my lawyers to transfer it to the trust. So now I've got nothing.'

'Except the people in the ashram. I thought you had a tight little community there.'

'It was like any other. The usual enmities, the little jealousies, everything that you have in any group of people. I stuck to it because I could test Buddha's stuff sitting there listening to people I didn't want to listen to, and I think it worked. I understood what it means to give from the heart, you know. But I never thought the ashram would get someone killed in the end.'

'Two things: did the ashram get Raju killed, and is this its end?'

He replies with two questions. 'Do you really think anyone

disliked Raju enough to kill him for his own sake? And do you think the ashram will ever return to what it was?'

'No, and no,' I tell him. 'That takes us back to the murder. To Gowda, and Uchil, and others who might eventually be responsible for your being in prison and Raju being dead.'

'Have you discovered anything new?'

'Yes. Gowda has a mistress, a whole chain of them, including maybe Smita Sharma, who complained about you. Uchil arranges their meetings. Gowda's wife doesn't like it.'

He smiles. 'So will you go public with that? A minister's sleazy affairs?'

'No. Not yet, anyway.'

He laughs out loud. 'Why is my sleaze sleazier than the minister's? I've been accused of stealing, sheltering fugitives, and attempted rape. The minister's been accused of stealing and worse, his own son is a fugitive, and he's got a mistress. On balance, he must be at least as sleazy as myself.'

'Having a mistress is no crime.'

'The rest of it? Come on, Bala.'

'He's no godman.'

'Did I ever claim to be one? I've never even claimed to be better than anyone else.' He smiles. 'Don't take offence. Never claimed to be better than an alcoholic journalist going downhill flat out.'

'No offence taken. It's just that you expect a politician to do all these things but not someone like you.'

'Are you saying I don't deserve the same leeway that Gowda gets?'

He's got under my skin now. 'Do you think I'd be spending half as much time with Gowda as I do with you? Am I being unfair to you?'

'Do you think any other journalist would do what you're doing?'

'Perhaps not, but I'm doing what I can.'

'I wasn't complaining. I'm doing what I can, too, spending time with you and being as honest as I can.'

I seek to avenge his digs. 'You might spend time with me but you're not really answering my questions, are you?'

He laughs. 'Bala, I've told you what I can. I know nothing about the murder or about who's behind this plot to get me in prison or to malign Krishnappa Gowda, so I can't answer your questions on those subjects. Ask me anything about myself and I'll tell you what I can.'

'Right. So I'm trying to write a story and you're telling me to look into myself.'

The warder interrupts. It seems there's another VIP to see Prakash, this time a lawyer. 'You'll think about it,' he tells me as I rise to leave. 'Some day you'll find yourself unable to run away from these questions … and come tomorrow if you can.'

Back in the hotel my mind turns to the chat with Gokul. I put the bottle firmly away and go down to lunch determined to spend it thinking out what might be happening behind the scenes.

As usual, I fail. I do think about the chat with Gokul, but not about Gowda or the story: instead, I keep going back to what he said about my marriage, that he always wondered what I saw in her.

Why *did* I marry her?

Of course, she was the best-looking woman around. She had learned to use cosmetics subtly, to give her a shine like a model. And I, like many others, was first stunned, then smitten, and eventually, disbelieving when she agreed to marry me.

Back then, I'd almost begun to believe in myself. If I could do this, I'd thought, I could do anything.

Do what?

Win her. Like a prize.

A prize? A trophy wife? No …

The troubles had emerged slowly, afterwards, with the steel beneath the burnished looks, with the ambition, with the intolerance. These receded during the months of her pregnancy, but resurfaced almost immediately after, when diaper-changing and sleepless nights with the baby were required and our budget wouldn't run to an ayah. I'd learnt over the next sleep-deprived few weeks to nap when I could, and to manage my share of caring for Pallavi with the demands of work and everything else.

Not that it was difficult. Pallavi was a sunny baby, and a happy child, when we were alone together, I remember, and my occasional bouts of irritation at her had never lasted very long.

The beast awakes. Disgust at my own stupidity overwhelms me. How could I have been so blind, I wonder. I cringe at the memory of my foolishness, my cowardice, then understand that I've been evading such questions, such memories, of things that make me cringe in shame now, though they seemed acceptable when I did them.

I sit unmoving for a while, watching the rain beat at the glass in the windows, helpless in the grip of the shame and the guilt that rise up in waves. The beast has me by the throat, and won't let go.

Time passes, I have no idea how much, and regret emerges as the beast loosens its grip. When did I lose Pallavi? We'd been so close until just a while ago, and the thought of her present indifference brings up a sour taste in the mouth.

By the time Pallavi was one, we had an ayah for her, an eighteen-year-old girl from Mohini's hometown, uncorrupted by Bangalore's version of urban rapacity. I'd been glad then, to catch up with my sleep, but found Mohini's suspicions harder to deal with than sleep deprivation. Matters came to a head just before lunch one day, when Mohini returned from a shopping expedition to find Pallavi and the eighteen-year-old and me indulging in what she thought was inappropriate activity: playing horsies, myself the horse, Pallavi the rider, and the eighteen-year-old walking behind to make sure the rider didn't fall off, laughing wildly all along. Mohini contained her explosion until we were alone, the gist of it being that my behaviour was unbecoming, that I would only encourage the maid to forget her station in life. The eighteen-year-old was packed off in tears the very next morning. I resumed my nightly vigil, and life continued with hostilities lurking just below the surface, until a lean, stern, middle-aged woman came along to take care of the baby.

I should have cleared it up then, the jealousy. She had no grounds for any such feeling. I should have explained, right away, that there was nothing going on with the poor girl. But Mohini wasn't willing to listen … in a flash, the beast is up. Coward. You were always a coward, and you're not going to change.

Was it cowardice? With spreading shame I realize it probably was. I took the easy way out. I was always the junior partner in the marriage, always beholden to Mohini for agreeing to live with me, always giving way … in a word, I was pussy-whipped. Coarse, but accurate.

There are the usual excuses. There was Pallavi, of course. And there was work, and as long as I was free to work I didn't really worry about what went on at home … so I made these small compromises, one after another, and ended up properly domesticated. It happened slowly, over the years, and, like the frog that died in water that got hotter slowly, ended up completely tied down.

And then, with a shock, I see it: those really are excuses. I used my daughter as an excuse to back down when I should really have stood up for her. For instance, with the eighteen-year-old, who did a much better job than her dour middle-aged successor. I let her down, I let my own child down, and now I'm wondering why she's distant.

Score one to Prakash.

What a fool you are, says the beast. But fighting the beast is no use, so I give up. More cowardice? Slowly the realization comes: it's all in the past, and there's nothing I can do about it. Shame isn't going to help, nor guilt.

What will, then? What could I possibly do that will get rid of that terrible weight from the past?

Did Prakash know this was going to happen when he said the day would come when I wouldn't be able to run from my questions?

The phone rings, shaking me out of the reverie, if such it was. Srini, demanding to know what progress I've made. He's putting on the pressure, but I'm relieved. It's easier facing him than going walkabout in the darker parts of my own mind. 'What's going on, Bala?' he asks. 'Nothing yet?'

'Getting a good story together takes time, Srini, and you know it. It's a matter of depth.'

'At the rate you're going, this one's going to be dead before you get anyplace.'

For the first time in some years – since the drinking got serious – I look at what he's been doing, and find a few lapses. 'Srini, you've done a great deal, but you also missed a couple of crucial points, okay, so now I have to double-check everything. Lay off.'

He does, immediately. 'Not blaming you, Bala,' he says. 'Just want you to do your best.'

'Leaning on me isn't the best way to go, then,' I tell him.

'In any case, given the Swami's attitude, I think he's innocent, but others are using him, and that's not going stop unless we get to the root of it. Gowda himself seems to be trying his best to get the Swami out of prison, and he's surely not gunning for the man. So let me repeat my question: who is Krishnappa Gowda's biggest enemy?'

'Straight answer to that: the chief minister himself.'

'Why?'

'Every chief likes to keep his underlings in place. Gowda might have been getting above himself. Raising a little power centre of his own, independent of the party's.'

'Do you seriously think this is the chief minister trying to keep Gowda under control? The murder?'

'No. It must be something else.'

'Well, then, work on it, please,' I tell him.

'Will do. Let me know what else you need.'

When I hang up I'm drained by that small confrontation with Srini, and, I discover later, the big one with myself. I lie down for a brief rest, and, strangely enough, go to sleep. I sleep deeply, and awake as the last of the sunlight disappears from the sky at the end of a long unusually dry day in the middle of the monsoon season.

## Chapter Eight

The nap has done me good. The chances are that Mohini hasn't got home so I'll be able to catch Pallavi on her own, to figure out a way to ask her how she thinks I let her down. I'm reaching for my phone to call her when the phone rings: it's Gokul. 'Shall I pick you up?' he asks. 'Jayanthi has told me to tell you that you're expected for dinner, and if you stand her up you'll be found in a dark alley with your throat cut. Just passing the message.'

'She can get my throat cut?'

'She can cut your throat herself. She's twice the man I am. So, I'll pick you up. Twenty minutes?'

'Half an hour,' I tell him, thinking of trying Pallavi while waiting for him, and then change my mind. I won't be able to face Gokul if the talk with Pallavi goes badly. Maybe I should think a bit more before speaking to her. As I hang up, I wonder how a man could hesitate so much talking to his own teenage daughter. More cowardice? I don't feel up to thinking about it so I get back to my notes just in case something pops up for me to check with Gokul.

Half an hour later we're in his jeep, heading towards his place, an unpretentious single-storeyed house not far from a beach next to one of the city's best-known temples. 'So, what have you screwed up now?' he asks, as we sit in a traffic jam at a bridge across the Netravati river south of town.

'Nothing,' I tell him. 'I've been discovering I screwed up long ago and I'm paying for it now.'

He grins. 'Don't take it so hard. It happens to all of us. Myself included.'

'What did you screw up?'

'My career. You have to have the right combination of thick skin and thin spine to do well as a policeman.'

'You don't have it?'

'No. So I didn't make it past that barrier that Sadashiv Uchil crossed so easily. Now, with retirement coming up, it makes a difference of a few thousand rupees a month. If I'd made it, the boys could have gone to better schools, and Jayanthi could have had time to do what she likes. But they don't blame me, and so I don't either.'

'Any post-retirement plans?'

'Nothing in particular, but there's plenty to do. Live by the beach. Read. Cook. Listen to music. Go on a pilgrimage. Travel. Learn some yoga. Teach the neighbourhood kids football.' He grins. 'Learn to keep out of Jayanthi's hair.'

'You seem to be looking forward to it.'

'I am. I'm not cut out for this job, but I've had to do it because there was nothing else available. And I think Jayanthi and I have got used to each other over the years.'

'What about the boys?'

We're at the gates of his house. He hops out to push the gate open before replying. 'They're gone. They'll visit when they find the time, until they get married, but we hope not to depend on them for anything. They'll lead their lives as they wish.'

At the steps to Gokul's house comes a vision of Mohini and me, retired, with Pallavi gone, leaving us with nothing to do but snipe endlessly at each other. It would be better to drink myself to death than to live like that.

With the vision comes a decision. No matter what, I won't have a future like that. When I go back to Bangalore, I'll tell her. With the decision comes a moment of fear, but it's a decision that seems to have come from deep within, and I cannot deny it, and the fear passes, relief taking its place, along with the realization that I've never disliked Mohini's bossiness, only my inability to handle it.

Jayanthi and I have known each other since they got married, but the last time I saw her I wasn't alcoholic, and she sees the difference. 'You're not well,' she says. 'Gokul said something about it.'

'Nothing like that,' I tell her. 'I'm fine now.' I do feel much better in the aftermath of the decision to leave Mohini.

'You've lost weight,' she says leading us into the dining room, where Gokul likes to take close friends, 'and you don't look healthy, but at least your face seems bright as it was … Will you have some tea, or start with your liquor?'

I can't help grinning. 'I already had my tea at the hotel.'

She bustles off to get the booze. Jayanthi is teetotal, house-proud, and independent, managing to keep her house spick and span with almost no help. Gokul has never been averse to housework, but she doesn't allow him to do much. Minutes later, she's left a bottle of moderately good whisky, a bucket of ice, a couple of small bottles of soda, a couple of plates of nuts and finger food, and a box of tissues before us. She herself is armed with a small glass of fruit juice that she finishes while bringing me up to date with their sons, both of whom have done well and are working abroad, one in the US, the other in Germany. The elder, the one in the US, has found an American girlfriend but isn't ready to marry yet, she tells me, shrugging, disappointed but unwilling to interfere.

Update done, she's about to disappear into the kitchen when Gokul stops her. 'This fellow might have a lot to say. Don't wait for us. Eat when you want.'

'Of course not,' she says. 'Take your time, just let me know ten minutes before you're ready.'

'What happened to you just now?' he asks. 'You looked miserable when we left the hotel, but now you're more … well, quieter.' He smiles. 'I can tell from the way you hold the glass and the way you drink.'

'I discovered something as we were turning into your gate,' I tell him.

'What?' he asks when I pause for a long moment.

I thought it'd be easy telling him, but it's not. 'You were talking about how you plan to spend your retirement, now that the boys have grown up and flown away.'

'Yes. I remember. Something about travel and cooking and staying out of Jayanthi's way.'

I nod. 'You didn't seem to mind the idea of the two of you spending your retirement together.'

'I don't.'

'That was when it hit me. When Pallavi goes away …'

'What?'

'There'll be just the two of us, Mohini and me, left, tearing at each other. I can't bear the thought.'

'So you're breaking up?'

'Yes.'

'Now?'

The words stick in my throat, but I force them out. 'As soon as I get back.' Then the tricky bit. 'As soon as I can work up the nerve.'

He grimaces, looks at his glass. 'You could consider what matters most to you,' he says after a moment's thought.

'I will,' I reply.

He shakes his head. 'You were saying you might be fired, and you're drinking too much.'

The question behind his thought destroys my newfound relief. 'Yes, and yes. So?'

'I'm worried, that's all.'

'So am I,' I admit. 'At the worst, I'll work with something in the print media. No TV. I'm not cut out for that. I'll survive if I don't drink too much.'

'You said it. That's a big if.'

I dredge a grin out of the darkness spreading afresh in my mind. 'You don't trust me, do you?'

'Not with the booze.'

'We'll see about that when we get there,' I tell him. 'Maybe I can get this story right. Make my way back.'

'I don't think so,' he says. 'You seem to like this Swami guy. Not good for a journo. Besides, I think all swamis are fakes.'

Gokul knows me far too well for me to ignore that. 'I'm sure he's innocent,' I tell him. 'Don't ask me how I got that feeling, but it's there, and I won't ignore it.'

'Okay,' he says. 'But I heard something else. He was questioned earlier today. About meeting the woman who's accused him of trying to rape her. It seems he didn't want to talk about what she told him when they were alone and the recorders were turned off. When they pressed him, he finally agreed. He said she told him she was ashamed because she'd had an affair with someone and afraid her husband would get to know, and if he did there would be unbearable consequences, the children would suffer, and so on.'

'So?'

'She's not married. She got a divorce three years ago. No kids. This is available off the internet.'

'Did you tell him?'

'I wasn't there. I just picked this up. Umm, office gossip.'

'Well, did his interrogators tell him?'

'Apparently they did. He replied that she looked to be in her thirties, and said she was a housewife, and he thought she was married. And he said he was sure she wore a wedding ring.'

'Did she?'

'They're checking. She doesn't wear one in any of the recent photos they've got, or in the TV interviews she gave after she filed her case.'

'Are there any photos at the ashram? Just before the audio recording was turned off?'

'They're looking for that kind of evidence. They have some photos, and they're making sure they're not faked. Also ...'

'Also what?'

'The woman used to be an actress. She never made it big: all she got were a couple of small roles in a TV serial, and then she got married and disappeared. So someone could have persuaded her to trap the Swami. And, finally, there's just one point on which their statements agreed.'

'A few minutes into the meeting, the Swami's assistant, Raju, knocked on the door, and the Swami asked him in. Raju said he'd probably left his phone behind, and could he look for it, and the Swami told him that the meeting was to be interrupted only in an emergency, and, since this wasn't an emergency, the interruption was uncalled-for. Raju left without looking for his phone. He must have retrieved it later. But that might have no bearing on the case because Raju is dead.'

'Right.'

'So it's his word against hers, and you know how the system works.'

I think a moment. 'I told Prakash – the Swami – that I told him that if the case went on he could find himself in prison. He said he was prepared for the consequences. Then he smiled and said, "Shit happens!" Didn't sound like a guilty man.'

'You seem to be close to him. Too close to have an open mind.'

This is the second time Gokul's saying this, and he doesn't repeat himself lightly. One of the things I like about him. I remember my concern for Prakash, and the empty offer to pay for a lawyer for him. It's hard to think of him as a rapist or a thief, and yet … he might be one. 'Possible,' I tell him. 'Now that you've brought it up, I'll make sure I keep it balanced.'

He nods. 'Good. You know as well as I do that it's not useful to have opinions about suspects.'

'Yes.' The conversation is getting too heavy for me. I need to unwind. 'Look, can we talk of something else now? I've had enough of this.'

'I can see that. How about some music?'

Gokul's father had spent a few years learning to sing Hindustani style as a youngster, and had to give up lessons because his parents couldn't afford it. Gokul grew up listening to his father's favourite songs, first on old records then on cassettes, and now on electronic media, and, though he can't hold a note, listens to a lot of Hindustani music, mostly vocal: a taste I share.

But when we listen, we listen, and we don't talk, except to discuss the music itself, or to point out notable bits. Jayanthi joins us soon after – she shares Gokul's tastes in music, at least – and listens as quietly as we do for some time before reminding us that we should eat.

Dinner is quiet, the conversation limited by something close to contentment: there's no need to talk, and we listen to more music. It's the first such evening I've had in a long while. At the door, thanking Jayanthi for dinner while waiting for Gokul to get the jeep going, I wish desperately that Mohini at least liked the kind of music that I do. Remembering that she thinks of music as at best a sort of background, I wish she liked any kind of music, so I could get to know it and like it. And then, with a wrench, I see that there is nothing

– not one single thing – about which we both feel the same with some intensity.

Pallavi?

The greatest surprise of all. I've always assumed that Mohini loved her with the same intensity I do, if not greater. Thinking back, though, I might have been mistaken. I remember times when she treated Pallavi more as a nuisance than a child. Were those just moments of irritation or times when her real feelings came through? I don't know, and I must find out. But another fugitive thought lingers at the edge of my mind, and I can't concentrate.

Gokul is sensitive enough not to try to talk, and we drive in silence to the hotel. At this time of the night, in the rain, there's little traffic, and when the rain comes down we don't see much past the area lit by the headlamps. At the hotel, in the portico, I turn to thank him, too, for listening. 'Any time,' he says, grinning. 'It's the simplest thing to do, listen.' The grin widens. 'It doesn't cost anything either. You should try it someday.' The grin fades. 'There was a time when you used to.'

Back in the room I find it's getting on for midnight, far too late to try to speak to Pallavi, so I check my email and discover that the results of the tests on Raju's body fluids have arrived, with a note confirming that datura is the source of the alkaloids that killed him. I write a brief note to the news editor of the TV channel, telling him what I've learnt from Gokul without naming my source, since it certainly is newsworthy. After that, perhaps out of habit, I turn on the TV to keep tabs on the news channels.

On all channels but ours, Prakash's reputation has been reduced to tatters, news shows including interviews with women visitors who claim to have found him 'creepy', and, though they don't complain that he tried any monkey business with them, hint very generously that he would have if he could. There's more speculation than fact, and I can't help wondering what new angles will emerge once the stuff that Gokul told me leaks out, as I'm sure it will.

I give up after ten minutes and decide to read my notes in bed, hoping they'll send me to sleep. They do, a few minutes afterwards, and without benefit of a nightcap, and as I drift off I wonder how I'll cope with the Chennai heat.

## Chapter Nine

I COME AWAKE at five with the shakes, severe nausea, and a headache worse than any hangover. I get out of bed and throw up, then get myself a large rum with just a splash of water, and then another, and everything settles down. The thought nibbling at the edge of my mind while Gokul was driving me back to the hotel emerges with a sort of thump.

I drink in anger, to hit back at Mohini. What for, I wonder.

It doesn't matter. There's no need for that any longer. Besides, I want to be sober when I talk to Pallavi later today, I think as I lie in bed, the burden of my unforgivable stupidity keeping me awake.

Meanwhile, the press have found a leak, and the questions in my mind last night are answered within three minutes of my turning on the TV before breakfast. The morning news coverage of Prakash's situation now includes the conflicts between statements made by Smita Sharma, the complainant, and Prakash: essentially, what Gokul told me last night. One single channel besides ours ends up saying that we have to find some way to get at what really happened during that hour that Prakash spent alone with Ms Sharma. The rest all imply that Prakash manipulated her into asking the recording to be switched off so he could have his way with her, and since the ashram was completely under his control, she had no way of escape.

To this are added further questions: Did Raju know what happened? Did Prakash kill Raju – or have him killed – to prevent him from backing up Ms Sharma's version? More motive for a shady character?

A strong flicker of revulsion at the way some of the press do their job leaves me shaken up. This, after all, is how I earned my nickname, all those years back. The unrelenting search for truth could be seen as hounding the innocent. I used to tell myself that these 'investigations' were never clearcut, because what mattered was why the digger digs. If the digging is to find out the truth, which is what I think I used to do, and am doing now in Prakash's case, then, well, a certain amount of persistence is justified. If, on the other hand, the idea is to crucify someone for the purpose of gaining readers – or viewers – then it's a different kettle of fish altogether.

Now I don't know, but I'm even more worried about the public hankering for some sort of a crucifixion. Much in the manner of the old Roman circus, though it's reputations being mauled on TV, not gladiators in stadia. It's a taste I don't share. I don't think I ever did.

Srini calls as I finish breakfast. 'I saw your mail from last night,' he says. 'We've got a little more detail than the others. That the police are looking for evidence that Smita Sharma might have misled the Swami by using a wedding ring, which she hasn't worn since her separation from her ex-husband four years ago. Good. But it's still nowhere near done. And we don't know anything about the murder beyond the poison that was used, and that everyone knows …'

'Yes.'

'Bala, get something. You're the only press person that the Swami talks to. Get him to open up.'

'He just refuses. You know he's even turned down a deal for a lawyer, or any other kind of help.'

'Tell him he's self-destructing.'

'I did. He doesn't seem to care.'

'Not care about life in prison? Fourteen years if he behaves?'

'Yes. I told him about the possibility, and … you've read what he said. "Shit happens!"'

'Okay, so push him some more. Today.'

'He's not easy to push. He's like water, that way. He just flows away from where you push.'

'Try. Keep trying. That's all we have, it's big, and we shouldn't waste it.'

'I'm heading to the prison soon. I'll tell him we don't have much more time.'

'Tell him whatever you think will make him open up,' he says. 'Find out what he wants, and we'll give it to him. If it's within reason, of course.'

'Okay.'

Anil, the cabbie, surprises me on the way to the prison. 'You've spent some time with the Swami,' he says.

'Yes,' I tell him.

'The day I first picked you up, you wanted to go to Belman to look for a bar.'

'Yes.'

'Don't misunderstand me, but you seem to be drinking less.'

'Why do you think so?' I ask, intrigued.

'Unless you've been going out to buy liquor on your own, or drinking in bars … I don't know for sure but you don't seem to have such a big headache this morning.'

Yeah? I don't know. 'It must be the clean Mangalore air,' I tell him. If only he knew how I'd begun the day.

He smiles. 'Or it could be the Swami.'

'I doubt it,' I tell him, laughing. 'The man's been a big headache for me ever since I met him.'

'You'll see,' he says.

'All right,' I tell him. 'Let's leave it at that.'

He seems to want to talk, so he changes the topic. 'What did Dr Hegde tell you about the death in the ashram?' he asks.

'Only that the man died of poison,' I reply. 'Datura. It grows everywhere.'

'Nothing to help the Swami?'

'No. Why?'

'I think the Swami is good, and he's helping people,' Anil says. 'No matter what they say on TV, I don't think he's involved in anything bad.'

'Neither do I,' I reply, 'but the Swami isn't defending himself. He refused to get a lawyer. I told him my office would pay, but he didn't want to owe anyone anything.'

'So he has nothing to hide. How can anyone believe that he's involved in stealing and killing?'

'I don't know,' I tell him. 'You've been watching the news. You know the gossip. You know what they're saying, and why they're saying it.'

'I don't understand it. I thought you might know. You have contacts.'

'Not really. They're my boss's contacts.'

He smiles. 'No, sir,' he says. 'I know that you're the only reporter that the Swami meets. There must be something special.'

'Just luck. Timing.'

Our arrival at the prison gates thankfully cuts this conversation short. Again, there's a little crush at the door and I wait outside while a few people trickle out. Among them, tucked away in the middle of a little cloud of thickset men with bushy moustaches, is Sadashiv Uchil. What's he been up to, I wonder as I step up to the warder at his desk inside.

A few minutes later, Prakash and I are face to face. For the first time, I notice that Prakash's demeanour is a little different from what it was before he was arrested. He no longer looks as rested and fresh as he used to. 'Prison life seems to be catching up with you,' I tell him as we sit.

He smiles. 'This morning has been a rough patch. That's all. It'll pass.'

'Does Sadashiv Uchil have anything to do with the rough patch?' I ask. 'I saw him leaving as I entered.'

He shakes his head. 'No …' He thinks for a moment. 'Your rough patches have only to do with you.' Suddenly his brow clears. He smiles the clear smile I've got used to. 'It's passed.'

'What do you mean?'

'Nothing. The rough patch has passed. It came from vanity.'

'Vanity?' I ask, taken aback. 'Your vanity?'

'Yes.'

'You're the least vain person I've seen in a long while.'

'I ran into a spot of my own vanity back there.'

'What kind of vanity?'

'The most dangerous kind. The kind that makes you think you make a difference.'

'You're bullshitting me!' I tell him.

'No, no,' he says, shaking his head. 'I'm serious.'

'What did Uchil tell you?'

'Nothing of importance,' he replies. He smiles. 'Nothing that'll change anything.'

'Is it something about Raju's death?'

'No. Why?'

'It's strange he's come visiting you so soon after the autopsy report on Raju.'

He laughs. 'Strange? If the connection you're trying to make between Gowda and Raju's death really exists, it's natural. The opposite of strange.'

'What connection?'

'That he's involved in Raju's death, and perhaps responsible for it in some way.'

'Isn't he?'

'He didn't tell me,' Prakash replies. 'He's never opened up to me.'

'But what do you think? Is he involved in it? Did he order it? We both know he's capable of it.'

'I don't think about it,' he replies.

'What do you know about datura?'

'Very little, except that it's poisonous. Why?'

'Raju died of it.'

'If that helps us find out who killed him, very good. Otherwise …'

'Smita Sharma, who filed that complaint against you, is one of Gowda's former mistresses … he must have some reason for wanting you in trouble.'

'I can't think of any.'

'Look, you're not helping yourself.'

'I thought we'd agreed I'm having a holiday.'

'Okay, but you do want to get back to your ashram, don't you?'

'Not particularly … look, why don't we talk about you instead?'

'Why?'

'You look as if you've been having, umm, revelations.'

'I have, but that's not relevant to the story.'

'So? Tell me about them anyway.'

That brings up the belly-beast in quick time, and I barely manage to keep my voice level. 'Why are we doing this now?' I ask.

'Is there such a thing as the right time for a revelation?' he asks in return. 'Whatever it is, it's still fresh in your mind.' He pauses, and smiles briefly. 'Is this about your marriage?'

'Yes,' I tell him.

'So what's the trouble?' he asks.

'Look, what's this got to do with the story?'

'Humour me, Bala,' he says. 'For a little while. Answer the question.'

'All right,' I tell him. 'I discovered I've no common ground with my wife. Over the years, as a result of a series of small compromises, I've become henpecked. For the sake of peace in the house I've left my daughter almost entirely to her. I think she's managed to persuade my daughter now that I'm not a good person to trust.' I pause, gathering sarcasm. 'Good enough for you?'

'Yes, Bala, very good,' he replies. 'And you discovered all this after we last met?'

'Yes. Last night. While I was with a friend.'

'And have you decided what to do about all this?'

'Yes. When I go back, I'll tell her. There doesn't seem to be much choice.'

'Ah! I see your point.'

I decide to open up just a little. 'I've always wondered why she married me,' I tell him. 'Even that first time we met, when you asked me about her, I wondered about that, and whether those reasons still stand, and so on.'

'I got that impression,' he says, slowly, 'but that seems incomplete, doesn't it?'

'What do you mean?'

'Have you asked yourself why you wanted to marry her?'

'Of late, I've been asking myself that very thing. All the time. Many times a day.'

He shakes his head. There's a grim look in his eyes I haven't seen before. 'You haven't. You've just been kicking yourself for having done it. You have yet to ask yourself that question without deciding beforehand that it was a mistake and you were a fool to do it. Ask yourself honestly and see what you get.'

'What do you think I'll get?'

'If I tell you, you won't be able to get an honest answer out of yourself. You'll have to see it for yourself. Like last night: you got some real insights into yourself.'

'Okay, so I'll work it out.'

'Just remember that whatever insight you get isn't a conclusion. There's always more to go.'

'Fine … Now can we talk about your case? Your options?'

'Must we? I thought we were all done. I think we're all done anyway.'

Something in his tone takes me aback, and I blink at him in surprise. 'That sounds a bit like a farewell … as if you won't be telling me anything, listening to anything from me.'

He hesitates for a moment. Then, 'Yes, you're right. I think you'll move on by yourself now, without me trying to push you onward.'

'But what about your case? The story I'm supposed to do?'

'What about them?'

'Your case is stalled, and I've got nowhere yet on the story.'

'I don't know about the case, because that's up to the police. The story is yours, so you decide where it is. But ask yourself, what is this really to you? Do you know what matters and what doesn't? If you do, all these things will take care of themselves.'

'What do you mean they'll take care of themselves?'

'Just that. Whatever will be will be.' He smiles. 'I thought we'd been through that before.'

'You can't just drop out in the middle like this!' I'm near panic. Losing contact with him will mean losing my edge, with the story, with Srini, even with the job offer.

'All right,' he says. 'What do you want from me?'

I blurt it out. 'Something to prove you didn't try to rape that woman. The rest of what you've been charged with is insignificant: small amounts of money shifted elsewhere, and the possibility that a fugitive hid in your ashram.'

He shrugs. 'About the woman, your Ms Sharma. As things stand, it comes down to her word against mine, as you had said.'

'Why are you doing this to yourself?' I ask. 'Why are you giving up? I thought you'd have more nerve.'

'Nerve?' he asks, smiling. 'What's that?'

'Exactly!' I tell him. 'You don't even know!'

The smile widens. 'Don't be angry, Bala,' he tells me. 'It's a ghost. Courage is a ghost. Only fear is real.'

'This is urgent, Prakash. You could spend years in here if you don't get to work on your defence.'

'No,' he says. 'Not years. Three months. Ninety days, unless they have more evidence. After that they'll have to let me get out on bail.'

I sit back. He's not totally disinterested in his fate, as he makes out. 'So you're prepared to spend three months here?'

'As long as it takes. I'll be fine. You worry about yourself.' He pauses, then smiles again. 'It's been good chatting with you.'

'Yes. I wish we could keep at it. Not about your case, the other stuff.'

'There's nothing new in what I say. You know, I used to make notes all over the place, about the *Vivekachudamani* and all those other things I used to read and think about. I didn't throw any of that away ... Actually, it was Raju who used to collect all that stuff, and then I got into the habit.

'Anyone who really wants to know what I think is welcome to my notes. Yourself included. Tell Narsimha. Help yourself.'

'Where are your notes?'

He shakes his head. 'I don't know. Probably in my room at the ashram, where Narsimha might be persuaded to hand them to you.' Then, apologetically, 'If the police haven't taken away everything for evidence.'

'I'll check. I should be able to get copies from the police if they've got your papers.'

'Yes. You know people with influence.' A pause. 'One last suggestion, if you're willing to listen.'

'Of course.'

'Your focus might be misplaced,' he says.

One of those riddle-type statements he makes from time to time, I think sourly. 'Possible,' I tell him. 'You could help a bit more if you tell me where I should focus.'

'That's really for you to decide, Bala.' He rises, dismissing me. He does a namaste. 'I wish you the best, always,' he says. 'Be well.'

I, too, stand. 'If that's how you want it …'

'It is.'

'All right, then,' I tell him. 'You too be well. I'll see you around.' But as he turns and leaves with the warder following, I get the distinct feeling I won't see him again.

## Chapter Ten

ON THE WAY back to the hotel I consider my options. They are few, and uniformly discouraging.

I can hang around here for some time, try to get Prakash talking again, and explore other avenues, perhaps with Gokul's help. I can go back to base, do my research from there, and wait for things to happen, which will take time. I can quit, and take up the print media job, and try to keep going on this story. If they won't let me work on the story, well, I'll …

That clears up what I intend to do. I'll work on this story, on my own, if need be, with whatever help Gokul can give me without risking his job. Now I'm struck by an overwhelming feeling that there's something to be completed before I give up. And yes, I've been focusing on the wrong thing. I've been focusing on getting Prakash out of prison, where he's perfectly happy. I should be looking for the real crime here.

Raju's murder is at the centre of it all, but I don't know how. Catch the killer and it'll all fall into place. Perhaps not the person who administered the poison: I'll have to find out who arranged it.

I need to talk to Gokul and Srini.

Pallavi. I'll speak to her towards evening, before Mohini gets back. Why couldn't I have done this before? Talk to my only child alone?

Srini first. 'Are you sure you didn't piss him off in some way?' is his first question when I tell him that there won't be any more jailhouse chats with Prakash.

'Yes. The parting was peaceful.'

'But you said he's always like that. Peaceful.'

'Well, I don't think I pissed him off. But I did see that thug leaving the jail as I entered.'

'Which thug?'

'Sadashiv Uchil.'

'You think your pal's under threat? From this guy Sadashiv?'

'He could well be. We need to find out who killed Raju, and why. I'll stay here for a couple of days, following up on the murder – I'll need your help with access to the interrogations – and see if I can talk to Prakash again, just in case he's changed his mind.'

'You can bring copies of the papers here. Whatever material you want, I'll have delivered here, so you can come back as soon as you check with your pal Prakash.'

'Fine. In that case, if Prakash refuses to meet me, I should be back home the day after tomorrow.'

'Right … Bala, how's the booze going?'

'It's still going down well, but in smaller quantities. I don't know why, but I've been drinking less after I got here.'

'Keep that up when you get back.' He hangs up.

Gokul is on his way home for a late lunch when I call him. 'You were right,' I tell him. 'I was looking out for Prakash, not the truth.'

'It happens to all of us. Now that you know, I suppose you'll dig in the right places.'

'I hope so … but there's a little problem.'

'What?'

'Prakash won't speak to me.'

'Did you quarrel?'

'No. This morning I saw Sadashiv Uchil walk out of the prison just before I went in. Then Prakash said we won't be having any more of these jailhouse chats.'

'Look, I can't make him see you.'

'No. I wouldn't like to see him under duress, either. But that leaves me without a reason to stay here.'

'When are you going back?' he asks.

'Perhaps the day after tomorrow.'

'So I'll pick you up today. Another social evening?'

'I don't know.'

'Don't hide,' Gokul says. 'You know what, bastard? You might soon be unemployed, broke, divorced, alienated from your child, and still a boozehound, but you won't get me off your back.'

The belly-beast rises, hot and strong, but Gokul's directness has speared it through the heart, and I'm left drained of feeling and words for a moment. Then I feel like weeping. And then, I manage, a little hoarsely, to ask, 'Is it all right if I'm a little late?'

'Yes. Call me whenever you like.'

Pallavi gets home at half past four. She takes half an hour after that to wash and change and eat and I don't want to disturb her then, so I'll call her at maybe a quarter past five, when she's settling down to her homework before spending an hour – limited strictly by Mohini – watching TV.

It's only half past noon now, and a quarter past five seems an eternity away. Somewhere I find some resolve I didn't know I had, and decide to spend that eternity without a drink. I need to be razor-sharp when I speak to her. If she asks me whether I've had a drink or two I want to tell her, without lying, that I haven't, that I stayed sober for her.

So I will. Stay sober, that is. Shakes or no shakes, fever or no fever.

Anil is waiting downstairs. I call him to the lobby, and, when he arrives, ask him where I can find a good restaurant where you don't get booze. He recommends a place in the heart of town, not far from the railway station, and we go there. It turns out to be a Punjabi restaurant trying to be ethnic cute, with greeters in turbans and lungis, and loud Punjabi music. It's full, though, and the air is full of the mixed aroma of spices and milk sweets. I'm surprised for a moment that my sense of smell has survived all the booze, and, a moment later, even more surprised that I haven't noticed these smells all these years.

The lunch, however corny the ambience may be, is tasty, and the servings generous. I plough my way through about half of what they place on the table before giving up, and leave without a dessert. My watch tells me that it's only half past one, with over three hours to go. I didn't feel this jumpy even when I was waiting for the next time I'd see Mohini back in the days before we got married.

I don't want to spread my impatience around so I tell Anil to drop me off at the hotel, and, after he leaves me at the entrance, decide to take a walk around. I get caught in a brief squall of rain a kilometre away from the hotel and rush back sopping wet but happy to have something to occupy the hours until I can speak to Pallavi.

When at last I call her, she picks up the phone at the first ring. 'How was the day?' I ask.

'What do you really want to ask, Dad?' she asks in return. 'I've got a lot of homework to do before I can relax.'

Did I desert you, I want to ask, did I leave you at the mercy of your mother's whims? What do you hold against me most, I want to ask, and what can I do to make up? But I can't find the words for any of it. 'Nothing,' I tell her, faintly, 'Nothing. I just wanted to talk to you, to hear you, that's all. I didn't want to disturb you.'

'You sound different,' she says. 'Worried. Are you?'

'I am.'

'Dad, are they going to fire you from your job?'

'Most likely yes,' I tell her, trying to be as honest as she is.

'But then you don't like your job much, do you?'

How did this girl get to know so much, I wonder, and why didn't I ask myself this years ago, realizing with a rush that I don't like my job at all. I hate it. I've hated it for years now, and myself besides for not leaving it. The rest follows automatically. 'I'm going to quit soon anyway so it doesn't matter.'

'What will you do, Dad?'

'Take a break, maybe ...' The next bit is hard to say, but I manage it. 'Spend some time with you, maybe. Get to know you better.'

'I don't believe in fairy tales any more, Dad,' she says.

'No, really. We'll go off somewhere. Vacation.'

'You'll either be drunk all the time or something'll happen and you'll be off chasing it.'

'Do you think I'm drunk now?'

'Umm ... no. How come?' A pause. Then, quietly, 'Dad, are you in trouble?'

'I stayed sober to talk to you,' I tell her. 'And yes, I am in trouble. With the job, which you already know.'

'Will you get another job?'

That's one I can answer quite easily. 'Yes. But not in Bangalore.'

'So what are you going to do?'

'We'll see when I get back.'

'When are you coming back?'

'Perhaps the day after tomorrow. Why?'

'Umm ... nothing.'

'Fine,' I tell her. 'So I'll see you soon. Maybe we can talk at home.'

'Yeah. Dad, can I have an iPhone?'

I begin to give her my usual answer – ask Mom – and change my mind. An iPhone is too damn expensive a toy for a teenager who should be concentrating on her forthcoming exams. 'Not now,' I tell her. 'Maybe later.'

'Okay,' she says.

She doesn't seem particularly put out, so I ask, 'How come you're taking this so coolly?'

'I asked Mom,' she says. 'Mom said no, so I didn't expect you to say yes.'

After I hang up I realize that this is the best conversation I've had with Pallavi this year.

Score two to Prakash. Shame.

I haven't spoken of it to anyone. Not one person. It shows me in a light that forces questions about who I am, questions I'm not prepared to face.

Well, if I want to make things right with Pallavi, I'd better face them now. Maybe Gokul ... Gokul will listen. Gokul won't judge. So I call him, and discover that he can be free in an hour. He hangs up after promising to pick me up at seven.

I close my eyes and sit back and try to remember the details. It's easy to remember, but hard not to cringe at the memory.

Imagine this. You're a drunk. You have a friend who became a drunk before you did, and your wife suspects led you into more drunkenness, if he didn't start you on drunkenness in the first place. Your wife can't stand him, and you never invite him home. In all fairness, you don't like him much either because when he gets drunk he keeps talking nonsense that stopped being funny about a decade ago, but you put up with it because you have plenty of memories of him from the good old days when you were young and irresponsible. In even more fairness, you stick with him partly because your wife wants you to shed him.

One day he meets your daughter out shopping. She's with a friend. The three of them, your old friend, your daughter, and her friend, are all in a lift. There's a tiny little glitch with the electricity supply, and the lift is stuck between floors for about a minute, or a little more, before the electricity is restored, before the generators get going.

In that brief interval, a battery-operated emergency lamp is supposed to provide people in the lift illumination. The battery, for some reason, is down, and the lamp only gives out a ghostly nebulous glow in which everything is reduced to shadows.

Your daughter's friend, being mildly claustrophobic, begins to panic. Your friend, the drunk, who is drunk at the time – your daughter, who, thanks to your own efforts, has a trained nose, can smell the whisky off him from many feet away – attempts to comfort the panicking teenager and puts an arm around her shoulders.

This is how it started. The drunk is, of course me, and the drunk friend a college-mate called GK. Pallavi's mildly claustrophobic friend is a girl, Sumitra, nearly a year older, but in the same class at school.

From here on, their narratives diverged. There are three versions of what happened in that lift when the lights went out. Pallavi's friend Sumitra, said that my friend, GK, tried to kiss her, and patted her bottom as well. GK, admitting that he had breakfasted on several large whiskies, and was drunk enough at a quarter to noon to be a little unsteady on his feet, swore that he was only trying to calm Sumitra down, and, what with the darkness and booze, might have misjudged distances. Pallavi said throughout that it was so dark and things happened so fast that she didn't know quite what happened.

From here on, the narratives merged. Sumitra shrieked,

the lights came back on, and the lift resumed its stately upward journey. Sumitra and Pallavi cowered in one corner of the lift, while GK, taken aback at the shriek and the return of the light, staggered backwards into the opposite corner.

When the lift doors opened, the girls fled, without completing their shopping, to Sumitra's home, whence Pallavi returned to her own home after lunch, and from there called Mohini to narrate the events – Sumitra's version and her own – of the morning to her. Mohini, reacting in outrage, returned home immediately, after calling me and telling me to do the same.

We met at home, a little after three, in a cloud of recriminations built around Mohini's firm and repeated assertion that none of this would have happened if I'd dropped GK when she'd told me to some years ago. I called GK, who arrived as fast as he could, still drunk, and narrated his version of events. By about five in the evening, we all convened at Sumitra's house, where her parents were now up to date.

The courtesies were starkly absent at the meeting. No tea or coffee, no snacks, just a cold and hostile gathering around a coffee table. Sumitra, who had earlier been questioned by her mother alone, admitted to being a little unsure that GK had in fact tried to kiss her, or feel her up. She didn't like the man, she said, because he leered at her. He looked kind of lecherous, and smelt of booze, a smell she didn't like.

Mohini intervened a couple of times to say that Sumitra should just go ahead and tell everyone what happened, that there was nothing to fear, but Sumitra remained unsure. Mohini turned to Pallavi, then, and told her the same thing, that she should come clean without worrying about consequences, but Pallavi, too, stuck to her story: she didn't see anything untoward, but probably wouldn't have seen it anyway in the gloom.

In his turn, GK said he probably did smell of booze, he was just smiling and didn't know his smile was a leer, that he had indeed leaned close to Sumitra – for which he apologized profusely – and that he hadn't been too steady on his feet. He said that his hand had indeed brushed Sumitra at what he thought was waist height, but that was also an accident, that he was only trying to calm her down.

He had no history of misbehaviour, and had in fact confessed to me a few years previously of 'whisky droop', his term for erectile dysfunction. As for the leering, well, he leered at everyone, even at me. I tended, on the whole, to think that he really had made a mistake in the dark, but couldn't quite eliminate the possibility that he did it on purpose. I told Sumitra's parents exactly that, and left it to them to decide what follow-up was required. They hemmed and hawed, and, thinking of the consequences of filing a police complaint against GK and probably having their name dragged through the mud in a court of law, decided against legal action, much to GK's relief.

And much to Mohini's disappointment, which she expressed in controlled terms to Sumitra's parents.

By the time we left Sumitra's house it was getting on for ten, and I was itching for a drink. In any case, as far as I was concerned, the matter had ended there, with Sumitra's parents deciding not to file a complaint against GK. But not, apparently, for Mohini. In the car, on the way home, with Pallavi in the rear seat, she repeated what she had told me many times before we sat with Sumitra's parents, that none of this would have happened if I'd eliminated GK from my list of friends when she'd first told me to. Back home, even before packing Pallavi off to bed, she exploded into fullscale war. 'What would you have done to that bum if it had been Pallavi in Sumitra's place?'

'I might have filed a complaint against him,' I replied. 'I'd certainly have tried to find out more.'

'You'd give a drunken bum's word as much weight as your own daughter's!' she screamed. 'Maybe all you drunks are the same. Maybe it makes no difference any longer whether you're dealing with your own daughter or someone else's.'

I was about to start on Sumitra not being a hundred per cent sure, and so on, but saw that Mohini was past listening. I really didn't know what to do, so I left. I spent a good hour walking around the neighbourhood before returning home to find Pallavi gone to bed and Mohini stalking up and down the living room waiting for me to expend the rest of her anger and frustration. I poured myself a drink – I admit it was more to spite Mohini than anything else – and sat down to drink it, while Mohini raged on. When I didn't react to what she said – which was mostly along the lines of what she'd been saying before – she grabbed the glass out of my hand and threw the contents in my face.

I raised my hand to strike her, but couldn't bring myself to do it. Instead, I wiped my face, told her I wasn't going to listen to any more of this stuff, and went to bed, lying sleepless through the night. She came along a couple of hours later, and lay on her part of the bed, back to me. She spent most of the rest of the night crying, and I listened, without trying to console her.

There was, of course, no question of making love, or having sex. By then we were mostly off it. We did it rarely, joylessly, and as quickly as possible. After that night, we stopped altogether. That was the beginning of the war, the point at which I realized that things between us were never going to be all right again.

The bitter taste of regret fills my mouth as I consider what might have led Mohini to lash out at me as she did. The taste deepens as I consider also that I abdicated my position as Pallavi's father that day, and did it to hit out at Mohini.

Also ... was that when I started drinking to spite Mohini?

Gokul arrives on time, calling me from the parking lot below, and I join him. 'What's the matter?' he asks, putting the jeep in gear. 'You look as if you've been beating yourself up.'

'I spoke to Pallavi,' I tell him. 'That cleared up a lot of doubts.'

'Like what?'

'Like I'm going to quit my present job anyway, and split with Mohini, but mostly that I've been stupid. Or blind.'

Gokul grins. 'Humbles you, doesn't it?' he says. 'You need to go through this regularly. Helps you tell what matters from what doesn't.'

'Yes, and yes.'

By now we're in traffic and he has to concentrate on his driving so I shut up until we draw up at the gate of his house. Inside, Gokul tells Jayanthi, 'There's something fishy going on here. This man hasn't had a drink today.'

'Really?' Jayanthi smiles at me.

'Really,' I tell her.

'Why?' she asks.

'I wanted to find out whether I could talk to my daughter without having a drink beforehand.'

'Was it useful?'

'Yes. She put me in my place.'

She laughs. 'That's what children do best. The boys do it to us all the time.'

'I can see that.'

She leaves Gokul and me alone after making sure we're supplied with enough to eat and drink. 'Out with it,' Gokul tells me after she leaves.

'There was this thing last year …' I begin, then falter. 'A friend of Pallavi's, a little older than her, accused a friend of mine, who's also an alcoholic, of feeling her up in a lift when the power went off for a minute.' I tell him the rest of it in dribbles, using a large rum-and-coke-and-soda to lubricate my throat, which is suddenly dry.

'Follow your gut,' he tells me. 'You've been talking to people for years. You must have acquired a fairly accurate sense of who's lying and who's not.' He grins. 'Like a policeman.'

'I think I did follow my instincts, but I left it to Sumitra's parents to decide whether to follow up … I think they felt the same. I just wondered why Mohini got after GK so badly.'

Gokul takes a sip before answering. 'How do you know she was really going for GK?'

It's the same damn thing all over again. I've been so stuck in Mohini's sustained detestation of GK that it never occurred to me that she was hitting at me through GK. Only now does it sink in that it's like that incident with the eighteen-year-old maid, that she was actually getting at me through the maid.

I toss off the rum in my glass and put it down. 'Enough,' I tell Gokul. 'I've had enough for the night. You go ahead, though.'

He shakes his head. 'I'm trying to cut it down. I'd like to stay fit after I retire. That's what I'm trying anyway … You look like you got hit by a thought. Not very different from being punched in the face, is it?'

I grin at that. 'Yes.' Then, 'I might shift to Chennai after this.'

'Why? The new job?'

'Yes. A new magazine. Print and internet only. No TV.'

'Back to square one. Like you were all those years back when you started up with Srini.'

'Yes.'

'There's no going back. This won't be the same.'

'I know.'

'And it won't work if you don't lay off the booze. Do they know about it?'

'Yes, they do, and I think I can handle it.'

He looks at my empty glass. 'Go for it, then … and Pallavi?'

'I have some fences to mend with her. I'll start on it when I get home. Probably the day after tomorrow.'

'Don't hurry. It's not all your fault.'

After a quiet dinner he drops me off at the hotel. 'When do we meet again?' he asks.

'I have unfinished business here,' I tell him.

'Raju?'

'Yes. There's a whole lot more here than we can see.'

'There is. Just remember what I told you about Sadashiv Uchil.'

'I will … And Gokul, thanks for everything.'

'Wouldn't you do the same for me?' he asks, grinning.

'Well, yes … I wouldn't take you home, though.'

'It's the thought that counts … look, take care of Pallavi, okay, and go slowly and carefully.'

'I will.'

In the room I prepare to go to bed wondering how I'm going to face Mohini. A thought intrudes then, perhaps laden with hope, that she, too, will be relieved to see the last of me, and on that pleasant note I drop off to sleep.

## Chapter Eleven

I CAN'T SLEEP. Soon after midnight, I come awake with the shakes and nausea, the same as yesterday. I can feel my heart hammering inside my chest like it's going to burst. I've never felt like this before, and wonder if I'm having a heart attack.

Then the penny drops. Withdrawal. I've read about it. GK told me about it.

I remember the treatment for it from a conversation with GK: lorazepam. I go down to reception, discover that there's a large 24-hour drugstore a few kilometres away, and call a cab to go there. At the drugstore, the helpful assistant tells me that he can't sell the lorazepam in any quantity without a prescription. I remember more from that conversation. I tell him I'm from Bangalore, an alcoholic, have been prescribed it by a psychiatrist treating me, and forgotten my supplies at home, one two-milligram tablet every eight hours, so just two tablets will see me through to evening, when I will see a doctor. He sees my unsteady hands and sweaty face and relents, giving me just two tablets, brand name Ativan. It doesn't matter if it makes me drowsy because I won't be driving anywhere.

I don't sleep. Instead, after a deliberately large breakfast, I start the working day with the usual visit to the prison, to find instructions that Prakash doesn't want to see any visitors. Enough, I decide, and call Srini. 'I can't see the Swami. He's not seeing visitors.'

'Then you'd better get back here.'

'Only when I get copies of whatever the police have about Raju's murder.'

'Okay. I'll make a few calls.'

'Copies of transcripts of interrogations, forensic reports, the FIR itself, and of any papers that the police might have collected from the ashram.'

'Yes. I'll take care of that.'

Afterwards I head for the ashram, to talk to Narsimha. Not a single visitor waits in the area outside the hall where Prakash used to meet people before his arrest, but a few white-clothed men hang around, chatting. Inside, it appears that more than half the residents of the lodge behind the house are still around, as are all the volunteers: everyone hopes to see Prakash out of jail and back in the ashram soon, though there's no reason for believing that anything of the kind will happen.

Narsimha is enjoying himself. As one of the acolytes leads me to him, he emerges from inside leading a young man in black pants and a pale blue shirt, carrying a heavy bag. Turns out he's from the washing machine repair service: Narsimha has apparently decided to junk the old machine and get a new one. The guy from the washing machine service tells him the new machine will be delivered in a couple of weeks' time.

They have something to discuss, so Narsimha gets someone to lead me to a small office in the lodge to wait. One of the old ladies who served lunch the first time I ate looks in, recognizes me, and smiles. 'Where's Narsimha?' she asks. She's in her mid sixties, greying, thin, and simply dressed. I vaguely remember someone calling her Kamalamma.

'I don't know,' I tell her, 'but he'll be here soon.'

She shakes her head, looking angry and upset. 'He interferes in everything. I came to tell him that I want to leave. I'll go back to my son's house.'

'Why?' I ask.

'He pokes his nose everywhere ... now that Swami is away and Raju is gone. And he likes to show off.'

'And what does he like to show off?' I ask.

'He had a phone that he showed everyone.' Her laughter is a cackle. 'Then he dropped it in boiling rasam and spoiled it. He got this new gold watch. He likes to pretend to be a big man.' When I don't react, she goes on. 'Do you know when Swami will be back?'

'No,' I tell her. 'I couldn't meet him today, and he didn't say anything about it yesterday.'

'Is he all right?'

'He seemed happy. He told me it was like a holiday for him: no visitors, no work.'

Narsimha walks in. 'Come back in ten minutes,' he tells the lady. He turns to me as he sits behind the desk. 'What can I do for you?' he asks me.

'Prakash said I should ask you about some books and papers in his room.'

'The police have taken quite a lot of things from that room,' he tells me, steepling his fingers. 'They told me not to take anything without asking them.'

He's got a gold watch on his wrist, all right: it looks like a Rolex. Then I see the sweep second hand ... hey, that is a Rolex. Where would Narsimha get something like that? 'That's all right,' I tell him. 'I don't need the papers, just copies. I'll take them at the nearest photocopy shop.'

He makes his background clear. 'See,' he says, 'It's not so easy. What if there are papers of financial importance? What if there is something about ashram matters? Swamiji was sometimes a little careless with these things. The papers have to be inspected before they go out of the ashram. Also, I cannot let an outsider take the papers. Someone from here must come with you when you take them.'

'All right,' I tell him. 'If you could arrange to have the papers checked, and send someone out with me ...'

'That will take time,' he replies. 'Someone responsible must check the papers. Then, people here have been assigned duties. It's not so easy finding someone who can come out of the ashram with you for a few hours.'

'All right,' I tell him. 'So when can you have everything checked?'

'You come after ten days. I think I will have to check the papers myself, and I have a lot of things to do now.'

'But I'm leaving tomorrow.'

'You leave your address here. I will have the papers copied and sent to you.'

It's clear he has no intention of doing any such thing. I have a last card up my sleeve. 'Perhaps you can speak to Deputy Superintendent Gokul Rao. He's a friend.'

It works. 'All right,' he says grudgingly. 'I'm busy now. Can you come at three in the afternoon?'

'Look, why don't we finish it off now?' I ask. 'There's power now. We don't know if there'll be power at three, and if there isn't we won't get the photocopies done ... you know how it is. I can promise you I won't use any financial information in those papers. In any case, the police would have taken anything that held the faintest promise of anything about financial misconduct.'

He agrees, after a little more dithering, and sends a youngster out to Prakash's room with me. I look around, and find a couple of notebooks full of Prakash's writing, and a copy of the *Vivekachudamani* and a collection of Upanishads lying around. They make a three-inch stack on the desk. I hand them to Narsimha, who leafs through the papers without looking at their contents, as if taking stock.

Laxman, the man who found Raju unwell, knocks and

squeezes himself into the little room. He smiles when he sees me. Narsimha looks up from the papers and asks him, 'What is it?'

'Kamalamma has a pain in her leg. She can't clean the kitchen today, so I told her to rest.'

Narsimha interrupts him in a high, sharp voice. 'You don't have the authority to give people time off. You should have asked her to see me first.' Laxman doesn't respond, but I can see he doesn't like being scolded in my presence.

'Why don't you give Laxman the papers?' I ask. 'I'll take him out, and he can copy the papers for me.'

Narsimha makes sour a face but Laxman speaks up. 'Yes,' he says. 'I've nothing else to do.'

Narsimha finds himself unable to refuse. He tells Laxman to be careful while he gets the books and notes photocopied, and not to let them – or me – out of his sight, and Laxman agrees. Anil finds us a shop in Belman with a shabby old photocopier, run by a young woman who seems to pay equal attention to her cellphone as she does to us. When we finally explain to her what we want, she tells us to come back in three hours because she's in the middle of a rush job.

I look inquiringly at Laxman, who seems a great deal less rigid than Narsimha. 'All right,' he says. 'We'll come back in three hours.' He looks at his watch. 'That's half past three o'clock.'

The girl, who's speaking into her cellphone again, takes her mind off the call to nod at us, and we're off. At the cab, I ask Laxman, 'Shall we go have lunch somewhere?' It's nearly half past noon and I want to talk to this guy about what goes on in the ashram. He might give me a worm's eye view of it.

He hesitates. 'I should be going back,' he says.

'I can drop you off,' I tell him, 'but what will you tell Narsimha? That you left the papers with a girl who's more interested in her cellphone than her job?'

He sees the point, and, though his native honesty urges him to go back, accepts it. 'What would you like to eat?' I ask, assuming that he finds the food at the ashram wholesome but uninspiring.

He shakes his head. 'Nothing,' he says. 'No preference.'

'All right,' I tell him. 'What do you eat at home?'

It turns out he's from Eluru, in neighbouring Andhra, where the food they eat would set an outsider's mouth on fire. I don't know of a single restaurant in this area where you get anything close to what this young man must be used to so we go to a vegetarian Andhra-style restaurant where they serve watered-down versions of what he likes. 'Are you sure you want to eat here?' he asks when he sees the sign.

'Of course,' I reply.

'But they don't serve liquor here.'

'I noticed.'

'But …' His voice trails off.

'I don't drink all the time,' I tell him.

'But everyone says you're a drunkard.'

That pinches me more than it should. 'I am,' I tell him, 'but I've been drinking less than before since I came here.'

'Because of Swami?' he asks eagerly.

'I don't know. But let's go in anyway.'

Over the meal he opens up. He's been with Prakash for eight months, having given up a job with a call centre. His plans depend largely on Prakash's fate: he says emphatically that with Prakash gone he has no reason to continue in the ashram, and will return to his job in Hyderabad, which his former employers have kept open for him.

What difference does Prakash make, I ask him, and he replies at length, with some confusion. It seems Prakash's presence makes the place come alive, and yet go quiet. Of course, he's the provider, but even so … and then, out pops something useful. Raju took care of Prakash. Narsimha only wants to rule. He didn't dare open up in Prakash's presence, or Raju's, but with both of them gone he's become a petty tyrant who nitpicks endlessly without really doing anything. In fact, he's told everyone at the ashram that they should cooperate with the police, and answer all questions truthfully, but not to volunteer any information. 'He just likes to think he's a big man.'

'What will you do if Prakash goes to jail?' I ask.

'I think he is a good man,' Laxman replies. 'I don't think he would do any of those things that they say. But if he did, he should go to jail ... If he goes to jail, I will go back to Hyderabad. But I don't think he will.'

'So you'll go back to the call centre in Hyderabad?' I ask.

'Yes ... I will find some serious NGO working for children, spend my spare time helping out. That much I must do.'

Very worthy. 'What about marriage and so on?'

He smiles sunnily. 'No hurry. My parents will take care of it. I'm sure they can find me a girl from somewhere near Eluru.'

'Did you ever talk of these things to Prakash?'

'Yes,' he says. 'Even last week. He told me I should go back to Hyderabad whenever I feel like it.'

'How did you hear of him?'

'From Rajuji. Rajuji used to do voluntary work before he came here. He is a distant relative.'

'Aren't you upset at his death?'

'Of course. But death comes for all of us.'

'Don't you want the killer found?'

He shakes his head. 'Whatever is to happen to you will happen. Thinking you can change it is a mistake ... that's what Swami says.'

'I know. But do you really believe that?'

He gives his head another shake. 'No … I don't know. Yes, I do want the killer found and punished. Rajuji was a good man.'

'Have you talked to the police about it?'

'Yes. They came and asked us all questions. Over and over, the same questions. Then they took our signatures on some statements. They took away a lot of papers and other material, and they sealed Rajuji's room, and Swami's. But they've not come back to tell anyone what they found.' His voice trails off. It sounds as if he started to tell me something but decided not to.

'What haven't you told the police?'

'Well, nothing … nothing important, anyway.'

'Would you like to tell me?'

'I heard you met Swami a few times in the jail.'

'Yes.'

'What did you talk about?'

'All kinds of things. Books. His notes. Beliefs. Raju's death. The woman who's accused him of trying to molest her …'

'He didn't talk to anyone else, which means he trusted you.'

'Yes. In fact, he told me to ask Narsimha for his papers.'

'He did?'

'Yes. I have a recording if you want to hear it.'

'No, no, nothing like that …' He seems to consider what I've told him. 'There was this copy of the Gita in which Swami had made notes, that Rajuji kept. I borrowed it from him the day before he died. That and some other papers … I kept them. I haven't told anyone about them.'

'Would you mind giving me copies of those?'

'Why copies?' he asks. 'I'll give you the papers and the book. When we go back to the ashram, after we get the copies.'

'Are you sure? I don't want to deprive you of anything useful.'

He smiles. 'I don't understand much of it. See, when Swami explains, you see it, you understand it. Sometimes when you think of the same thing afterwards, you don't understand it, sometimes you do. So just keeping the books and papers is useless. You keep them. You give them back to me when Swami returns.'

'Do you think he'll return?'

'I hope so ... What do you think?'

There's a plea in his voice, but I tell him what I think. 'He could get himself free of all this but he's not working on his own legal defence.'

'Why is that?'

'He says he doesn't have the money. For lawyers and so on.'

'We can all raise enough,' he says.

'I told him that. In fact, I offered him a deal from the office: we pay for the lawyer if he gives us the story first. He refused. No deals he said, and people like you and I have better things to do than waste money on his defence.'

'Why didn't you try to change his mind?' he asks.

'I did. He refused. As simple as that. You know him.'

He nods. 'But we can't leave it at that. I'm going to speak to people at the ashram. Does Narsimha know?'

'I think so. He's been in touch with Prakash.'

'Why doesn't he do something? He's running the ashram. He knows some of the people who can help.'

'Ask him,' I say. 'Perhaps Prakash had told Narsimha not to try.'

Laxman grins wryly. 'Narsimha would be happy to be told that.'

'Be careful what you do. You don't want to be thrown out.'

He shakes his head. 'I don't care. If Narsimha throws me

out I'll go, and return when Swami comes back. Swami will listen when I tell him why I went. If Swami doesn't come back, I won't come back either.'

It's getting on for two now: driving out here, and looking for a restaurant, and ordering, and being served, and so on have taken quite a chunk out of the three hours the girl told us to wait. Getting back there will take another half-hour, so we have another half-hour or so to kill. 'I'm leaving tomorrow,' I tell him. 'I might come back for more information … I don't know what's going to happen. But I think Prakash has some powerful enemies, and Krishnappa Gowda is somehow tied up with them.'

'Maybe,' he tells me. 'There are some things at the ashram that Swami might not know about.'

'Like what?'

'Visitors coming to hide, I think. They come early in the morning and leave after dark.'

'What kind of visitors?'

'Different. It's hard to say. But they're not like the other visitors who come to see Swami. Some of them looked like … they looked like criminals, but I'm not sure. A lot of good people look like that.'

'Has this been going on for a long time?'

'Ever since I first came here some months ago. Just one or two at a time, never more than that, and not every day, but they were there.'

'Did Raju know about them?'

'I think he did. He didn't like them coming here, but he thought that we shouldn't turn away anyone who comes in daylight and doesn't mean us harm. The same as Swami.'

'Why do you think no one told Swami about it?'

'I know why Rajuji didn't want to tell Swami. He thought Swami had too much to do. He was very protective …'

I remember Raju's warning not to take too much of Prakash's time, and about Prakash not getting enough sleep. Maybe prison *is* a holiday for the man. 'I know,' I say.

'Besides,' Laxman continues, 'he didn't think there would be serious problems with those people. He was planning to get in touch with the police about them. Just to keep watch.'

'Did he do that?'

'I don't think so. There were many other small problems to be solved. I don't think he got around to it. Because if he had, the officer who came to arrest Swami would have come to the ashram to follow up.'

It's time to move on. When we get to the photocopy shop at three the girl behind the counter tells us to wait another ten minutes, the job's nearly over, and returns to what seems to be the same conversation on her cellphone that she was on when we came to give her the papers to be copied.

Nearly forty-five minutes later, we're back at the ashram gates, to drop Laxman off. 'Do you want me to come in and see Narsimha?' I ask at the door of his room, when he hands me the Gita and a few sheets of writing paper with Prakash's notes on them.

'Not necessary,' he says. 'I'll just give him these papers we copied. I already checked them, and I don't think there's anything missing. He won't have anything to complain about.'

'Well, I hope you don't get into trouble for anything you've done now.'

'No trouble. I've already said, if they kick me out of the ashram, I will come back when Swami returns. That's all.'

'Thanks, Laxman. Give me a call if you're leaving.'

'I will,' he promises, and we exchange cellphone numbers before I climb back into the cab to return to the hotel.

# Chapter Twelve

FROM THE HOTEL I call Shafiq to tell him I'm leaving tomorrow, and then get myself a ticket on a late-morning flight to Bangalore that'll get me there for a late lunch. The plan is to go straight to the office, talk to Srini, get off a couple of hours early, and try to get home in time to talk to Pallavi before Mohini arrives. I don't know what I'm going to say to her but meet her I will.

Dealing with Srini will be simplest. I'll just tell him I'm quitting, that he needn't put up with me for the rest of the three months that he offered me before I came here. If he asks me why, I'll tell him I've got a job with a newspaper and no TV. I'm sure his eyebrows will rise at the idea: at a time when most journalists are trying to get from print to TV, I'm going to quit my job for one that pays half as much and has only print and internet editions. Well, I am. My contract specifies a notice period of a month, so I'll give him a month's notice and tell him I'll work on Prakash's story until I quit.

The last and certainly the toughest job will be telling Mohini it's over. I cringe at the thought of her exploding in my face when I tell her. I wish for a drink, but more and more I see that drinking only led me to postpone what needed to be done. In desperation I call Gokul. 'What's the matter, bastard?' he asks.

'I'm free this evening as well,' I tell him. 'I'm booked on a mid-morning flight out tomorrow.'

He pauses for a moment before answering. 'Look, check out of your hotel in an hour. I'll pick you up, bag and baggage, and you can stay over and leave from my house.'

'If you're sure that won't be a bother, yes,' I tell him.

'It'll be less of a bother than having to drop you off at the hotel at midnight,' he assures me.

Instead of waiting for him I take a cab to the shrink that the drugstore assistant pointed out. There's one patient with him, and another waiting outside, and I get to see him after a twenty-minute wait. He's a plump little man with shuttered eyes behind rimless spectacles. 'What can I do for you?' he asks.

I tell him straight. By now the shakes have returned and I show him my hands. He checks my pulse and blood pressure, asks about my drinking habits and when I last had one, and I tell him honestly. Then I tell him about my morning's Ativan. He smiles bleakly. 'You shouldn't have done that.'

'What could I do at five in the morning?' I ask.

'Gone to a hospital. They'd have checked you out properly and called a psychiatrist if necessary. Your withdrawal symptoms can get worse fast: you could go from tremors and panic to delirium tremens in a short while. Next time, do it right.'

'Okay,' I tell him grumpily.

'Also, the symptoms could peak a few days from now if you don't drink. A peak five or six days after stopping is common. Be prepared.'

'Sure,' I tell him. 'Just give me a prescription'

'Wait. You have to get yourself monitored every day. I'll give you a prescription, but the dosage decreases tomorrow. Take it for another three days, that's all. You'd better go to a doctor tomorrow or day after at the latest.'

'Fine,' I tell him. 'I'll do that.'

I give him the three hundred rupees – quite a bit, I think, for a doctor here – he asks for, and leave with a prescription for six one-milligram tablets that I get at the same drugstore. If I need more, I tell myself, I can always get some in Bangalore.

Half an hour later we're in Gokul's jeep, heading home. I try to explain. 'I don't want to drink and I was getting restless and if I'd stuck around in the hotel any longer I'd have gone out and bought a bottle and crawled into it.'

'I understand. Good you called me. We can talk at home.'

Jayanthi is welcoming when she sees that I'm sober, and leaves us alone as usual. 'You're making waves,' he tells me.

'Where?' I ask.

'In the department.' Meaning the police department.

'How so?'

'You asked for copies of everything that the police took from the ashram. Copies of transcripts of interrogations, of the forensic reports, and so on ... People are saying there's going to be a media trial.'

'Well, people are wrong,' I tell him. 'I want to find out what happened, and I'm not going to print a word until I'm reasonably sure. No exposés without backing, without some kind of proof.'

'Why?'

'Because I'm sure that working out who killed Raju and why will lead to who's put Prakash behind bars.'

'Is that it?'

'There's more, Gokul. If Prakash is innocent, there's someone framing him. Since there's at least one minister's henchman involved, there's got to be something bigger behind all this.'

'Some sort of political game, you think?'

'I have no idea. As you yourself said, we don't know who's running whom: Gowda or Uchil.'

He nods. 'Whatever it is, you'd better watch out. If you're going to investigate any further, don't do it on your own.'

'Do you think it's going to be that bad?'

'Yes. Having a TV channel backing you up would discourage anyone out to stop you. So don't quit immediately. Take leave – without pay, if need be – for as long as you need to chase this one. Stay here for the duration if you wish.'

'Will you get into trouble?'

'I can take care of myself,' he says. 'It's not that I'm hard to kill or anything, but I do have information on people.' He grins. 'Actually, I don't, but people think I do, which is good enough.'

'All right.'

'And, yes, you should be thinking of protecting your sources, especially if you're thinking of quitting. Anyone who gives you information is liable to be threatened or hurt. That's one way they'll discourage people from opening up to you.'

I remember Laxman with a wrench. 'There's this youngster in the ashram who's been telling me stuff about visitors taking refuge there.' I tell him what Laxman told me about the comings and goings of the men who weren't the usual type of visitor, who never tried to see Prakash, and clearly had no spiritual inclinations whatsoever.

'Do you think anyone will be able to figure out that he's been feeding you information on the sly?'

'Not unless he boasts of it or something.'

'Play it safe,' he tells me. 'Tell him to go away until your pal, Prakash, comes back. He's relatively safe in Hyderabad. Uchil's influence doesn't spread beyond a few districts here, and Gowda's party has no presence in Telengana.'

'I'll do that tomorrow … it's too late today.

'Do that before you leave.'

'Okay.'

'So what's making you so uneasy?' he asks.

'I don't look forward to facing Mohini …' I falter.

He grins. 'For all you know, Mohini's waiting for you to say it so she can dump you.'

I sit up straight. I really hadn't thought of that. 'What?'

'You're down and nearly out,' he says. 'If she dumps you, she might consider that she stands accused of driving you to drink and then ditching you. So she won't do it. Instead she'll make life increasingly miserable for you, until you do the splitting. For all you know, she might be relieved when you tell her.'

'She might be relieved,' I tell him, 'but she's not going to admit it. She'll make my life even more miserable, that's all. And brainwash Pallavi.'

'What can I say?' he asks. 'You brought it on yourself.'

'Yes. I'll deal with it. As soon as I can.'

Thanks perhaps to the lorazepam I sleep reasonably well and manage a good breakfast by seven.

Anil picks me up at half past eight and on the way to the airport I call Laxman. 'I'm busy,' he says. 'Narsimha didn't like my going to lunch with you. He said I should have stayed with the papers throughout.'

'So why are you busy?'

'Packing. I'm going home to Eluru, and from there I'll go to Hyderabad.'

'Good decision,' I tell him

'Why?'

'You'll be happier outside the ashram, and you'll be welcome back when Prakash returns.'

'How do you know?'

'I've spent a lot of time with him in the last few days,' I tell him. 'I've gotten to know him fairly well.'

'Okay,' he says. 'Should I go back to my job?'

'Yes.'

'Why?'

'Prakash might come back here on bail, but he won't be clear until the investigation and trial are over. That could be a long way off. Stay clear until then.'

'Yes. That's good advice. Thanks.'

'My pleasure … and look, don't go back to the ashram without telling me.'

'All right.'

After an uneventful flight I arrive in Bangalore with a feeling of something approaching dread. Then it strikes me that Srini will certainly be relieved that I'm leaving, and that Pallavi might be disappointed in me but I can make it up with her, so the meeting I fear the most is with Mohini, and I'm going to make it as short and quick as I can. Doesn't help. The beast makes its presence felt, and without the booze calming it down, eats into my equanimity with vigour and persistence.

One drink. Just one drink.

I force the thought away. That one drink will always lead to another and another and so on. I can't afford that.

I will not sit down to lunch, because that will lead me to a beer or something, and from there to a bottle of rum is less than a hop, skip and jump … I pick up a sandwich outside the airport on the way to the office and eat it slowly as we struggle through the afternoon traffic. It takes an hour and a half, and I'm worn ragged at the end of it, and almost relieved to find Srini in and not too busy to listen for a few minutes. He's on the phone when I walk into his office, and he waves me to a chair while he finishes his conversation. 'Not a fruitful trip,' he says.

'It needs a little more effort to become fruitful,' I tell him.

'Effort aimed at what?' he asks.

'Finding out who killed Raju. That'll tell us why, and

that in turn will tell us who's orchestrating this attack on the Swami. And, I hope, why.'

'So you assume he's innocent.'

'Nothing of the kind. He might have done everything he's been accused of but the timing needs explaining. For all you know, someone led him into thinking he could get away with skullduggery and nailed him down when he thought the time was right.'

'You sound like one of those conspiracy theorists. The CIA arranged the destruction of the WTC.'

'There's some reason for thinking this. And we do know that Raju was poisoned.'

'I'm not completely persuaded yet,' he says, 'but it's not impossible.'

'It isn't. So let me have the papers from the police. And ask your pals in the police to get the investigating officer to cooperate with me.'

'I can do all that.' He pauses. 'Where will you work?'

'Here, to start with. There's going to be a lot of reading, if I'm not mistaken.'

'As you wish,' he says. 'Remember, Bala, the clock's ticking. Three months less a week.'

Time to give him the news. 'Ah, yes,' I tell him, pretending to be cooler than I am. 'That was another thing I've been wanting to talk to you about.'

'You want more time? This story'll be over long before that, so the answer right now is, well, it's going to be difficult.'

'I don't want more time,' I tell him. 'Quite the reverse … Srini, I'm quitting after this story.'

He leans back, puts his hands behind his head. 'What will you do?'

'Go back to print.'

'Are you nuts?' He straightens up, fiddles with some papers

on his desk. 'It's that Swami guy. He's sold you something.'

'Not really, Srini. I'm a print man. Regardless of the lousy pay and the irregular hours and the lack of TV presence. I'm going back to what I should be doing.'

'Another way of looking at it is that you're refusing to look at your fear of TV. Be honest.'

'I'm not particularly afraid of it. I just think it's far poorer as a medium than either print or the internet.'

'That's your choice, of course,' he says. 'Do as you will. Come and have a chat sometime, though, after work.'

'Sure,' I tell him. 'After this story.'

'Okay.' He raises his eyebrows. 'And we'll keep your decision pending until then?'

'If you insist,' I tell him, 'but I don't think I'll change my mind.'

'Do you have an offer?'

I pause before answering. I've never played these games before, and won't start playing them now. 'Yes,' I tell him.

'Will you be looked after well?' he asks. 'I don't want to know any more than that.'

'The salary is poor, the contract is for a year, they'll not renew it if the booze keeps me away from work, and I'll probably have to shift.'

'And you think the quality of the work will be worth all this?'

'It's a gamble. I don't know how much longer I'm going to continue here.'

'I notice you're sober now. Stay that way and you'll find that question answering itself.'

'Yes,' I tell him, though I refrain from saying that the answer won't be the one that he expects. 'But like I said, we'll have that chat when I'm done with the story.'

'Okay.'

'One more thing.'

'What?'

'I need to get home early. By about five.'

'Sure. You're on your own for the time being. Do as you wish.' He probably senses something in my manner. 'Something big coming up?'

'Yes. I'm not sure about tomorrow.'

'That should be okay, because the papers from Mangalore will arrive tomorrow at the earliest, but more likely the day after, because they'll likely send them only today.'

'So I might take tomorrow off.'

'Sure.'

I remember that I might be without a roof over my head in a few hours. 'I might have to use the guest house for a few days.'

He gives me a quick look, and nods. 'Sure. Just call ahead and make sure there's someone around to take care of you.'

'I will,' I tell him, and rise to head for the door, and he stops me. 'Bala,' he says. 'Don't go back to the booze.'

I try to smile, but fail because of the weight of the coming sessions with Pallavi, and, more importantly, Mohini. 'I'll do my best.'

I'm home by half past four, a half-hour before I expect Pallavi to return. I shower and change into clean jeans and a T-shirt, wondering whether to take her out to to a restaurant where she might talk more freely than at home. She walks in at five, sees me on the sofa, idly surfing TV channels with the sound muted, and does a double take. 'Hi!' she says, taking a step back, dropping her schoolbag in surprise. 'You actually came back like you said!'

'How long have I been saying I'll do things and not doing them?' I ask.

'What?' she asks.

'How long have I been breaking promises?'

She bends to pick up her bag and I can't help thinking how ugly and uncomfortable the school uniform is. When she straightens up, she looks at me seriously and asks, 'What do you mean?'

'Get changed,' I tell her. 'Let's go out. Let's go to some nice place nearby and sit down and talk comfortably.'

She looks doubtfully at me. 'What will Mom say?'

'Whatever she says she'll say to me, not you,' I tell her. 'Do you have a lot of homework?'

'No, not really,' she tells me. She hesitates a moment before seeming to make up her mind. 'Okay,' she says. 'I'll be ready in fifteen minutes. I've got to shower and change and make a call.'

The call lasts close on twenty-five minutes so she takes three-quarters of an hour. 'I'm going out with Dad,' I hear her say as she hangs up, leaving the phone on the dining table as she runs to fetch her purse. Just outside the house, she says, 'Dad, I forgot my phone.'

'Leave it,' I tell her. 'We'll be back soon.'

'All right,' she says, and a few minutes later we're out by the road looking for an auto. 'Forget the auto, Dad,' she says. 'It's not so far. We can walk.'

'All right,' I tell her, and we stroll ten quiet minutes to the place she wants to go, a large bakery filled with the sweet aroma of baking, and small round tables for intimate groups.

'What did you want to talk about?' she asks after the lad taking our orders has disappeared into the kitchen.

'Nothing much. It's just that ... it's been too long since we did that, that's all.'

She nods. 'Yeah!' she says, her ponytail bobbing. She looks me in the eye. 'I've been home all along.'

I nod back. 'I know,' I tell. 'I wish ...' I run out of words and sit looking dumbly at her. She looks right back at me. After a few long seconds of this I get my voice back. 'There's been a lot of water under that bridge.' I run out of steam again, and stumble on after another pause. 'I'm not much good at this.' She nods, and I plod on. 'Okay, it's just this. I'm back. Okay?'

She nods again. Before she can say anything, though, the lad is back, with a sandwich and grape juice for her, coffee for me. We wait for him to arrange the paper napkins and the cutlery around her plate. When he leaves, I try to retrieve what I can from the disaster. 'Look,' I tell her, 'I only want to say I'm sorry I haven't been much of a father to you for some time now, and I've let you down a few times, maybe more than a few … I can't even promise there won't be more bad patches, but I won't let them go on so long. And you should feel free to tell me when I mess up.'

She doesn't say anything, just sits looking straight down at her plate picking at her food, playing with the fries and the bits of salad that accompany her sandwich. I gather my courage. 'Pallavi,' I tell her firmly. 'Look at me.' She lifts her eyes to mine. There's hurt there, beyond words, and the beginning of tears. My firmness disappears. 'I'm sorry,' I mumble. 'I didn't mean to upset you.'

She drops her gaze, and takes a minute or two to recover while I sip my coffee. By and by she begins on a french fry or two, and then her healthy teenage appetite takes over. Midway through her sandwich, she looks up. 'What about your trouble, Dad?'

'It's only just begun,' I tell her.

'What do you mean?' she asks.

'Somebody killed a man I knew in Mangalore a few days ago. I want to find out who did it, and why.'

'It was in the news,' she says, happy to find something less exhausting to talk about than the distance between us. 'At that ashram.' A pause. 'Won't the police find out?'

'I don't know.'

'What about your job?'

'I'm quitting after this story.'

'What will you do, then?' she asks.

'I have to talk to Mom about that,' I tell her.

'Is she going to be angry at you?'

'Yes, most likely. I'll know for sure tonight when I talk to her.'

Suddenly, reassuringly, her hand is warm around my forearm, and I find myself on the verge of tears. As I turn to look at her, pride fills my chest, and a thought fills my mind, that this is a fine child, this daughter of mine. I swallow and look away, lest she see.

We bump into a friend of hers in the lift, and the two girls stop to chat in the corridor while I unlock the door and let myself in to find Mohini pacing the living room. 'Pallavi's gone off somewhere and left her cellphone behind,' she says. 'Do you know where she is?'

'In the corridor,' I reply. 'She'll be here in a moment. I told her not to take the phone when we went out.'

'Why must you interfere?' she asks. 'Call her in. I want to speak to her.'

'Let her finish chatting with her friend,' I say. 'A few minutes won't matter.'

'I'll decide that,' she says, her voice icy.

This is Mohini at her least pleasant, and most formidable. 'I'm not so sure about that,' I say neutrally, my heart thudding, for the storm has begun. 'I am, after all, her father.'

'You?' she says, her voice rising involuntarily. She rarely raises her voice, so she's really angry. 'You?' she repeats. 'You must be blind drunk to think I'll let you interfere with her.'

I take a deep breath. I used to flee by this stage, but I can't any longer. Coward, says the newly-risen belly-beast. Coward. Coward. Shout her down if you have the nerve.

In the storm the thought of Pallavi steadies me out. With an effort I keep my voice steady. 'On the contrary,' I tell her, meeting her eyes with difficulty. 'I'm sober. Stone-cold sober.'

'Woken up at last, have you?'

'I don't know about that,' I tell her. 'But I do know that some things have gone on long enough.'

Her voice descends to its usual level of ice when she speaks next. 'Such as?'

In a moment of insight I understand what Prakash said about courage being a ghost. You're intimately acquainted with fear. Whatever gets you past your fear, well, that's more or less accident. 'Your picking at me.' I pause for a deep breath. 'Your picking at her.'

She sits down, which promises an extended session of unpleasantness. 'I'm not going to let a drunkard tell me how to deal with my daughter.'

'Our daughter.'

'In the last few years you've done nothing to justify that.'

'I haven't. But I'm getting back to it now.'

Pallavi chooses that moment to enter the house. She sees the two of us sitting facing each other, and jumping to the wrong conclusion, smiles. Then she senses the atmosphere and the smile fades. 'Haven't I told you a hundred times to take your phone along when you go out?'Mohini asks. 'Do you know how worried I got?'

'I didn't know you'd come back so early,' Pallavi says. 'In any case, I was with Dad, and when I forgot the phone he told me not to worry about it.'

'We'll deal with that later,' Mohini says, taking command smoothly as she usually does. 'Your Dad and I have a few matters to sort out. Go to your room and stay there.' She waits for the click of Pallavi's door closing before turning back to me. 'I don't care how sloppy you are, but you're not going to teach her those habits.'

I can't stop myself asking, 'Taking a teenager out for a twenty-minute chat and a sandwich is a sloppy habit?'

'She has homework to do, and other things as well.'

'You're being unnecessarily rigid with her. Besides leaving her alone most of the time.'

Her voice rises in anger. 'Is that my fault? At least I do justice to my career and try to do justice to my family.'

I've held the belly-beast in check so far and as it rises now I see that Mohini has her own belly-beast. A twinge of compassion takes me by surprise, and, to my greater surprise, the beast subsides. I look down for a moment before answering. 'Yes,' I tell her, slowly, quietly, and without an iota of sarcasm. 'I can see that. You did the best you could.'

My refusal to give in to anger takes the wind out of her sails. 'What are you trying to say?' she asks, wary, still a little surly.

'Something I should have said long ago.'

'What?' Impatience raises her voice.

'This marriage isn't working. There's no reason for us to stay in it.'

She lowers her face into her hands and keeps silent for a long, long moment. When at last she raises her face to reply, her voice is a whisper. 'Bala, you bastard, you utter selfish bastard.'

'What do you mean?'

She gives up all pretence of control, and shouts loud enough perhaps for Pallavi to hear. 'I gave you my youth, I worked to keep us going, I put up with your drunkenness, with your drunkard pals, all for the family, and you just walk in here and say it's not going to work. If that isn't selfish I don't know what is.'

An assault like this – not that I've ever faced anything this severe – should send me fleeing, but the thought of Mohini's treatment of Pallavi holds me up. As I sit facing her, a deeper truth emerges. I never really wanted this marriage. I never really wanted her. Prakash's question haunts me. Why did I marry her?

'Answer me, you son of a bitch,' she asks, still shouting. My silence seems to have unnerved her. Suddenly, I know. This is her beast, in full cry. It has her pinned to the wall. 'Nearly twenty years I've given you, and now this!'

'I've got nothing to say,' I tell her, rising. With the disappearance of my belly-beast, a sort of quiet begins to settle in. I hope it lasts, and fear it won't.

'Where are you going?' she asks, also rising, as if to stop me from leaving. 'You can't just walk off like this.'

'I can,' I tell her. 'I'm going to pack a few things. I'll take some of my stuff along now, spend the night at the guest house, and come back for the rest by and by.' The only thing she can find to throw at me is a glass vase on the coffee table right in front of her. I duck involuntarily, and it crashes into the frame of the TV set with a bang. 'That's not going to help,' I tell her.

To my surprise, she breaks down, weeping. 'Why are you doing this to me?' she asks, a strange, pleading note in her voice. She rarely cries, hating to be seen as weak. When I ignore her and walk into the bedroom, she follows me. 'Why aren't you saying anything?' she asks. 'Why don't you reply?'

'I don't have any answers,' I tell her, opening the wardrobe.

She straightens up. 'There must be someone else,' she says, wiping her eyes. 'Who? Who's the bitch?'

'There's no one else, Mohini. Get a hold on yourself.'

'All right,' she says. Her voice rises again, to a shout. 'Go. Go ahead. Get out. I'll see to it you don't get to see Pallavi again.'

The beast is awakening again, but when I look at her I see again the beast in her. She's vulnerable, too, and memories of good times flood my mind until I'm tempted to back down. I wait until my weakness passes. 'Don't you see what you're doing?' I ask. 'You're using Pallavi to hit at me.'

'Remember GK?' she asks. 'Remember telling Sumitra's parents you thought he didn't mean it? You let your fellow drunks wander all over your daughter's friends and then accuse me of using her to hit at you? What the fuck are you talking about?'

I speak as neutrally as possible under the circumstances. 'Your daughter seems to matter less to you than your anger at me,' I tell her. 'Think about it.'

'Go to hell!' she says, turning her back on me.

As I pack I look around at what amounts to my stuff in the room. There's very little, and what I'd miss if I lost it won't fill a small suitcase. So I pack a biggish suitcase of clothes and other necessities, and the small one with the objects I'd miss if I lost them, photos and such, and wonder how it's going to be wherever I go next.

I knock at Pallavi's door as I leave. She opens it quickly, as if she's been waiting for my knock. 'I'm not sure when I'll see you next.'

Her eyes are blank, reddened. 'I heard,' she says. 'You're not coming back here.'

'Probably not. But I'll come for you soon. After I see a lawyer. The next few weeks are going to be rough, but I'll make it up to you somehow. I swear I will.'

She nods. Her reserve breaks and the tears tumble down her cheeks. I put my arms around her and she hugs me tight for a long moment. Mohini moves up behind us. 'Move on,' she says. 'You're no longer welcome here.' I can't speak so I pat Pallavi on the back and turn to the door. 'Let me know the previous day when you want to come for all the junk you've left behind,' Mohini continues. 'You can come just once, no more.' I don't reply, but hesitate outside the front door and she slams it in my face.

# Chapter Thirteen

A CAB DROPS me off at the company's Indira Nagar guest house half an hour later The guest house is a large three-bedroom flat in an old block, with large rooms and highish ceilings. It's staffed by a cook and an odd-job man, both of whom stay on the premises, and are both around when I arrive. The one other guest, Harsha, the cook, tells me, is a colleague from Mumbai, who has gone out to dinner and will be back late. When I ask him what he's got in the kitchen, he offers chicken curry and rice and salad, which he can bring me in ten minutes. I'm tempted to send Edwin, the odd-job man, out for rum and coke, but manage not to.

The utter emptiness of life ahead strikes me when I lie down after dinner. I'm even tempted to give up and go back and beg forgiveness, especially when I think of what Pallavi might have to endure, but with me out of the picture Mohini might give up punishing Pallavi to give me a hard time …

I look for some kind of a gain, but don't find one. Instead, there are losses. I no longer have a place to call my own. I no longer have the possibility of regular contact with my daughter. I stand to exchange a well-paid job for a poorly-paid one, in a different city altogether, taking which will mean that the chances of my seeing my daughter often enough to make a difference to her will also diminish.

There are ifs, too, all uniformly bleak. If Mohini declares

legal war, I could end up never seeing Pallavi again. If Mohini declares war, I'm also going to be broke. If I can't stay off the bottle, I won't have a job, or even the option of living off the missus, as was the case just a week or so ago, when Srini first broached the topic of my being kicked out.

I go through all this once again, just to make sure I haven't missed anything: if I can stay off the booze, and if Mohini decides not to take me to the cleaners, and if I don't get kicked out of my next job, then I have a reasonable chance of living in straitened circumstances in a strange city and meeting my daughter a couple of times a year or something.

That, mind you, is the best case. Assuming that each of these ifs is like a flip of a coin, which is optimistic on the first two, I have one chance in three of a barely acceptable future. In other words, this is the second most monumentally stupid thing I've ever done in my life. The most monumentally stupid thing, being, of course, marrying Mohini, which I am in the process of rectifying, although many years too late.

The biggest, most formidable if of all: if Mohini decides to take it out on Pallavi … It doesn't bear thinking about. If I go back and beg, will she relent on Pallavi? She might. On the other hand, she might not.

Dear god, what have I done to my daughter?

That twinge of compassion when I saw that Mohini, too, has a belly-beast as difficult as mine, caused the damage.

In the small hours, with a mind full of disquiet, assisted by lorazepam, I sleep. In a dream that follows, I drift through a garden of flowers that I know are sweet-scented but can't smell, meet a woman I know but don't remember, and wake an hour later to the torment of the notion of having known the taste of honey and the fragrance of rose petals in the dream but not remembering them.

It's only four, yet I can't go back to sleep.

Focus. The one thing on which everything depends is my staying off the booze. If I can stay sober, I might be able to find a way to a less discouraging future. If I can't, I might as well put a pistol to my head, and Pallavi's as well. You put a pistol to her head years ago, idiot-coward, says the beast, newly risen unnoticed after that brief rest.

If you want your life to work, you can never have a drink again, it says. Never is a long long time. It's not next month, or next year, or any time in the future that you can see. If I could have just one now, just one, I'll stop with that, comes the thought. One drink isn't going to make a difference.

The hours pass slowly as I persuade myself that it will make a difference, and I get out of bed at six. Harsha brings coffee, and, after a break of five years or more, I go for a walk in the cool air of a July morning. There are joggers on the streets, and middle-aged couples in running shoes out walking, swinging their arms. It seems a different universe from the one I inhabited yesterday.

Harsha feeds me breakfast before I leave at half past eight. The buses are unendurably crowded so I look for an auto or a cab, but can't find one. When I call the regular cab service, the operator tells me it's peak hour and it'll be at least an hour before one of his vehicles can get to me.

I have to have wheels of my own. With my future as uncertain as it is, I don't think I can afford a car right away. Besides, the consequences of crashing it if I'm drunk could be really bad. And so, by half past nine, I'm waiting outside the gates of a Honda two-wheeler dealer, where I discover that they'll take at least a week to give me any kind of vehicle. I can't wait that long, so I go to the TVS dealers down the street, and find that they can give me a usable scooter the very next day. I give them a cheque and my driver's licence to copy, and move on hoping that I will continue sober enough from tomorrow to manage a scooter on Bangalore roads, something I haven't done in a decade.

I'm at the office by half past ten, early by my standards, and Srini, who sees me at the corridor, is surprised. 'What's the matter?' he asks, stopping in his tracks.

'Let's talk,' I tell him, waving in the direction of his room.

'Looks like you've stayed off the bottle,' he says as he settles behind his desk.

'Yes,' I tell him, 'but there's something else going on. Something much more important.'

'What?' he asks.

'Mohini and I are separating,' I tell him.

He nods. 'I knew you weren't as close as you used to be … Well, what can I do?'

'I might have to continue in the guest house for some time,' I tell him.

'Sure. What else?'

'Recommend a lawyer.'

He nods. 'I know a couple,' he tells me. 'I'll check with them and get back to you, by email, in an hour or two. I might take a little while to contact them … if they're at the courts, I might have to wait until lunch.'

'Fine,' I tell him. 'What about the reports from Mangalore?'

'Shafiq sent them yesterday. We should have them in a couple of hours.'

'Right.'

'For the time being,' he says, 'you'll keep your room. But at some stage Surya'll have to move in there, and you … well, that depends on how you do. If this keeps up we'll get you something better.'

'We can talk about that after the story,' I tell him. 'Nothing's going to change in the meanwhile, I guess.'

He nods. 'An eventful time for you,' he says. 'Like that Chinese curse: May you live in interesting times!'

'It's just something I should have done long ago,' I tell him. 'There's more to come. More cleaning up.'

He grins. 'Go for it.'

'I'm buying a bike,' I tell him.

His jaw drops. 'You can't be serious!'

'I am. I can't afford a car.'

'We'll get you one. You rate it, you know. But we won't get a you a new one, not until you've stabilized.'

'If I get drunk in a car I might run over people, but with a bike I won't even be able to stay on.'

'Doesn't sound too good, Bala,' he says. 'Think again.'

'I thought about it most of the morning,' I tell him, and leave.

My room at the office seems a different world now. Just before I left for Mangalore it was a safe haven: now it seems a stranger's workplace. The half-empty bottle of Old Monk still sits in the bottom drawer, and the photograph of Pallavi at age two still sits on a corner of the desk, but it all seems to belong to someone else.

There's this overpowering urge to empty that bottle so I wrap it in a sheet of newspaper, slink off to the toilet down the corridor, and, with a wrench, pour the contents down the sink. When I return, Surya is waiting. 'Bala, I didn't ask for this,' he begins. 'I asked for a raise, because I'm doing more than my brief, but I didn't ask to be given your job.'

'Don't worry about it,' I tell him. 'The future's still open.'

'This matters to me, Bala,' he says, 'even if not to you.'

Surya is normally unemotional, and I tend to listen when he speaks like this. Besides, I know he's covered up for me at least a couple of times in the recent past. Finally, and perhaps most importantly, I like him. So I sit back and nod. 'Go ahead,' I tell him. 'Say your piece.'

'It's not much of a piece,' he says. 'Srini and I went out

for a drink a few days back at the Press Club, and we both had a few.' They aren't alcoholic, by any means, but neither are they teetotal, and Surya doesn't hold his liquor well. 'I did tell him I wanted more money, now that my wife's no longer working. I don't remember what else I told him, but I was angry at you because you were … well, you seemed to be avoiding making some decisions on what to carry, so I was irritated. I don't know what I told him, but I did remember next morning that I ranted about you. So I told Srini immediately that I didn't mean any of that rant, that I was quite happy to go on with you.'

'Fine,' I tell him. 'I believe you.'

'But I did tell Srini that I wanted to move upwards …' He looks shamefaced. 'Look, Bala, I don't want you to think I got you in trouble.'

I can't help laughing. 'I'm in more trouble than you can imagine,' I tell him, 'and it has nothing to do with you. Don't think about it. Just do whatever you're doing as best you can.'

'There are rumours that you're leaving, that Srini's given you a deadline to get yourself straightened out.'

I nod. 'Yes, that's exactly what happened. My drinking has caught up with me.'

He shakes his head. 'Even at your drunken worst you're not that bad,' he says. 'I still have a lot to learn from you. Mostly about why, not how.'

'Thanks,' I tell him.

He rises to go, but stops. 'What are your plans, Bala?' he asks.

'I'm not sure,' I tell him, deciding that it's better to bring it out into the open rather than cause misleading rumours, 'because my marriage is history, and I have to deal with that first.'

'I'm sorry,' he says. 'It's going to be painful. And troublesome. Specially for your daughter.'

'Yes,' I tell him. 'I don't know how it's going to work out.'

'Take care, Bala,' he says, leaving.

Srini calls as he opens the door. 'Your Mangalore papers have arrived,' he tells me. 'Come and get them.'

Three large and heavy envelopes bearing a courier company's livery sit on the edge of his desk. Upon inspection, they turn out to be addressed to Srini personally, they've all been opened, and are all full of what seem to be photocopies. The envelope on top contains copies of the FIR lodged by Smita Sharma, the woman who complained about Prakash, as well as transcripts of interrogations of Prakash himself, of Raju, Narsimha, and Sarada, the woman who accompanied Smita Sharma until told to leave Prakash and her alone.

The second envelope contains papers on Raju's murder, and is much larger. There is the autopsy report, plus the lab report on Raju's body fluids, which is dated a couple of days after the autopsy. There's also the FIR, which doesn't name suspects, but just notes that the murder was committed by a person or persons unknown. There are some notes on the crime scene by the investigating officer and crime scene technicians, which are quite basic. The largest bit here is the collection of transcripts of interrogations, as well as statements from residents at the ashram.

In the third envelope, the smallest, are copies of papers confiscated from Prakash's and Raju's rooms at the ashram. Here are photocopies of a couple of books: a translation of and commentary on the *Kathopanishad*, and another of the *Vivekachudamani*. Right at the bottom is a copy of what seems to be Prakash's diary for the year, starting January 1, but with several dates missing.

Almost everything in the first two envelopes is in Kannada, almost everything is handwritten, almost everything seems in random order, and almost everything will give me a headache when I'm done with it. The papers are in a mess: someone has been through the lot and shuffled them around. I don't even know if they're all there – there's no tally sheet to help me confirm. Besides, I can't speed-read Kannada, so this is going to occupy me for some time … I have no idea how long.

I consider calling Gaurav Seth, my other policeman friend, for help, to get another set of copies independently, but then it strikes me that he, too, might be compromised … No, I decide, I'll keep it simple for the time being, and call him later.

I start with the rape charge, looking for some kind of connection between it and what I remember of the murder. I dig for the FIR, and find it somewhere in the middle of the stack, and then get hold of the transcripts of Prakash's and Ms Sharma's interrogations.

The complaint itself is simple. Ms Sharma was depressed, and spent some time at the ashram to try to recover, on the advice of a friend who had been there. She spent a few days at the ashram and found her depression worsening, until she couldn't sleep nights.

On her fourth night there, being restless, she began to wander about the corridors, and was found there by ashram volunteers, who took her to Prakash. She spent an hour or so talking to him alone, with the recording devices switched off at her request, and felt a little better for it. She did the same thing the next night, when the depression took hold of her again, and again felt better.

Until this point, the narratives converge. It's only with the next time that there's a difference.

The third time, though, according to her, fifteen minutes or so into their tête-à-tetê, when she started weeping, he hugged her, apparently to console her. In seconds, though the hug turned into something very different, and she found his hands running over her. She pulled herself free, and he apologized. She accepted his apology and calmed down, but he started grabbing her all over again, and she ran for it.

She left the ashram as early as she could next morning, scared and confused. She went straight back home to Bangalore, where she locked herself up for two days before meeting her 'spiritual advisor', who told her that she had to find her own inner peace. This she tried for several weeks before confiding in a friend, who later led her to an activist, who advised her to complain to the police.

She never went to a psychiatrist or a psychologist, only to advisors and friends. I can't help thinking, was she pretending? If she wasn't faking her ailment, was it depression or something else that can exhibit similar symptoms, like bipolar disorder or anxiety?

If only Prakash hadn't turned off the recording system.

Leafing slowly through the papers in the envelope, I'm surprised to find that Prakash has been talking to the police on the charge of attempted rape while he's been in prison: he was last interrogated the day after he stopped speaking to me. Right at the end of the stack is a transcript of this interrogation by the investigating police officer, conducted in the prison the day before yesterday.

The description of events in his answers to police questioning matches Ms Sharma's in almost every detail, down to the actual words spoken, all the way until the last fifteen minutes of their last meeting. Prakash says that he held her when she collapsed on him, in tears, and let go a moment later, when she straightened up. By his account, that's all the contact there was between the two of them.

What follows, though, more or less condemns him. He's mentioned what she spoke about: an extramarital affair, a fling with a young man, the guilt from which was weighing on her mind. She feared to tell her husband, terrified that it would damage her marriage irretrievably, shatter her husband, and alienate her son, but its weight was becoming unbearable.

Towards the bottom of the stack is a note from the investigating officer: enquiries show she has no husband, for her only marriage ended in divorce four years ago. There were no children by that marriage, and the divorce, in the eyes of the law, was amicable, for it was by mutual consent, and the couple had worked out the financial settlements before they went to the law.

If Prakash is telling the truth, then there has to be a conspiracy to get him. Otherwise, he's been up to tricks.

Likewise, if Raju's killing is tied to Prakash's arrest, it's likely someone's out to get Prakash. I turn, then, to the next envelope. This one is thick with statements from and interrogations of over a score of people from the ashram, inlcuding Laxman, Narsimha, and everyone who ate at the ashram on the day of Raju's last meal. The investigating officer notes, early on, that no one else felt any kind of gastric discomfort after eating, and that everyone agreed that Raju had had a bout of vomiting a few days earlier, before Prakash was arrested. The doctor, with whom Raju spoke on the phone, remembers prescribing lactobacilli for that earlier bout of vomiting.

When I look at my watch it's past two, and I'm hungrier than I've been in a long time. Almost inevitably I wish for a drink, and put the thought away before locking up the papers in my filing cabinet and heading out for a quick lunch. I avoid the regular joint and, conscious of the need to economize, go to a small vegetarian hotel that serves a comprehensive all-you-can-eat South Indian meal at a price I think I can afford.

Over lunch I realize that I've missed something in all those transcripts, some little detail that doesn't fit. Parts of my mind that seem to have stopped working while I was on the booze are kicking in again, and it's not really pleasant because most of the time they tell me about my mistakes. I look at the half-empty plate, discover I'm full, and flee.

Back in the office I go over the transcripts once again, starting with Prakash's interrogation. His answers are short and to the point: they contain no explanations or qualifications. He fails to answer very few questions, and all of those relate to details of exact words spoken, and exact times, and for each of those questions his answer is that he doesn't remember. Those 'I can't say' answers are few, and I can't help being impressed at his memory of an event that happened so long ago, involving someone he hardly knew.

Unless, of course, the charges are true, in which case the details would stick in his mind.

A sudden thought strikes me. He's never told me that he switched off the recording device on all three days, only the first. I look up his transcripts again, and find exactly the same thing. He's not said specifically that he turned off the recording on the second and third days. I look through them again, and find, yes, that he does say that he turned off the recording on the second day.

And then the questions come. The policeman didn't think to ask specifically if he had turned off the recording on the crucial day. Does Prakash have something up his sleeve?

Did Raju hear something while he was hanging around outside the door? Is that why they killed him? To eliminate the possibility of his testifying? Was there an earlier attempt to kill him, one that failed? If there was, then the timing of his death is not so crucial because it could have happened a week earlier.

I go back to the papers, looking now for the smallest inconsistency. I do the usual things: build a timeline, try to understand who was where at crucial moments, plot the movements of people who've been interviewed by the police. It all comes to nothing.

My cellphone rings. The caller ID says it's from Mohini's father's house, and I answer. Turns out it's the old gentleman, Chandramohan Venkatesh, himself. 'Bala, what's all this Mohini's telling me?' he asks in his rasp of a voice. Years ago, when Mohini placed me on his doormat to tell him that she was going to marry me, he was at first stunned, then furious. In those days he'd had a mildly crooked finger in many pies, mostly trading, and he was rich. He didn't think – rightly, as it turned out – that I could earn enough to keep his daughter in the style to which she was accustomed, and besides, he thought I had leftist leanings, which, for him, was like blasphemy.

Within a couple of years, the disapproval had been replaced by a wary kind of friendship that fell short of intimacy but carried no hostility. We circled warily at social functions, and occasionally visited each others' houses with fanfare, smiles, and caution. Afterwards he unbent enough to invite me home for a drink from time to time, trying to use my contacts to the benefit of his business, and failed. But in the process he did warm to me, telling me to call him CV, and inviting me home for drinks quite frequently. The warmth turned tepid when I became obviously alcoholic, and he is now lukewarm but civil.

'What's Mohini telling you?' I ask in turn.

'That you two are separating.' He doesn't mince words, and I appreciate that.

'Yes,' I tell him equally bluntly. 'We are.'

'We should discuss this, Bala.'

'There's nothing for the two of us to discuss,' I tell him, 'but if you want to mediate between Mohini and me I'm willing to listen.'

'Good enough,' he says. 'Come home today. As early as you can.'

'That might be difficult.' He lives a couple of peak-hour hours away, near the airport, in a large house set in what used to be a semi-pastoral acre-and-a-half fifteen years ago, but is now surrounded by apartment blocks with pseudo-colonial names like Windsor Residency and Victoria Park.

A moment's silence follows. Then, in a moment of unusual tact, he says, 'Mohini told me you're not very busy these days.'

'That was true until a week ago,' I reply, 'and might again be true in a week. But right now, I've got plenty to do.'

'Look, I'll send my car to pick you up. Please come.'

'I might be late.'

'It doesn't matter. I'm retired. I don't have to go anywhere.'

'All right.' I look at my watch and find, to my surprise, that it's already half past four. 'Send your man right away and let him call me when he gets nearby.'

'All right,' he says.

'What about Pallavi?' I ask.

'Pallavi will be here soon,' he says. Mohini's mother had a stroke six years ago. Ever since, because her grandmother can't travel, Pallavi has spent at least one weekend every month, and often two, with Mohini's parents. She enjoys that because it's a break from the drunkenness, mine, and the rancour, both Mohini's and mine, that she gets at home. 'So will Mohini. We'll wait for you.'

When CV's driver calls an hour and a quarter later, I'm still going through the papers. I stuff them back into their envelopes and the envelopes in my briefcase – lying unused for many years now – and head downstairs to the lobby. There, waiting on a sofa, to my great surprise, is CV himself. He rises when he sees me, and puts out a hand to shake. 'I'm happy you could make it,' he says. He gives me a keen look, but says nothing. 'Let's go.'

'What brought you out here?' I ask.

'I thought it might be useful to talk to you alone,' he says. He gives me a wry smile. 'I know, I know, you told me we've got nothing to discuss, but still ...'

'I don't mind talking to you,' I tell him as he leads me out to the car. 'It's just that any talk between the two of us might be useless without Mohini.'

He nods. Then, as we settle down in the rear seat of the car, 'Put on your seat belt.' He's always insisted that you can never tell when you'll crash, so you have to be prepared, you have to have belts and air bags all over the place. I click the buckle on and sit back and he continues, 'We've had difficult times. When Mohini first brought you along I wasn't impressed, but I found you were honest and hard-working and as good a husband as anyone else ... then you started drinking.' He looks at me again, to see how I react. When he sees I don't, he continues. 'Then I heard you were in trouble at your job.'

'From whom did you hear of that?' I ask.

'At first from Mohini ... I didn't know how serious she was, so I checked ... There's your retired finance man, Ahuja. I invested some money with his son, for a gym, you know.'

'It's all true,' I tell him. 'I'm in trouble at work, and I'm alcoholic, though I haven't had a drink for a couple of days.'

'Are you splitting up because of that? You shouldn't worry too much about the work, you know. If you cut down on the drinking you should have no trouble getting work.'

'I know that.'

'And I can keep you going for a while. An investment, that's how I think of it. Not in you, in my granddaughter's future.'

'No, that shouldn't be necessary.' Now that I've got to tell him, I can't find the words to say that it's his daughter I can't stand, and that, to my surprise, I like him better than I like her.

He speaks again, perhaps sensing me hold back. 'Is there another person involved? For either of you?'

'Not for me,' I tell him, honestly enough. 'Not for her, too, as best I know. You should ask her.'

'She won't tell me.' He shakes his head. 'I thought not, too. Neither of you seems the type.' When he looks at me again, there's a world of worry in his eyes. 'Is it because she's … spoilt? Bossy?'

We're inching through traffic. A shower has flooded part of the road and we're down to two cramped lanes now instead of the usual three. He's given me an easy way out but I don't want to take it. How can I tell him that his daughter, of whom he thinks the world, isn't above using her own daughter to punish me? I take evasive action instead. 'That's part of it,' I tell him.

He looks out through the window at the line of traffic stretching ahead and behind. 'Her business is … it's more or less gone,' he says. 'Before the crash, when the economy was booming on false hope, it was fine. After that it's been up and down. More down than up. Then, last year, she thought it was going up, and invested. It went flat, not up. Now she doesn't know what to do. It took a lot out of her.

'She didn't tell me all this until this morning, but I'd guessed. I'm not blind. She should have told me earlier, checked with me before investing, but she's grown up and she goes her own way.' He looks at me now, pleading. 'Don't be too harsh on her, Bala. She's also had a hard time. What with her business failing, and you drinking the way you do … it's been difficult all around.'

She hadn't told me either, and CV knew it. I, too, should have guessed.

He continues. 'You're losing your job, Mohini's business is sinking, leaving her in debt. Your flat is collateral for her loan. I suppose you didn't know that either.' There's a break in his voice. 'What happens to Pallavi, Bala? She's my only grandchild. Don't you think I have a right to ask you about her future when the house she lives in will be taken by the moneylenders?'

'What do you want me to say?' I ask.

'I don't know,' he replies. 'I can understand some of your problems, and some of Mohini's. I won't interfere between the two of you, and I won't take sides. For Pallavi's sake, I'll bail Mohini out. I'll support you as long as you need to get back on your feet. If you stay together. After I'm gone, everything goes to you three.'

'And if we don't?'

'I'll still bail Mohini out. I'll do what I can to make sure Pallavi grows up without trouble. As for the rest of it … I don't know, Bala. I'll probably help you anyway.'

'Why is that?' I ask. 'Don't pretend you like me all that much.'

'No pretence, Bala. You're right, I don't like you that much. But Pallavi needs you as well. You don't see it, but she does. If I do it, it's for her sake, not yours. If you do split up, I'll make sure Mohini doesn't harrass you, for the same reason.'

'I do see it. I spoke to her about it yesterday.'

He smiles a bitter smile. 'Mohini doesn't know about some kinds of trouble. She's learning. Unfortunately, she's making Pallavi and you learn with her … If only she'd come to me two years ago.

'When I saw you in the lobby I was hopeful. You looked like you used to, when you were on a story. Intense. I hoped …'

'What did you hope?'

'I've hoped for many things. Before Mohini brought you home I hoped for a rich young man who'd continue to spoil her as I did. She got you instead. When I got used to you I hoped that Mohini's business would do well and you'd stick to your job. Then you dropped out of sight on the TV channel and started drinking and I hoped you'd straighten out. Then Mohini's business began to go down and I hoped that it would go up. Now … now I just hope Pallavi does all right.

'You know, Mohini used to be proud of you. You were the brain. The one who didn't care about anything.' He smiles. 'That name came later. Bloodhound. By then I didn't mind you so much. You didn't want to ask your contacts to help me. You argued with me. Pallavi adored you. I thought you weren't such a bad fellow … where did it all go, Bala, that we can't get it back?'

'Maybe it was never ours to start with,' I tell him.

He gives me another keen look. 'Maybe you're right.' He sits back. 'I've said what I wanted to, Bala, and if you want to say anything to me alone you should do it now, before we get home. You might not get another chance soon.'

So I tell him about the eighteen-year-old maid that he sent us, and the jealousy that lurked beneath the surface.

He nods. 'I remember that incident. We picked that girl because she seemed to like children. Mohini told me vaguely that she wasn't happy about her, though I couldn't see why, and I didn't know …' He pauses. 'Are you sure you didn't give Mohini any cause for it? Absolutely sure?'

'As best I can recall, yes. Before or after that incident.' I think some more. 'I can promise you this. I never looked at another woman after we married … No. After we got together.'

'And before?' he asks.

'I don't know if that's relevant,' I tell him.

He nods. 'I shouldn't have asked that.'

'It's all right,' I tell him. 'You just won't get an answer to it. I know you don't want to pry.'

'Good,' he says. 'She was really happy in between, you know. There you were, an up-and-coming newsman. Then you people got into TV and she was really proud. She said you were going to be South India's best TV news editor. You'd have your own show on that channel. Things like that. None of it happened.'

'I didn't like TV. I still don't.'

'I thought as much … You know, people talk of trophy wives. Well, you were a bit of a trophy husband. But the shine wore off.'

This is the first I've heard any of this. 'I didn't know Mohini expected all that from me,' I say weakly.

He looks at me directly with a challenge in his eye. 'And you, Bala, what did you expect of Mohini? Having a beautiful wife with a rich father certainly wouldn't have done you any damage.'

My hackles go up. Then I realize it's the beast come visiting. I wait a moment and tell him, 'Perhaps you should rephrase that question.'

'I'm being straight with you, Bala,' he tells me, not backing down. 'You didn't marry her for my money. I know that. But did you have a trophy in mind?'

'As much as any man married to a beautiful woman, yes,' I tell him. 'But I also misjudged her. I thought she was spirited and independent. She isn't. She just likes to do things her way, and her way has to be different, that's all.'

'Isn't that being independent?'

'There's a difference between being independent and looking independent. I didn't catch it in time.'

He sighs and nods. 'I understand. We'll leave it at that for now. You talk to Mohini. I will be there if you both wish it. Think before you decide anything. A week or a month doesn't matter when you look at the rest of your daughter's life.'

'Okay.'

'It's strange. I have three brothers, two sisters. The sisters are gone, one brother remains. One of them has three children. Everyone else has one child or two. But when we were young and working for the future we thought we were working for large families, that we'd each have a dozen grandchildren. That's not happened. The family's shrinking …

'I could have retired ten years before I did and still had enough to look after Pallavi. A waste of time and energy. And health.'

'If there was something else you wanted to do, well, yes, it was a waste. Otherwise …'

'I should have spent more time with my family, that's all. With Mohini. Things might have been different.'

We're home. There's a watchman to open the gates and a moment later we're in the porch with mosquitoes attacking us. We go inside and find Mohini's mother, Amma, sitting slack-jawed on the sofa. I do her a namaste and she nods and smiles her bright lop-sided smile. She doesn't talk much because she slurs and knows it. Besides, her hearing is going, and she doesn't like using a hearing aid because she finds it intrusive. So she gets by with sign language and signs and the occasional grunt, and manages pretty well, mostly because of that bright smile.

Another car draws up outside, one with a diesel engine that's running a little roughly. The doors slam, and there are female voices outside. Mohini and Pallavi. Amma shows no sign of having heard. She raises her brows at me, gives me an inquiring look. 'Mohini and Pallavi,' I tell her, loudly and clearly.

She watches my lips and understands. She smiles, points at an ear, shakes her head to say she hasn't heard.

It comes in a wave, then. There's something wrong with

Narsimha's statement. I must go back to it and find out what. He's claimed to have heard something he couldn't have, even in the dead of night. Easy enough to find out what he said he'd heard, and whether it was possible for him to hear it.

But he's an ashram stalwart, a staunch believer in Prakash's other-worldliness, if not holiness. Why would he lie about something at the ashram? The questions keep tumbling out of my mind until Pallavi's eyes light on me and she comes running up for a hug.

This is straight out of old times, though she's six inches taller. The last time she did it she buried her face in my chest: now it's my shoulder. After a moment, though, her head comes off my shoulder, and she asks the question we've all been asking: 'Dad, what are we going to do?'

There's nothing to do but hold her for a while, and tell her it'll be all right, we'll work something out, and other such meaningless phrases. I look up to find Mohini glaring at me with a concentrated venom I haven't ever seen before, and know that we're not going to work anything out, that Pallavi is going to be a shuttle bouncing back and forth between the two of us. Out of a corner of my eye I see CV, whose powers of observation haven't dimmed with age, coming to the same conclusion.

CV takes charge. Pallavi disappears into her room, which is up the stairs, and Amma's minder wheels her away into her own domain thirty feet away, where she will spend the rest of the evening in front of a TV set running the minder's favourite shows.

That leaves three of us around a coffee table, Mohini and myself facing each other with CV refereeing from the side. Mohini's venom, I can see now, is her beast displaying itself. 'What have you got to say for yourself?' she asks me.

'Nothing, really,' I tell her.

'I put up with you and your drunkenness all these bloody years and you have nothing to say for yourself.' She turns to CV. 'That's gratitude for you,' she tells him. 'That's his commitment to our daughter. I told you it was going to be useless talking to him.'

'Calm down, child,' he tells her.

'Don't you "child" me, Appa,' she tells him angrily. 'Are you on my side or his?'

He faces her calmly, with the air of man who has nothing to lose. 'Neither,' he tells her. 'I'm on Pallavi's side.'

'Then why are you talking to him?' she asks, her voice rising. 'He walked out on Pallavi too last night.'

'Please don't shout,' he tells her. 'I might be old, but I can hear well, and I am, after all, your father.'

'I don't believe this,' she says, lowering her voice automatically. 'He doesn't care.'

'Then why did she run to him as soon as she saw him?'

'He's spoiled her, that's why,' she says forcefully. 'Every bloody chance he gets he takes her out, pretends to be the fun dad, makes me the wicked witch. Ask him what he did yesterday, as soon as he got back. He interrupted her homework, took her to some stupid fast food place, fed her junk, ruined her schedule, and walked out on her. Go on, ask him.'

'I don't have to ask him,' he replies. 'Pallavi told me.' He looks at me. 'Pallavi didn't go to school today, and Mohini didn't go to her office. I was hoping we'd be able to talk without too much bitterness but I was wrong. Maybe it's too early. Maybe I'm in too much of a hurry to sort things out because I don't have as much time left as you do.

'But let me warn both of you. Time flies. You'll wake up one day and find it's too late. So whatever problems you have, fix them without putting my granddaughter through too much. I'll be here for you, of course, but I'll leave it to you.' He rises, turning to me. 'I'll have you dropped off wherever you want to go.'

'Thanks,' I tell him. 'I'd like a moment with Pallavi before I leave.'

'Okay,' he says. 'I'll have her called here.'

'Appa!' Mohini begins.

He cuts her off. 'I told you, I'm on Pallavi's side. I think she needs to see him before he goes.' He looks directly at Mohini. 'You will not interfere. You can say what you like to Bala when Pallavi is not around, but in her presence both of you will be civil to each other.' And while she stands pale and shocked, he walks off to the kitchen to tell one of the maids to call Pallavi down. He'd have liked to do it himself but his painful knees don't let him negotiate the stairs easily.

I hug Pallavi goodbye in the porch, while Mohini stands watching, silent, nursing her rage like a second child. CV hangs back, ready to intervene if he thinks necessary. 'When will I see you again?' Pallavi asks.

'As soon as possible,' I tell her.

'Come whenever you like,' CV says. 'Just be sure to call me before you come.'

'I'll do that,' I tell him. Perhaps I misjudged him, too, as he did me long ago. But he's corrected his judgment, while I haven't. I turn at the top of the steps to offer him my hand. 'Thanks,' I say, and go down to the car.

Back in my room at the guest house I dig out the papers, and find the transcript of Narsimha's interrogations in both cases. I put both sets together and find the potential lie on the third page of his interrogation on the rape charge. 'What were you doing in the corridor when Raju was waiting outside Prakash Shastry's room?'

'The noise of the washing machine woke me up,' goes

Narsimha's reply in the transcript. 'After that I couldn't sleep so I got up for some water. I thought I heard voices so I went to check.' How did partially deaf Narsimha hear the washing machine, or those voices? Hassan told me they all knew about his deafness but didn't mention it in his presence for fear of offending him. And how did his deafness escape the notice of the cops who interrogated him? From the transcript, it seems that they spoke to him alone. If there was only one policeman interrogating him, Narsimha could have got by on his lip-reading skills, without the cop ever noticing the deafness. The transcript carries the name of only one cop, the investigating officer, but I do know that there are at least two cops at these sessions, one sometimes only to observe.

I sit back with a feeling of relief. Every investigation, whether carried out by a policeman or a reporter, depends for its success on the first inconsistency. That first little chink in the armour into which you insert something sharp to pull the whole suit apart. This is it, that first little chink.

Gokul will be able to find out the details of how these interrogations have been carried out ... in any case, we can always find out whether Narsimha's hearing is good enough to hear that washing machine, and voices in the corridor.

If it isn't ... what if the interrogation was meant to be this way? What if the investigating officer doesn't want Narsimha's lie exposed?

Would Narsimha go creeping down the ashram corridors late at night on his own initiative? He doesn't have any initiative because his years of government service killed it. Someone must have put him up to it. Prakash is being framed.

By whom, and for what?

## Chapter Fourteen

MORNING BRINGS WAKEFULNESS, a headache, and deep concern for Pallavi. It only gets worse because I can't find the remaining lorazepam and I'll have to get through the day on my own because there won't be time to see a doctor and I'm certainly not going to a hospital. I lie around for a while, then try to meditate, and then give up and get ready.

Harsha puts together an egg-and-toast breakfast before I remember I've got to collect my transport from the dealer in the morning.

By the time I'm done with breakfast, the shakes have gone and the headache is passing and I'm at the dealer's at ten, only to find the scooter hasn't been registered yet. 'I'll take care of it today,' the salesman assures me. 'You can collect it in the evening.'

'What'll I do today?' I ask.

He looks shamefaced, then says, 'We have a standby that we can give you for the day, but it's not the same model.' Apparently the one I'm getting is the one with all the bells and whistles while the standby is basic.

'Doesn't matter,' I tell him. 'I'll take the standby.'

The standby turns out to be a battle-scarred black machine with racing stripes and a pronounced dent in front. It used to belong to the man who owns the dealership, and it's spent a few years being test-ridden by prospective customers, the salesman tells me as he hands me the documents. Apparently its insides are fine, and only the outside is beaten up. The engine buzzes happily to life when he turns the key, and it sounds fine to my undiscerning ear. I purchase a basic helmet, hop onto the scooter, and, briefcase between my legs, putter to the petrol bunk a few hundred yards away for a tankful. No hidden glitches announce themselves other than a loud squeal from the brakes. With the tank brimming, and with no more practice than the brief ride to refuel, I pitch myself into the city's homicidal peak-hour traffic.

Forty-five minutes and a dozen brushes with death later I turn into the office parking lot, dusty and trembling but mildly exhilarated at the thought of having avoided being knocked down by sundry buses, trucks, and cabs. The watchman, who knows me, grins as I go by, and tells me to get a parking permit later in the day.

Got to keep busy all day, I tell myself, because being busy is one way to keep the withdrawal at bay. I had to concentrate so hard all the way to the office on the scooter I didn't have the time to worry about withdrawal symptoms.

Srini is out at some meeting or other but Surya grins toothily at me as I stride by him, briefcase in hand. Alone in my room, I call Gokul. 'Call me in an hour,' he tells me. 'Busy.'

An hour later, he starts the conversation with, 'What is it this time, bastard?'

'Info on procedures,' I tell him. 'There's this transcript of an interrogation.' I give him the date and time and the name of the policeman conducting it and the name of the interrogatee, Narsimha, besides the case reference. 'This guy has hearing troubles. He's partially deaf; I don't know how bad the deafness is. He gets by in normal conversation by lip-reading to supplement what he hears, if at all he hears anything. Can you find out if the policeman doing the interrogation knew about the deafness? Can you ask him to check if Narsimha can hear the washing machine in his bedroom, and voices in the corridor, like he claims to?'

'It's not my case,' he tells me, 'and nowhere near my jurisdiction. I know the investigating officer, but not very well, and I know that he's not known to be corrupt. I'll ask him about the deafness, but I can't say for sure whether he'll follow up.'

'Can you at least find out if he knew of Narsimha's deafness?'

'Yes. I'll call you in the evening.'

I need to check with the ashram's doctor whether he knows about Narsimha's deafness, but I don't have his number. I do have Laxman's, so I call him. He's in Hyderabad, taking a couple of days off before returning to his old job, and seems relaxed and happy. 'Good morning, Bala,' he says. 'What can I do for you?'

'Tell me how I can get hold of that doctor in Belman,' I tell him.

'I'll send you his number after I hang up,' he says.

'Thanks,' I tell him. 'How are you doing?'

'Fine, fine,' he says. A pause. 'Eating well. I really missed this.'

I laugh. 'Enjoy while you can.'

A moment later he texts me the doctor's home, clinic, and cellphone numbers. The doctor, one Rangaraju, is in his clinic. 'I know Narsimha,' he says, 'but I'm not allowed to tell you anything about him unless you get an order from a judge or something like that.'

'I just want to ask you about his deafness.'

'Okay. I've discussed this with others in his presence, so I can tell you. He is moderately deaf, meaning that he would have trouble following normal speech in most conditions, a hearing aid would be useful, but he doesn't want a hearing aid because he says it's uncomfortable.'

'He lip-reads quite a bit.'

'Yes. If you look for that, you will understand that he is deaf. Otherwise he can disguise it quite well.'

'Are you familiar with the ashram?' I ask.

'Of course.'

'Do you know about their washing machine?' I ask.

'The one that sounds like a bus?' he asks. 'Yes.'

'Would Narsimha be able to hear the washing machine from his bedroom?'

'You'll have to test for it. There are lots of factors. Ambient noise, time of the day, the frequencies of sound, and things like that. Some sounds, like car horns, are pitched so that most people, even partially deaf ones, can hear them. So it all depends.'

'Did you recommend a hearing aid?' I ask.

'I can't,' he says. 'You have to go to an ENT specialist for that. And there are some technicalities with hearing aids. You need to find out what kind of hearing aid suits you best. It's not as simple as going out and buying one.'

'Thanks very much,' I tell him. 'May I call you again?'

'Of course,' he replies. 'Any time.'

I go back to the transcripts. The same officer is investigating Raju's death and the case against Prakash which makes sense, and if he's doing even a halfway honest job, and if the two cases are linked, he'll find that out. But then, if Gowda's trying to interfere with the investigation, it makes it easier for him because he only has to bullock one policeman, not two.

What a mess!

When I check again, Srini is back, and available. When I knock on his door, he tells me to return in five minutes.

When I return to his room he's wound up his meeting and is showing the visitors out, and I'm surprised to see that they're money men, quiet, discreet investors. 'Yes, Bala,' he says as soon as I enter, 'I see you're still dry. Good.'

'Yes,' I tell him. 'Look, there's a possible inconsistency in the case.'

'What?' he asks.

I tell him about Narsimha and his deafness and the story of him being woken up by the washing machine. 'Okay, we'll get it checked out,' he says. 'I'll talk to someone in the police about it. Anything else?'

'I want a good background on this Smita Sharma. I want to dig some more.'

'Sure. You want to talk to people who've worked with her on TV shows?' He grins. 'It can be a vicious world, entertainment TV. Worse than news channels.'

'Maybe. But I need your contacts.'

'Sure. I'll try to set up something by evening, but you might not get the right people immediately, specially if they're shooting somewhere out of town.'

Back in my room I turn to the third envelope: copies of Prakash's books and whatever papers they'd collected from his room. To this I add the copy of the Gita and the other papers that Laxman gave me. I can't think of anything useful coming out of these things but since I have nothing else to do I grit my teeth and go at them anyway.

I find most scriptural texts arcane, tedious, or banal, and not just the Hindu scriptures: they're all like that, except possibly some Buddhist texts. I start with the copy of the Gita that Laxman gave me. It's not really a book: Prakash seems to have downloaded the material from a bunch of internet sites. It's a thick pile, one page to a sloka, each page containing the original Sanskrit text, and its English translation. There's plenty of space on each page for notes, which Prakash has made in his neat hand.

The first few slokas are banal, but then comes the big question. Arjuna, the peerless bowman, stands between the armies, sees his relatives arrayed against him, and, refusing to fight and perhaps kill them, throws down his weapons. Krishna, his charioteer, explains why he must fight.

Inserted into this are some slokas about the caste system, and about 'loose' women having the potential to destroy a clan. Prakash dismisses these emphatically as nonsense, and I wonder why.

The essence of the Gita is in the second chapter of eighteen. The self that we think the self is an illusion, Krishna tells Arjuna. There is no such thing. The real self is eternal, neither born nor killed. Therefore, the thought that you kill or are killed is meaningless.

Prakash has some notes here. Three different schools of thought sprang from the second chapter of the Gita: advaita or non-duality, dvaita or duality, and visishtadvaita or qualified non-duality. Advaita says that you're god. Dvaita says you're not, but you and god are both eternal beings. Visishtadvaita says you're different from god but part of him as well. They're three different ways of looking at the relationship between you and your maker.

Prakash's notes go straight to the point. In essence, he says, the exponents of the three schools argue about the nature of the ultimate self from interpretations of the Gita and other texts. The Gita itself claims that this same ultimate self is within reach. None of the three speaks from experience of this ultimate self. They're all fumbling, along with the rest of us, looking for answers in texts rather than in themselves.

Isn't this proof that they don't know this ultimate self? If they knew what they were talking about, would they have any reason to talk? Doesn't this actually throw doubt on the very existence of the ultimate self? It's provocative stuff, the kind of thinking that generates lynch mobs from among Hindu fundamentalists. Now he's got me. I can't help reading on.

My phone rings: it's Srini, who tells me that the guy who produced the last serial in which Smita Sharma acted is out of town, that he'll fix up a meeting as soon as the man returns. I turn to Surya, who has his own set of contacts in the universe of TV serials. Surya doesn't know this producer but instead an actress who's worked with Ms Sharma earlier, and is currently resting between shoots. 'I'll give you her number,' he tells me after a few minutes. 'She's available. You can set up a meeting yourself.'

'Thanks,' I tell him.

'Bala,' he says, as I begin to move on. 'No recording. You can't quote her. She won't want to get involved with the police in any way. I promised.'

'Fine,' I tell him.

I call to set up a meeting, and find the lady – one Swarna Rao – available right away. 'I'll talk to you,' she tells me, 'if you can come home right now. My son is down with a fever and I don't want to leave him alone.'

She gives me her address, and I board the little black scooter and proceed to battle with the traffic to her house, which is five kilometres away, forty-five minutes in the city's traffic. She lives in a large, florid second-floor flat in an expensive tightly-guarded apartment block. She turns out to be comfortably plump, in her late thirties, about the same age as Ms Sharma, and voluble enough. Her sitting room is full of photographs of herself in various roles or at weddings or parties, in full war paint and showily dressed.

'Surya told me you'd come,' she says, in Kannada. 'You wanted to know about Smita. About that case against that man in the hills.'

'Yes,' I tell her. 'I'd like to know more about her.'

'He told me this is just for you. No police, nothing.'

'Yes,' I reply. 'I won't record this, and I won't quote you.'

'I've known her for twenty years,' she says. 'I know all about her career, from the time she used to act in college plays.'

'I haven't heard much about her,' I say. 'I don't know how successful she was, or how good she was as an actress.'

She laughs. 'She couldn't act very well. She got only small roles for older people.' She preens. 'The first time we worked together, she was my older sister, ten years older, even though we're the same age. After that she had no hope of getting a young woman's role.'

'Did she have many fans?'

Another laugh. 'Every actress has fans. Many … I don't know. But she didn't get much on Facebook or Twitter. She wasn't so popular. We all knew how she got her roles.'

'How?'

'She would do anything to get roles … it didn't matter. That's why her husband left her. You know what I mean.'

'Umm … yes.'

'She was with that minister for some time. Then he got fed up with her because she kept asking him for presents. He gave her some. He gave her a car, and some jewellery, and then he stopped. I don't know what happened after that. But I know that she didn't like him. He drank too much, he smelt bad … he was useless.'

'Were you surprised at the rape charge?'

'Yes. I never thought she would care so much about it … you know, she isn't very good-looking anyway, without makeup and all.' She smiles happily. 'But the Swami might have been desperate, no?'

'Did she tell a lot of lies?'

She takes her time replying. 'In this business you have to keep up appearances. We all lie. Even if I don't have work I say I have offers. We lie about age. About money. Now I am going to retire, which is why I'm telling you all this. No more work.'

'Why?'

'Too much competition,' she says. 'And I have my boy to look after.'

I don't ask her if she's got offers. Instead, I ask, 'Was Ms Sharma thinking of retiring?'

She shakes her head. 'No. She wanted to keep acting as long as she got offers. She would retire only if she stopped getting offers.'

'Was she any good on stage?'

'Yes. Actually, she might have made a better stage actress than a TV actress. It's different, you know. But there's more publicity for TV people, more money.'

'I know,' I tell her. 'And was she depressed from time to time?'

'It happens to many actors,' she says. 'She was depressed quite a lot of the time. She used to talk about it all the time.'

'Did she talk of suicide?'

'Not directly … she used to say, so-and-so will miss me only when I'm dead. But I never knew her to speak directly of killing herself. Never.'

'Was she on medication for depression?'

'I don't think so. She would have told me …'

There's not much else to ask her, so I start to give her my thanks but she interrupts me. 'Acting is not what you think it is,' she says.

'What do you mean?' I ask.

'If you act seriously you learn to observe.' She smiles, a hint of mischief in her eyes. 'All the while you were wondering how I could say what I did about someone who's my friend. Everyone thinks like that.'

I find myself embarrassed, and manage a kind of smile. 'I don't mean to judge,' I tell her.

'I could see that,' she says. 'You've seen much worse than this, but you can't help reacting.'

She laughs. 'You should know that we're not very different from other people. Maybe more honest in some ways, that's all.'

Still embarrassed, I say my goodbyes and return to the office, stopping on the way for a light lunch. The waters are as muddy as before: it's difficult to establish the truth of either Prakash's version or Ms Sharma's.

Back in my office I settle back down to his notes on the Bhagavad Gita and find nothing more of interest. I move on then to his diary, looking for entries starting about the date on which Smita Sharma first met him. He's made notes, saying that she seemed genuinely sad but was covering up the reasons for the sadness. There are more details, all of which confirm what he's said about the three meetings. The air of falsehood remained right up to the last meeting, he says, adding in his notes the next day that Raju was relieved that she was gone. No mention, in any but the notes on the first day, of recordings being switched off or left on.

That's not conclusive, either. No one would mention groping a woman depending on him for emotional support.

After noting Raju's relief at Ms Sharma's departure from the ashram, Prakash notes more details about Ms Sharma. Why did she come to him for her depression rather than go to a mental health professional? There's a more general question, after that: why are people such suckers for godmen?

The notes started about two years ago. If there's a hint in here of why anyone might be after him, it would be much earlier than Ms Sharma's arrival, so I go right to the beginning.

It starts with an intriguing entry. 'Godmen are suckers: Patanjali warns of it. The key to it is in the Gita. Krishna tells Arjuna that those people on the other side will die when their time comes. Whoever thinks he's the killer is fooling himself: he is only the instrument of god. In other words, the politically incorrect conclusion that you have no free will. It's the same with godmen. They and their followers might think that the godmen did it. It's just fate.

'Godmen are deluded or false.'

About ten days later, on a Monday, he notes, 'Yesterday was spent looking over numbers on success. Very revealing. One Bombay-based investor converted a thousand rupees into a thousand crore rupees over twenty years of speculation on the stock markets. With a base of a hundred million or so investors, it's very probable that one or two investors make such profits over a couple of decades. More than that would be suspicious.

'I would be a fool to offer anyone advice.'

There's an intriguing entry from about five months ago. 'Krishnappa Gowda and his colleague, Sadashiv Uchil, spent some time here. Raju used the mikes to eavesdrop. After they left, he told me that he had some changes in mind. I told him to do as he wished, because I would like to withdraw from these matters.'

Other entries make him seem vulnerable: 'The ashram is a burden, but I learn from visitors. The gratitude of visitors is a bigger burden than the task of running the ashram. They don't see that I'm just as hollow as they are. I look forward to leaving it.' Was he planning to leave anyway?

'I wish for a guide. A guru, actually. I wish there were a city of gurus with a gurukul where you could just walk in and ask … For what?'

'I want to teach young people physics. A rigorous

education in physics makes you question things without losing touch with reality.'

And then I get to the last entry, on the day I first met him. 'A guest for lunch, a journalist. He's far less respectful than most other visitors, asking questions about all kinds of things despite being lost in alcohol. Maybe we have something to learn from each other.'

He's observant and he's been learning all the time. I wish I could look at his original notes, rather than these copies: I want to know if he goes back to the old entries, and which ones he revisits most.

Gokul calls at four, just when I'm wishing I had a drink, just as the shakes return. 'Got something?' I ask.

'Nothing,' he says. 'The officer who questioned Narsimha, one ASI Venkatachalam, is quite a jolly type. Loud and cheerful. A half-deaf man would have no trouble hearing him. There were two policemen present, and they both agree on the transcript. Venkatachalam is very straight, as far as I've heard, and unlikely to give in to pressure on what questions to ask.'

'Can we check if Narsimha's hearing is good enough to hear that damn machine?'

'It'll be easier to persuade Venkatachalam if there's medical opinion to support your view that he's partially deaf.'

'The doctor in Belman says he's likely to be moderately deaf, meaning that he'll have trouble hearing conversations. He's learnt to lip-read. Everyone at the ashram knows about his deafness but no one mentions it because it hurts him.'

'Let me see what I can do. It shouldn't be a problem.'

I tell him we don't have much time because Narsimha has ordered a new machine which is due to be delivered soon. It strikes me now that that in itself is suspicious. 'It's the only possible inconsistency I've seen so far. I hope it works out.'

'Yes … How're you dealing with the booze?'

'It's under control so far,' I tell him. Suddenly I open up. 'You know, it's different if you set a time limit. You can count the days or the hours or even the seconds until your next drink. But never ... that's a different feeling altogether.'

'Yes. Take it day by day.'

'I will. Today should be better. I'll try to spend some time with Pallavi.'

'Good. Have fun.'

'I will. We're closer than we've been for years.'

I get back to the papers and to wishing for a drink but not for long because Gokul calls again. 'Neither Girish Kavoor nor Venkatachalam would mind verifying whether Narsimha could have heard that washing machine. Venkatachalam thinks the simplest thing would be to test it out at the ashram. He'll do it late in the evening, after their dinner, before they go to bed. There's not much ambient noise then, to give Narsimha an excuse. He's busy today, but he can take care of it tomorrow.'

'Good,' I tell him. 'But is Narsimha at risk? What if the guy behind this, umm, well, disappears him?'

'I don't know,' Gokul replies. 'Only Kavoor and Venkatachalam know about the test. You spoke to the doctor about it, so he might have guessed that Narsimha's deafness might be a factor, and might pass on the word. No one else could possibly know. If he fails the test, we can have him taken into custody for further interrogation. I don't think they'll try to finish him in prison.'

I remember telling Srini about Narsimha's deafness, and my suspicions, and mention it to Gokul. 'If you want to be certain,' he replies, 'you'll have to doubt everyone. That includes Srini and you and me, too.'

'Okay,' I tell him, but in the back of my mind that niggling suspicion pops up again: Srini? Unthinkable!

Time to call Pallavi. 'Hi, Dad,' she says. She's in her grandfather's car, on her way to his house. 'Mom's at home. She'll be back late. She told me to go to bed if she isn't back by nine-thirty.'

She doesn't know that home isn't likely to continue to be home. I wonder how Mohini will tell her. She probably won't: she'll leave it to her father.

'I see,' I tell her. 'I'll see you later today, even if it's only for a short while.' I can make it, though it means travelling a couple of hours or more to spend half an hour with her. It suddenly hits me, the time that you lose having a few drinks every day. There's never any question of going out in the evening alone after starting off on the booze.

At six, eyes aching from reading handwritten Kannada through most of the day, I pack the papers neatly away in my briefcase and leave it in my filing cabinet: no more reading for the night. Then I call CV. 'I'd like to visit,' I tell him. 'To see Pallavi.'

'I'm not going anywhere,' he tells me. 'Come whenever you like. Stay for dinner if you can … Mohini will be back late.'

'I know. Pallavi told me.'

I bump into Srini in the corridor just outside his room, and tell him my plans for the evening before leaving. It's drizzling outside but traffic is worse than usual and I buy a raincoat before venturing out on the dented old TVS. What with the poor visibility and the traffic and the hidden potholes – they're full of water now, and you have no idea how deep they might be – and the rust on my riding skills, it's past seven when I pull up outside CV's house. The watchman doesn't recognize me until I lift the helmet's visor, and then waves me through, grinning. I can't help wondering why all the watchmen I know grin when they see me on the scooter.

CV leaves Pallavi alone with me as we sit in the cavernous sitting room faced with tea and large plates of hot snacks. CV belongs to the school of thought that children just back from school need a big meal before being made to do their homework and I watch while she digs in with a pleasure I rarely saw at home, or even at that fast food joint where we last ate together. 'Did you have a lot of trouble coming here?' she asks. 'And why were you on a scooter?'

'No trouble at all,' I tell her. 'A scooter's all I can afford. I might be out of a job soon.'

'Dad, what's going to happen?' she asks. 'Are we going to be thrown out of our house?'

'I don't know,' I reply, wondering how I can think of her as a child because her worries seem about the same as mine. 'Your mother used the flat to get herself a loan from a bank, and I have no idea what she did with the money, or how she's going to pay it back, so the bank might take the house.'

'But isn't the flat yours as well?'

'It is,' I reply, 'but I might have signed some papers for her without asking why. I don't remember.' I do remember, though, with considerable shame, at least three occasions on which I signed, without question or even reading, papers that Mohini placed in front of me. I also remember that she used to do this sort of thing when I was already sunk in guilt for something else, drinking or missing an occasion or something ... CV will intervene, I know, but I shouldn't have let this happen in the first place. 'When I was drunk,' I add, in explanation.

'You aren't drunk now, are you?' she asks.

'Not at all.'

'You've been like this since you got back from Mangalore? Did the Swami do something to you?'

I can't help grinning at the thought of Prakash 'doing

something' to me. 'Not that I know of,' I tell her, 'but he's a good man all the same.'

'So have you cut down on your drinking like you used to promise Mom all the time?'

I stop myself from explaining to her. 'No. There's no question of cutting down.' I pause. 'I have to stay totally off. If I have one drink I'm gone.'

'But don't you feel like a drink sometimes?' she asks.

'No,' I tell her, 'not sometimes. All the bloody time. And it's not just wanting a drink. I ... well, I ache for a drink most of the time.'

I suspect she gets a sense of what it means, this notion that in all the hours and days and weeks and months and years to come I'll never ever be safe having even one little drink. It must be worse for her because she's a good thirty-five years younger. In any case, she holds my hand in sympathy for a moment and the ache decreases just a little bit for a little while.

'Are you going back to Mangalore?' she asks.

'I have to,' I tell her. 'The Swami – his name is Prakash – is in prison for something I don't think he did. A few days after they took him away his assistant was murdered. There's something very unpleasant going on there and I want to find out what it is.'

'Won't the police do it?' she asks.

'The police have already made one mistake,' I tell her. 'Besides, they're usually overworked, so you have to keep pushing at them to get a case solved.'

'How do you know they made a mistake?' she asks, a little sceptical.

I explain about Narsimha's partial deafness and his statement that he heard the washing machine. She hears me out in silence, then says, 'You know, Dad, you're quite smart.'

I think of the hours spent poring over those photocopies of handwritten Kannada – and that I have to get back to it tonight – and don't feel at all smart. It's quite hard to have an honest conversation with a teenager unless you're used to it or very determined. But CV marches up, and saves me the trouble of a response. 'Dinner will be ready whenever you want it,' he says. 'Do you mind if I join you?'

'No,' I tell him, knowing what's coming.

He sits. 'Your transport, Bala. You should have told me.'

'Why?'

'You're not safe.'

'It helps me stay sober.'

That shuts him up for a moment. 'Better to have you drunk and alive than sober and dead.'

Pallavi pipes up in my defence. 'Come on, Granddad, he's okay. Everyone uses scooters.'

He quells her with an angry look. 'You know how many people get into accidents? You know that your risk of death or serious injury on a two-wheeler is ten times more than if you're in a car? You know your father hasn't been on a two-wheeler in … in fifteen years?'

'Easy,' I tell him. 'It's all I can afford.'

He doesn't even hear it. 'Take one of my cars. Take a small one if you like. You won't get wet in the rain. You won't fall off. You won't go into a ditch if a car hits you.'

I raise my hands. 'Enough,' I tell him. 'Let's change the subject.'

He gives up. 'Okay.' A smile lights his face. The one thing he appreciates about all this is having a chance to spoil his granddaughter, and he does it shamelessly. 'I've got you some clothes,' he tells her. 'Some of those things you wanted. Go try them out. They're on your bed.'

She looks at me, pleading. 'Go if you wish,' I tell her, lightened by her enthusiasm. 'I'll wait for you.'

After she rushes off, he turns to me. 'Bala, I just wanted to tell you this. If you and Mohini get back together, I will do what I can to make sure that your flat stays yours. Otherwise, they live here.'

'Why?' I ask.

'Because Mohini by herself will not be capable of bringing up Pallavi when she's at a critical stage of growing up. Once Pallavi goes to college, it doesn't matter, especially if she goes to a hostel, but in any case it's only for the next three or four years, and I do expect to live that long.'

He's anticipated some of my questions. 'Okay,' I tell him. 'Looks like that's what'll happen. I don't think I want to get back to Mohini.'

'That's very frank.'

'You deserve the truth. You seem to be taking care of them, and you need to know what's in store for them.'

He nods. 'I thought so. Bala, I'm sorry this became such a mess. So many regrets, all for old things … What are your own plans?'

'I'll probably shift to Chennai, to another job with a newspaper … No TV.'

'That's a step back.'

'Only if you want TV.'

'What about money?'

'Poor to start with, but there's hope.'

'Is it new, this newspaper?'

'Yes.'

'You like startups, don't you?'

It's strange, an insight like that coming from him. 'Y-yes,' I tell him. 'Though I never thought of it like that.'

He nods and changes the subject. 'What about Pallavi?'

'If she's going to stay with you, I'll just pop in as often as I can. Once a week, if I can. Chennai's not that far away, and I needn't be office-bound.'

'Right.'

'Let me be honest. Your presence is a relief. Pallavi will be okay with you. Perhaps ...' My voice trails off when I begin to voice the thought.

'Perhaps what?'

I force it out. 'Perhaps better off than she would be with either Mohini or myself alone.'

He laughs. 'It's funny,' he says. 'You and I are just about beginning to get along and your marriage to my daughter is breaking up.' He rises. 'Come and eat. Consider borrowing one of my cars. Buy it, if you like. I'll give you a good price.'

The belly-beast is up in a moment, flaring at the thought of taking his charity. Then I see the worry in his eyes and, for the first time, the beast disappears without resistance. It's not charity that he's offering. A smile emerges. 'No,' I tell him. 'I'll get by.'

We eat when Pallavi returns in a fresh T-shirt and jeans that look no different from the ones she was wearing before, but she's all aglow so I tell her the new outfit is pretty and we move on to dinner. Pallavi digs in as if she's forgotten the stuff she ate only an hour and a bit ago, talking all the while to her grandfather, and I watch with mixed feelings, pleasure at her freedom and regret at having missed so much of it.

Then the notion that a drink would go down very well enters my mind and the evening falls apart. There's no question now of looking for a doctor and medication and so on: I have to have a drink.

They tell you the desire for a drink is only in your mind but it's an avalanche all the same. You can't get away from it, and it blows you off your feet. After all these days without one I've been feeling mildly virtuous but the avalanche buries the virtue under twenty feet of snow. When Pallavi asks me when I'll know for sure about the job I don't hear her at first and she has to repeat the question twice before it gets through.

Dinner seems interminably long and when Pallavi finally gives up I jump to my feet and announce that I need to get moving. 'Did you suddenly remember something?' CV asks.

'Yes,' I tell him, glad for the excuse, and move off to the scooter.

I emerge onto the highway home without looking right and left and a large Volvo bus blows past, horn blaring. The rush of wind and the receding wail of its horn bring me back to earth momentarily, and I discover I'm not really competent to ride back to town so I find a lorry moving steadily and not too fast in the direction I want to go and follow thirty feet behind it. Soon a lady on a scooter much like mine, but with its shiny bits intact, pulls along behind, obviously doing the same thing, and, further on, another little delivery van joins us.

It's past ten, and the booze shops are all closed. I'm in a hurry to get that drink but I don't want to drink in a bar so far away from the guest house because there are occasional police checks for drunk drivers. After the fifth closed liquor shop, I notice that the van, which can travel much faster, has continued at the tail of the procession for several kilometres, and risk a quick backward glance to note its number, an ordinary jumble of digits.

Near the guest house, though, I remember that I left my stocks of booze in the flat when I moved out. I still have a key to the place, and unless Mohini's changed the locks I should be able to retrieve a bottle from there.

I find my way to the flat, and find our next-door neighbours, Shyam and Savita, at the door of their flat. Shyam just nods at me but Savita walks over. 'What are you doing here?' she asks, standing arms akimbo, looking for a fight. 'Mohini told me she threw you out.'

'She did,' I reply. 'I've just come to pick up something of mine.'

'She said you'd come back once, just once, after telling her. Have you told her?' Her voice is rising, and Shyam tries ineffectually to restrain her.

'It's not your business,' I tell her. 'If you don't like me entering my own flat, tell Mohini. Or the police, if that's what you prefer.' I duck into the flat and slam the door shut in Savita's face. My only aim now is to get back to the guest house as fast as possible, and I leave in under a minute, the precious bottle safe in an old bag I've slung over my shoulder. Savita is still outside, speaking shrilly, but I ignore her and moments later I'm heading for the guest house, in a fever of anticipation, the helmet's strap flapping loose around my chin.

A drizzle, gaining strength quickly in a strong wind, takes me by surprise. With no raincoat, I'm soaked in a couple of minutes. Thinking only of getting out of the rain and into the bottle, I speed up. A kilometre away from the guest house, through the rain now driving horizontally into my face, I see a delivery van coming up in the rear-view mirror. It seems like the one that tagged me from CV's house, and it's catching up fast. When it's within a few feet, I panic, and speed up some more. I misjudge the distance to the next curve, and take it too fast.

One moment I'm leaning hard into the turn, and the next I'm on my side on the road, without knowing quite what happened in between. Out of a corner of my eye I get a glimpse of the van speeding away. I'm not sure if it hit me: if it did, it was a very gentle impact, just a nudge, but enough to throw me off balance. Lying on the road, trying to get a hold of myself, all I can ask myself is, why the bloody van didn't finish me off. Then I remember Prakash talking about letting go so I let it go and sink into the rising dark.

The next thing I know there's someone trying to get my

cellphone out of my pocket. He notices me stirring, says, 'Accident. Whom can I contact?'

The first name that comes to mind is CV's. 'Look for CV,' I tell him blearily. There's a numbness spreading up my leg and when I try to touch it my arm doesn't obey orders and there's a pain in my shoulder too. There's the smell of alcohol in the air: the bottle must have broken in the fall. What a pity, I tell myself and slide off again.

I become aware, very dimly, of more confusion, of hands picking me up, and a pain in the shoulder that makes me cry out, but I feel too weak to speak so I give up. Then there are lights and small bumps and a cool clean sheet and people bending over me. The pain keeps me awake through the journey and the transfer to a gurney at what I presume is a hospital is excruciating and I cry out again. Then there are needles going into me and more movement and I black out again.

When next I awake I'm in a room with dark green curtains keeping out the light. There's a terrible taste in my mouth, a bad pain in my leg, and aches and little pains all over. My throat is completely dry and when I try to speak all I can produce is a croak, but it looks like there's someone watching because a brighter light comes on and in a few minutes someone in white comes up and holds a glass of water to my mouth, swallowing from which makes my throat infinitely better.

Then I remember falling off the scooter and sinking into the dark and with the return of that memory some of the aches and pains take a more definite shape. But by the time I can begin exploring them another figure turns up, apparently a doctor, for he's got a stethoscope around his neck. 'Do you know who you are?' he asks.

'Balaram Kamath,' I tell him.

'What day of the week is today? What's the date?'

I can't seem to remember but it doesn't matter. I tell him I don't know, and he asks me a few more questions, none of which seem important, but I answer whichever I can and slowly drift off to sleep again.

The next time I surface it's daylight but I can hear the rain spatter on the window panes. The same terrible taste lingers in my mouth and I have a splitting headache, and my left leg and shoulder are painful. There's a tube sticking into my wrist and the discomfort in my groin indicates they've stuck a catheter in me as well. I try to sit up and discover that my back aches, too, but it's all bearable. Someone sitting close by watching me stands up and comes to the bedside. He's vaguely familiar but I can't place him. 'Where am I?' I ask. 'And who are you? I've seen you but can't remember your name.'

He smiles. 'You're in a hospital: Lakeview Clinic, Ulsoor. You were brought here after you had a fall from your scooter. I am Ramnath. Mr CV sent me here to make sure you are all right. I'll call the nurse and we'll see.'

I remember the fall quite clearly now, and the van. 'What about the van?' I ask Ramnath.

'I don't know about any van,' he says. 'I'll get someone.'

He disappears for a while and returns with a nurse who checks my pulse, gives me more water, and leaves to find a doctor. The doctor arrives twenty minutes later with another nurse in tow. He's an authoritative-looking silver-haired man about sixty years old and behaves as if he owns the place. He wishes me good afternoon. 'What time is it?' I ask, surprised. I thought it was morning.

'Around three,' he says. 'I'm Dr Baliga, and this is my clinic. CV is an old friend, and he's asked me to look after you. How do you feel?'

So he does own the place. I dredge up a smile. 'I have a

bad headache, my shoulder hurts, and I have a few aches and pains, especially in the left leg.'

'Do you remember what day it is?' he asks.

I can't seem to figure it out. 'Is it Friday?' I ask.

'No,' he says. 'It's Saturday. You had your accident on Thursday night.'

'I've missed a whole day?'

'You've been in and out of consciousness. You're on painkillers and mild sedation, and we'll keep you that way for another couple of days.

'You concussed your head when you fell. Your helmet was lying four feet away from your head when they found you. If you'd strapped your helmet on properly you wouldn't have been here. But then, if you hadn't been wearing one at all, the damage would probably have been worse.'

'Okay,' I tell him, 'I'll be careful in future. What's the damage?'

'Nothing very serious. You have a grade IV concussion, that's what they call a traumatic brain injury, and your headache is probably a result of that. You might find parts of your memory unreliable, you might have trouble balancing, you might have nausea sometimes, and you might be irritable at times. You might find your sleep cycle upset.

'You have a deep gash on your left thigh, and lost a lot of blood … I don't know how much, but we had to give you a transfusion. That loss of blood has left you weak. You dislocated your left shoulder, on which you landed. You're lucky not to have broken your collarbone. But the shoulder is immobilized because you have damaged ligaments which will take a couple of weeks to heal. You might find that the pain of your injuries keeps you awake, so you've been prescribed painkillers and a tablet or injection to help you sleep.'

'Right now I could do with a drink. That'll help me sleep better than any tablets.'

He shakes his head. 'No. Drinking will retard your recovery from the concussion. I'll keep you here under observation for a few days during which you won't be able to drink. Even after we discharge you, you should stay off alcohol for at least a month.'

'It's just a concussion, isn't it, and some cuts and damaged ligaments?' I ask.

'The concussion could be serious. Sometimes the symptoms take months to go. They usually go in a few days, or weeks, but sometimes they last. You have to be careful. I'll personally review your condition every day from now on.'

'Look, can I at least go to the toilet on my own?' I ask angrily.

'Of course,' he says. 'Slowly, carefully. No jerks.' The nurse removes the tube going into my wrist – the cannula stays, though – and then, gently, withdraws the catheter. She draws back and I sit up. My head and back ache a bit more, but that's all. I swing one leg off the bed without trouble, and then the other, but when I try to stand the world begins to spin around and I sit back with a thump. The nurse is at my side, and lowers me gently down.

'Try again tomorrow,' the doctor says. 'With someone watching, so you don't fall again. A second fall before you've recovered from your first can do a lot of damage. Sleep as much as you can. The rest will do you good. I think we'll put the catheter back. You'll need it if you want to sleep in peace.' He smiles. 'You're lucky, you know.'

'Why?'

'Back in the old days, they didn't let concussion victims sleep for more than a few hours at a time. They'd wake you up every few hours to make sure you hadn't gone into a coma. Now we have things like CT scans so we don't need to do that any more.' A pause. 'We don't want your phone to disturb you, so we've given it to Mr Ramnath here. If there's anything urgent for you, he'll tell you.'

'Hey, you can't do that,' I tell him. 'I'm in the middle of something.'

'Whatever it is can wait a few days,' he says ruthlessly. 'We'll review your condition tomorrow.' He stalks off with his retinue and I'm left with the smiling Ramnath to face my aches and pains and restlessness for the remainder of the day.

The regular nurse gives me a shot and takes a few minutes over a fresh catheter. After she leaves I lie around helpless and then drift off without knowing it, in the daylight. There are periods of wakefulness after that, and dreams, all accompanied by a delightful feeling that none of it matters. None of what, I ask myself, and get the answer: not even that.

Then comes a blur of a nightmare that I can't remember. I come awake sweating in the dark, unable to remember where I am, but with old buried memories refreshed and a lump in the throat with the stiffness and nagging pains from a dimly remembered fall long ago. I try to put the pains aside but the memories swamp me very quickly.

Mohini, my wife. Mohini all those years ago, before we went sour. Mohini beautiful and soft and smiling her brilliant smile. In a passing moment of clarity I remember that Prakash asked why I married her. I'm beginning to drift off again and smile thinking it was the wrong question. What was the right question, then?

The right question? It rises without warning to my mind: whom did I want to marry? Whom did I love?

Mohini, of course.

Still drifting, I tell myself that's bullshit! And then comes the answer, with another round of wakefulness. After all these years I remember, more clearly than ever before.

I'd spent a miserable two months after being turned down

by a woman I'd chased for a year: she liked me all right, but not enough to marry me. I responded by throwing myself into my work and discovering a taste for it.

The woman I'd loved so much – her name, Shobha, emerges with reluctance, her face barely at all, and the depth of my feeling for her is incomprehensible now – had introduced Mohini to me at a restaurant where I used to lunch occasionally, when I had something to celebrate. After those two months of misery, I bumped into Mohini at the same restaurant. She was with a group of friends, and invited me to join them. I told them about the story I'd just finished, due to be published the following Monday. The story made the front page, and a crooked corporator lost his job in the fallout.

The next time Mohini and I met was at a new year's eve party thrown by an up-and-coming businessman, to which our money affairs correspondent dragged me along. Also present were CV and Mohini, CV being the businessman's friend and one-time mentor. Mohini introduced me to him as the man who brought down the corporator, a poor beginning, for the corporator had done CV an official favour in return for cash. His hackles went up, as did mine, and Mohini, I think, enjoyed needling him.

Another story – but no resignation – later, Mohini and I began to meet regularly. Since I had a rather prominent byline, accompanied, in those days, by a photograph, many of her friends recognized me when she said my name. Three months later we were engaged, and married after another three months.

Shobha came to the wedding, to wide smiles and nasty little messages from bride and groom: Mohini to say that she could steal Shobha's suitor without effort, and me that I could get myself someone prettier and altogether more desirable than her …

The first cracks began when I discovered that money, for her, was a weapon. She earned more than I did, and had no qualms about taking more from CV without telling me about it. Soon I found myself surrounded with 'comforts' I didn't particularly want, in a flat too big for the two of us. Worse, I found myself spending time with people who left me cold, and my work suffered, because Mohini had no idea that you don't know in advance which story will turn out good, so you chase lots of them in the hope that a few will work out. I tried to explain to her a few times, and gave up because she never did seem to listen.

Then came Pallavi, and my life turned inside out. In the hospital I held her tiny swaddled form in my hands and something inside me seemed to break. All went well after that, until the eighteen-year-old …

Looking back, I'm surprised we lasted as long as we did: the only reason we did was Pallavi. But for her, the marriage would have broken up in a couple of years, if not less.

But the thing is, it's as much my fault as Mohini's. It's a humbling thought, but it washes away the bitterness I have for her.

I remember Prakash saying something about your own greed, your own temper, your own vindictiveness, your jealousy, all being reasonable to yourself. Others see you better than you see yourself.

Now I understand why Prakash dismissed some of the Gita as nonsense. Men wrote most of the scriptures, and their own jealousy would have seemed reasonable to them, so they blamed women for it, and got it all backwards. Women tend to hold clans together, and jealous men tear them apart. So do men like me, who marry for all the wrong reasons.

How could I have been so unbearably, unutterably stupid, I ask myself.

I must have spoken out loud, for Ramnath, dozing in a smaller bed along the opposite wall, stirs and wakes up. He turns on the light, looks around, sees me moving, and gets up to ask if I want anything. When I ask, he tells me it's past nine at night, and when I ask him if it's possible to get coffee, tells me to wait and takes off. He returns ten minutes later with a large cup of very strong coffee, which hits the spot: only a large double rum with coke could be any better. I feel a little guilty about his spending all his time tied to my bedside, but when I say so he only laughs. 'Anything for CV sir,' he tells me. 'No problem.'

Something nags at me. I get it as I drink the coffee. That van. How come it was following me around? It disappeared when I went home, and reappeared when I was going to the guest house. Of course, I could be mistaken, but if I'm not, who sent the van after me?

With a sinking feeling I realize it could well be Srini. Srini knew I was going to CV's house. Unless, of course, it had been hanging around near the office and had followed me out to CV's house. That's unlikely, because I made much better time on two wheels in the heavy traffic than any van could.

Then comes a thought that should have struck me when I first saw the news of Prakash's trouble on our TV channel. How did they scoop it?

They have no major resources in Mangalore: Shafiq is good in a plodding sort of way, but he's not particularly good at sniffing out news. It must have been someone with sources in the police. Some policeman must have let Srini know that there was trouble coming. Or was it the guy who caused the trouble?

Did Srini make a deal with the bad guy?

The need for a drink nearly overwhelms me again, but this time I manage to keep it down. I have to stay alive.

I consider calling Gokul and ask Ramnath for my phone, which he hands over. I discover it's in silent mode, that Ramnath seems to have ignored calls: it says I've missed a call from Laxman. I call him back. 'I was about to call you again,' he says.

'What's the matter?' I ask.

'I remembered something from the ashram,' he tells me. 'Narsimha … Some months ago he got an iPhone, the latest version available. I never expected him to get something like that: his old one was a cheap Samsung. The iPhone gave trouble all the time, and he couldn't get it serviced easily, so he used to borrow cellphones sometimes. He borrowed mine three or four times, and when I looked at the number he dialled, it was always the same. I didn't tell the police because I … it slipped my mind, that's all.'

'We have to find out whose number it is, and this could well be the crucial link. To Raju's murder, the case against Swami. Text it to me. Do you remember anyone else whose cellphone Narsimha might have borrowed? Someone who's still at the ashram?'

There's a moment's silence after which he replies, 'You could try Rajiv Shanbag,' he says.

'Thanks very much,' I tell him. 'Keep in touch. May I call you for more details?'

'Of course,' he says. 'If it helps find the killer, no problem.'

I call Gokul immediately after I get Laxman's text, and explain to him what Laxman told me, giving him Rajiv Shanbag's name as well. 'Let me pass this on to Venkatachalam. He might have to talk to you, or to Laxman.'

'Sure,' I reply.

'How're things with Mohini?' he asks after a little pause.

'We've separated,' I tell him. 'She and Pallavi are with her father for the time being.'

'And you?'

'In a hospital with concussion.'

'Did you get drunk, bastard?' he asks.

'No,' I tell him. 'I was stone-cold sober when I fell off the scooter.' On an impulse I tell him about the van and my suspicions.

'Did you get the registration number?' he asks.

'Yes,' I tell him. 'I'll text it to you.'

'Fine. I'll check it out.'

It's getting on for ten now and I ask for a nurse to remove the catheter so I can try once again to limp to the bathroom and get ready for the night ahead. My knees are weak and my back hurts and the dizziness persists even when I sit up but I decide to try anyway and just about make it to the sink before throwing up. I stand leaning on the wall while Ramnath stands by, and eventually gets me back to bed. 'Give it another couple of days,' he says. 'Try to rest.' The nurse replaces the catheter, and I lie back. From the speed of her response, I guess I must be getting VIP treatment.

She has one more shot for me when she's done, and as I wait for it to take effect, I remember the scooter lying on its side by the pavement. 'What happened to the scooter?' I ask after the nurse leaves.

'We found out about it, and returned it to the dealer. They say you'll have to pay the difference between the insurance payment and the actual cost of repairs, which seems reasonable. But there's no hurry. CV sir will take care of it. Your new scooter will be ready when you are all right.'

'Why don't you go home?' I ask. 'I don't think I'll have an emergency until morning.'

He nods. 'Yes. I'm waiting for Rattan, who will relieve me soon. We have orders not to leave you alone.'

'CV's orders?' I ask.

'Yes.'

'Let me talk to him.'

He looks at his watch to check whether it's too late before handing me the phone. I call CV's number and he picks it up at the first ring. 'How are you feeling?' he asks.

'All right,' I tell him. 'I just wanted to say thanks.' I notice Ramnath sloping off, I wonder where.

'You don't have to do that,' he says.

'You don't know what I'm thanking you for,' I tell him.

'What?' he asks warily.

'For not rubbing my nose in it,' I tell him.

He laughs. 'I thought about it. You weren't drunk when it happened, it was night, there was no traffic, and I thought I should ask you how you fell before saying anything about how you could have avoided it.'

'I misjudged a corner, that's all,' I tell him.

'I came to see you in the hospital, but Dr Baliga told me not to try to talk to you. You were incoherent, you had hurt your head and lost a lot of blood, so he told me to keep off.' He's silent for a moment. Then, 'Bala, sometimes you play with powerful people. Things have changed in the last few years. Crime is much better organized now. But we can talk about it later, face to face.'

He's more perceptive than I thought. 'I want to see Pallavi,' I tell him.

'She wanted to see you but I told her you have a headache and you're dizzy, that she can see you when you're better.'

'That should be tomorrow.'

'We'll visit you tomorrow. How are they treating you?'

'Very well. I get VIP treatment.'

'Good,' he replies. 'I know everyone there. I lent the hospital some money a few years ago.'

'Have they paid you back?' I ask.

'Not yet, not fully,' he replies. 'But they will. Meanwhile, any friend gets the best. It comes in handy.'

'I don't need a nursemaid,' I tell him. 'Ramnath and his pal can go home.'

'They'll be with you throughout,' he tells me. 'You can't get to the toilet on your own, and the doctor says that another fall before you've recovered from the concussion can be very much worse. So get used to them.'

I bite back a retort and then decide to let it go. It's only a couple of days anyway, and they might be able to help me get hold of my papers from the guest house. I wish him good night and hang up, only to have the phone ring almost immediately. It's Surya. As I respond, Ramnath walks back in with a nurse in tow, carrying a tray. It looks like I'm due for another round of medication. 'Will you call again in a few minutes?' I ask Surya.

'Sure,' he says, and hangs up.

The nurse hovers while I have the medicines, and, over the next few minutes, I become aware of the aches and pains fading away. Then the phone rings, and Rattan – Ramnath has left in between – hands it to me. It's Surya. 'You don't sound very well,' he tells me. 'You're tired.'

'Just sleepy. They gave me a shot just now.'

'I'll call later, then.'

'No, it'll take a few minutes to work.'

'You have any serious damage?'

'No. A cut leg, a bang on the head, a dislocated shoulder.' Drifting a little, I add, 'I broke an unopened bottle of booze.' He laughs awkwardly, unsure of how to handle liquor jokes with me. 'Look, Surya,' I continue, 'I'm beginning to believe you when you said you didn't ask Srini for my job. I must have misunderstood something Srini said.'

He takes a moment to think, searching perhaps for a

trace of sarcasm, and, when he finds none, brightens up. 'I'm glad,' he says. 'I wouldn't stab anyone in the back. Not you, of all people.'

'Good,' I tell him. 'Leave it at that.'

'Look, Sunil told me to tell you something when I called.' Sunil is the new bean counter, Rajesh Ahuja's replacement. 'He said to tell you not to worry about the hospital bills. He wanted to put someone from the office in here, one of the boys, to look after you but your father-in-law insisted that his people would do the job.'

'Tell him thanks,' I say. I'm relieved, because I don't want to owe CV these bills.

'He'll talk to you directly soon,' he says. 'Get well.' He hangs up.

Srini. What the hell am I thinking, I ask myself. Srini is my oldest friend, but these little things coming up … I still can't believe that he's doing all this. Something niggles at the back of my mind but I can't pinpoint it.

My mind turns to the stacks of paper, Prakash's notes. The sheer size of the pile defeats me. I decide now that whenever I get back to them I won't look at any of the regular notes, only highlighted bits, and his handwritten notes on printed matter. That should ease the work dramatically, but there'll still be a large pile of paper remaining.

As I decide this the pains recede further and my mind goes fuzzy and the last thing I remember is reminding myself to check with the doctor whether I can read while I'm in hospital. I'm sure CV can get me one of those tables on which you have breakfast in bed, or use your laptop while lying around.

The next thing I know, my cellphone is ringing. Rattan, who's on standby duty, hands it over: from the caller ID I see it's CV. 'How are you getting along?' he asks.

'Still unsteady,' I tell him, 'but I think I can sit up in bed.'

'Very good,' he says.

'Yes,' I tell him, 'because if I can sit up and you can get me a little table to keep on the bed and Rattan or Ramnath can get me some papers from the guest house I should be able to work in here. I have a lot to read.'

'Let me check with the doctor. Reading a lot might not be very wise when you have a concussion.'

'Okay.'

'I called to ask if I can bring Pallavi there later. I'll have her dropped off from school, and she can have dinner with you. I'll have her brought home late. She can afford that once in a while.'

'That's fine,' I tell him.

'I'll arrange for something better than hospital food,' he tells me.

'That would be nice. Ask her what she wants.'

'I'll take care of all that … If the doctor says you can read I'll have a table sent across.'

'Thanks.'

'I have other people to meet, otherwise I'd have come myself.'

'Don't worry about that,' I tell him.

There's a lot of unfinished business that keeps me awake. I call Gokul. 'I traced that number,' he tells me. 'It belongs to a motorbike. Either you were seeing things or someone put false number plates on that van.'

'I don't think I was seeing things,' I reply. 'I used to make a living out of observing little details like that.'

'Then it was a false plate, which means that guy was out to get you. Maybe only give you a scare, force you into a fall, get you out of the way for a few weeks. Look, leave your scooter parked for the duration of the story. Get a car. It's a whole lot safer.'

'Are you serious?' I ask.

'Of course. Your risk on two wheels is a hell of a lot more than it is on four, and much more if someone's out to do deliberate damage.'

I give in. 'All right,' I tell him. 'I'll borrow a car from Mohini's father.'

He hesitates for a moment. Then, 'Look, you dumb bastard, if you're short of money, tell me. I can get someone to lend you a car for a few weeks.'

I laugh. 'My soon-to-be-ex-father-in-law made me exactly the same offer.'

'What's so funny about it?' he asks.

'Not funny, ironic. It's only now when his daughter and I are splitting up that we've got friendly.'

'He's being friendly? After all these years?'

'Yes.' I explain how we've learnt to put up with each other, that it started because of Pallavi but now we're finding other common ground as well. 'So all I have to do is call him.'

'Do it,' he says. 'Use the old bugger as much as you can.'

'Right. Any progress with those numbers?'

'Yes,' he tells me. 'I nearly forgot to tell you. We got Narsimha's phone: the iPhone that gave him so much trouble. Turns out he dropped it in his lunch one day, and it started malfunctioning after that. We checked out the SIM card, and found it registered to someone else … The number Narsimha called from Laxman's phone: it was assigned to a dead man, a gangster who died in a brawl a year ago. They used his driving licence to get the SIM card, forging his signature on the forms.

'This is typical of gangs. You use a dead man's driving licence to get a phone whenever you like. Or you get a prepaid phone with a false driving licence, which is easy to get if you have a few thousand rupees to pay off a tout. The licence gets you as many prepaid phones as you wish.

'But we got a lucky break. Someone recognized Purshottam Rao applying for the SIM card. It's not confirmed, and whatever we have now won't stand up in court, but Venkatachalam can follow up and look for another link that'll hold up.

'Another bit of news. Venkatachalam visited the ashram to check Narsimha's deafness. Narsimha seems to have been lying when he said he heard the washing machine. We'll send him to a good ENT specialist at the Wenlock if we need a better evaluation. Again, this might not stand up in court.'

'Good work,' I tell him.

'Not really. We just followed up. You're the one who worked out Narsimha's deafness and got us these telephone things to put together. Venkatachalam should thank you, in fact.'

'You know, it just happened. Okay, I figured out that bit about Narsimha's deafness, but the thing about the phone just fell into my lap.'

'I'm sure it didn't. You must have made friends with this Laxman chap. You got him to trust you though he knew you were a drunk.'

'Yes, I did.'

'I'll get back to you about all this. Perhaps at night, because I have a couple of meetings to attend.'

I take a chance and call Gaurav Seth on his cellphone, and discover that everything about him – except that cellphone number – has changed. He's quit the police force, he's quit Bangalore, and is now a partner in a large private detective agency in Mumbai. 'I heard about your accident,' he says when I call him. 'I was wondering if you were in any shape to talk.'

'Most of the time, yes,' I say, 'but I sometimes have these terrible headaches.'

'I spend at least ten days a month in Bangalore,' he says.

'Lots of useful contacts, some good clients. I'll see you next time I come.'

'Call ahead,' I tell him.

'Maybe not. I sometimes have to travel at a few hours' notice, so I'll just drop in and take a chance.'

Lunch, from the hospital canteen, is insipid, but I eat just because there's nothing else to do. I eat too much and feel heavy afterwards and then the medication puts me to sleep and I come awake at four in the afternoon, disoriented and confused, with blurred vision and a bad headache. I ask Ramnath – who has switched places with Rattan – if he can get me my papers and Ramnath tells me that since he's not allowed to leave my bedside he'll ask Rattan to pick them up on his way to the hospital at night. I agree grumpily – because of the headache, knowing that I won't be able to read anyway – and manage a cup of tea and a tablet for the headache before the door opens and Pallavi bounces in.

Ramnath's presence inhibits her not at all. She hugs me, careful of the sling on my shoulder. 'You should have taken the car,' she says, finally. 'How could you have been so stupid?'

'Last time we met you were telling me how bright I am!' I protest. 'Besides, you supported me when I said I didn't want the car. Everybody uses scooters. Remember?'

'That was before I understood what a lousy rider you are,' she says. 'There was no traffic, and you weren't drunk or anything, and the scooter was all right!'

'Out of practice, that's all,' I tell her, afraid to let her explore further possibilities, with the headache easing and my mind beginning to drift.

My fear is unnecessary. Her teenager's mind has already jumped to more important matters. 'You look cool with that stubble,' she says. 'Even though it's pepper and salt.' She reaches forward and scrapes her cheek across the stubble like she used to until a few years ago. Until the booze got to me, actually. 'Keep it. You look really cool, all relaxed, not wound up like usual.'

I nod sleepily, peacefully. How true!

She comes to the most important thing on her mind. 'Granddad's not letting me watch Star World,' she tells me. 'He says I'm too young for those serials.'

'I don't know about the serials but he does treat you like a ten-year-old.' Our neighbours in the apartment building included several nine- and ten-year-olds, and I remember her complaining about them: in her book, being ten years old is the worst possible state to be in. Of course, nine-year-olds and below don't even count as human.

'Yeah!' she says, settling down beside me on the bed. 'I didn't know you'd noticed.' I'm glad to see her and content to sit holding her hand while she chatters on, taking a break occasionally to check for messages on her cellphone. Only ten minutes later do I notice that her phone is actually an iPhone, which she definitely didn't have when I left for Mangalore. 'Where did you get that phone?' I ask her.

'Granddad.'

Up comes the belly-beast, but perhaps because of the on-and-off sedation it doesn't dominate me as completely as usual. 'Granddad's spoiling you,' I tell her quietly. 'I'll speak to him about TV serials for you if you tell him you don't want any more expensive presents.'

'But he likes giving me things,' she says. 'He even likes giving you things. He wanted to give you a car. He told me he's going to get you one.'

I remember his offer of a car, remember thinking that he likes to buy loyalty. But then I also remember the concern in his eyes and when shame twinges I understand that my anger is not at him but at myself for not being able to give this child what she wants. But why should I give her whatever she wants, comes the thought. Because some of the rich kids in her class get these things? To compete with the parents of her friends?

Of course not. Whatever I get her I get her because I don't want her to feel deprived. But I don't want to spoil her.

Bullshit, says another dry voice in my head. You don't want to lose her love.

Will she stop loving me if I can't give her an iPhone? Of course not, says the voice. She's a better person than that.

It's not about letting her get used to expensive things, either. If CV does as he promises – and he does keep his word – then she's going to be well off for all her life, because she's going to get everything he's got. She's going to be richer than Mohini ever was, richer than I ever dreamed of being. She's going to be able to buy me iPhones in my old age, if ever she and I feel like it.

It's yourself that you doubt, not her, says the dry voice. You think you're hollow, you're a coward, you're stupid, you're weak, you're a liar, you're dirty, you stink, and you're entirely unfit to be loved.

This is the lair of the belly-beast. It's got nothing to do with her, or with anyone else. It's all about me.

The belly-beast always misleads you, away from its lair, where it hides the lies it tells you. Now you've found it, kill the beast. But the beast is nowhere in sight. But now I do understand what Prakash said, about fearing what people will think of you if you screw up more than the screwing up itself.

I come sharply awake at that, and so do all the dormant aches and pains. Pallavi's presence eases the pain: I remember the feel of her cheek against mine from just a few minutes ago and feel better for it. Forget the money, I tell myself, go to Chennai. I hold on to her hand a little more tightly. 'What's happening, Dad?' she asks, squeezing back. 'Something hurts?'

'Just a twinge,' I tell her. 'Getting too old to be falling off things.'

There's a knock on the door and Ramnath and CV's chauffeur come in with a package and a folding table, which they proceed to set up by the bed. It's dinner.

While they set it all up and Pallavi goes off to the bathroom I lie thinking. On the available evidence, Narsimha is involved in Raju's murder, if he's not the murderer himself. Narsimha might also have orchestrated Ms Sharma's complaint. But I find it hard to consider Narsimha, for all his meanness, the murderer, or even a party to it. But if Narsimha has done all this, there's someone behind him and that someone is after Prakash.

Srini is involved in this, to what extent I don't know. He let somebody know my plans for last evening. It's hard, no, virtually impossible, to imagine Srini thinking of physical harm to anyone, or knowing people who could do that kind of harm. But, apart from Gokul, he was the only one whom I'd told I was going to CV's for dinner.

And if Surya's telling the truth, then Srini has been lying to me, twisting things around. He's also been messing with the papers the Mangalore office sent me: has he hidden something? But I've known Srini almost as long as I've known Gokul …

There must be something tying this whole mess together. What? Who's behind it? The same guy must be after me through Srini.

Purshottam Rao and Sadashiv Uchil are involved, which might mean that Krishnappa Gowda, the minister, is in it.

Could Gowda himself want to go after Prakash? I've assumed otherwise. When I spoke to him, Gowda tried to persuade me that he was Prakash's benefactor, and himself a victim of the scandal. He could be lying.

Why would he do that?

The second time I had lunch with Prakash, just before the police arrested him, he said something about Gowda being responsible for his being where he was. What did he mean?

Did Prakash mean that Gowda was responsible for the whole damn mess? But why? He said something about strings attached to everything. Did Prakash refuse to respond when Gowda pulled a string?

A wave of fatigue rises from deep within, and the aches and pains light up again. The doctor had said I must relax, give my brain a holiday, but I find I can't do that.

Dinner's all set up but my appetite has fled and I pick at my helping of bland biryani. 'What's the matter, Dad?' Pallavi asks, noticing.

I raise the wrist with the cannula still on it. 'Liquid diet. Only it's the wrong liquid. Dextrose, not rum.'

She giggles. 'Come off it, Dad,' she says. 'You've been off it for a long time.'

'That was accidental,' I tell her.

She looks at me sharply. 'What do you mean?'

CV hasn't told her everything about my fall. 'I was hurrying home with a bottle when I fell. The bottle broke, so I got here staggering but stone-cold sober.'

'Oh!' she says.

'But don't worry,' I tell her. 'I'm not going to risk a crash for another bottle. I'm determined to quit.'

Her phone rings intermittently throughout the meal and she spends almost all her time chatting with friends but I don't mind because her presence does lighten up the room and I don't have to worry about sustaining a conversation. When she finally hugs me goodbye I'm restless from the discomfort and when everything's been cleared away I tell Ramnath to tell the nurse I need a painkiller.

The next day I get worse. The headache deepens and I can't concentrate and I find myself raising my voice at people like Ramnath and Rattan and the nurse and if their goodwill survives, it's only on account of CV. I begin to throw up comprehensively and the nurse soon hooks up the intravenous feeding tube. The doctor changes his prescriptions and warns me that there can be more ups and downs. 'Concussion is special,' he tells me. 'There's injury to the brain but it doesn't show up on any scan. So we have to treat it symptomatically, and go by the numbers. I warned you the first time I told you about your concussion.

'But if you insist on reading and working your brain instead of resting it, you can be sure that you'll get worse before you get better.'

CV calls, and I grouch half-heartedly at him. He tells me he's been in touch with the doctor to make sure everything that can be done is done. Afterwards I feel mean and small but haven't the courage to apologize. At night the nurse gives me more medication for sleep and that ends the worst day since the accident.

After a good night's sleep I wake up with the headache almost gone and the other aches and pains bearable. Most important, I make it to the toilet with only one stumble, and declare myself free from the bedpan.

I persuade Rattan to call Ramnath and tell him to bring me my briefcase of papers from the office on his way to the hospital because I can't endure another day of daydreaming. Rattan protests, but very mildly, and when Ramnath arrives at ten he's got the briefcase. I open it and take the papers out and decide eventually to read Prakash's notes in Sankara's *Vivekachudamani*, in the chapter about finding a guru.

What I read in it is enough to have him shunned ten times over by fundamentalists. 'This guru-shishya thing is nonsense,' he's written in his neat hand along the margins of one page. 'We all have something to learn, and something to teach. We are all shishyas, we are all gurus. For some I am a guru, for others a shishya.'

And then, out of context, 'If I had something to teach, I'd go to where the gurus live, find myself a gurukul, and wait for people to ask.'

And then, towards mid-morning, my cellphone buzzes in Ramnath's pocket. Ramnath looks at me and decides I can handle a call or two, and hands it over. It's Sunil, the accountant, the one with the spending habits Rajesh Ahuja couldn't stand. 'Good morning,' he says. We don't know each other very well, but he's been professional and neutral in all my dealings with him.

'Good morning,' I reply. 'Surya delivered your message the last time he called. About the bills.'

'Very good,' he says. 'I should have told you myself but Srini said at the last meeting that it's better to leave you alone.' Sunil is very formal. Even when drunk, as he was at the party. 'Half the board have been asking about you.'

'Good to know,' I tell him, letting some anger surface, 'specially considering that they wanted me sacked ten days ago.'

There's silence. Then, 'That was Vish's idea. He was quite vehement about it.' Vish, who smirks when he rubs somebody out. No wonder he was smirking at Rajesh's farewell party. Vish and I don't get along because he's got the attention span of people who get their news only from TV.

Of late, Srini has been going Vish's way. Vish mostly does what Srini tells him to.

'Didn't everyone agree?' I ask.

'No,' he says. 'Some didn't. I didn't, for instance. You'd have known if you'd bothered to attend.'

'Thanks,' I tell him. 'I wasn't quite sure of that.'

'Well, now you can be.' He's a little abrupt, miffed at what he considers my rudeness, but seems to sense my anger. 'We can discuss this face to face when you're better. Until then, just relax.'

'Sure,' I tell him. 'Thanks again.'

'Let me know when we can meet,' he says. 'I'll come and see you.'

'Great.'

I lie back after he hangs up. So Srini *has* been lying. Well, he's been spinning things, if not lying. That still leaves me uneasy, because wanting to see me out of the firm is one thing, and wanting me scared off is entirely another. Besides, the Srini I know is capable of the first, but perhaps not the second.

So what's going on?

As I sit considering Srini, the cellphone rings again. It's Gokul, with news. 'I thought you should know,' he tells me. 'Narsimha's been arrested.'

'For what?'

'Conspiracy to murder. We don't have much, but there are those calls to shady numbers and his lies about hearing the washing machine.'

'So is he in prison?'

'No. A lawyer turned up to represent him. An old friend, he claims. Got him out on bail.'

'So what are you doing?'

'Not me. Venkatachalam. He's investigating. Narsimha was jealous of Raju. He thought he deserved to be the Swami's second-in-command. He's older, and has known the Swami longer. Hot on seniority.'

'What now?'

'His story's got holes in it. We'll get him back for interrogation. Try to break him.'

'And the lawyer?'

'The lawyer knows how interrogations work, so Narsimha will end up coached. As things stand, we don't have material for a prosecution.'

'What about the witness who saw Purshottam Rao apply for the SIM card?'

'He's not sure. That was a long shot. And there's more. Your pal, the Swami: he got out on bail. His case came up for review yesterday and the prosecutor didn't oppose bail.'

'That's good.'

'Listen. He turned up at the ashram last evening. He seemed just the same as always. But this morning, he, too, was gone.'

'Gone?'

'Yes. Just disappeared. The thing is, he could have something to tell us about the murder.'

'But he was in prison when it happened.'

'True, but he could have background information. Besides, the rape charge hasn't been dropped yet … We can't find him.'

'He skipped bail!'

'Yes … How are you getting along?'

'Yesterday was really bad, but I'm better today. The doctor says I should be resting.'

'Take it easy then,' he says. 'I'll call you when I have good news.'

And then, in the afternoon, when I'm about to doze off after lunch, Srini calls. 'How are you?' he asks.

'Up and down,' I tell him, hesitantly.

'We have things to discuss,' he says, 'about the story and your future both.'

'Yes,' I tell him. 'The doctor says I should be on holiday.'

'Tell me when we can meet then.'

'Any time. Meeting you isn't going to be very stressful.'

'Okay. I'll see you when I'm done with the office. I'll call ahead before I leave.'

His call has woken me up properly and I won't be able to get back to sleep so I turn to the stack of papers in the briefcase in the corner. Some instinct draws me to Prakash's notes in Sankara's book. There's something hidden in it. Some of those notes about gurus or teaching or godmen contains a clue. It sits in the back of my mind, nagging me, but I just can't get hold of it.

The rest of the afternoon passes in a haze of frustration as I go over the notes again and again, but find nothing. I break for coffee at about four, and get back to it afterwards, but can't put my finger on it.

Gaurav Seth takes me by surprise ten minutes after I start on the paper. 'I arrived here this morning,' he says. 'I was ten minutes away so I thought I'd drop in. As threatened.'

'Very good,' I reply, not knowing what further to tell him.

'I got some details about your crash,' he says. 'I still have friends in the department. You might have been knocked down. You're playing with fire again.'

'It's possible,' I tell him.

'I came looking for business,' he says, grinning. 'You want a bodyguard?'

'Heavens, no!' I laugh. 'But how did you know about playing with fire?'

'Friends in the department,' he tells me. 'Like you, I have to protect my sources. Let me pretend to be a know-all. I knew that you were going to Mangalore before you did.'

'Can't be!' I tell him.

'Well, I'm not telling you any more,' he says. 'I just wanted to find out how you are. Also ... well, I heard you've got over your drinking. I wanted to tell you how happy I am to hear that.' He looks me up and down. 'You don't look too good.'

'I'm better,' I tell him.

'I'll be moving now. I won't take more of your time.' He rises and makes for the door. He turns with his hand on the knob. 'All kidding aside, if you need help, call me. I have some pretty high-tech people for support. Don't think about the money.'

'I will,' I promise.

Srini calls at seven and arrives an hour later, alone, just when a headache begins to hammer on the left side of my forehead. He looks weary, and sinks into a chair as I ask Rattan to wait outside if he doesn't mind. Rattan doesn't, and tells me he'll be in the canteen, to call if I need him.

'How are you?' Srini asks when Rattan leaves. 'I hate to say this, but I did tell you so about the scooter.'

'You did, and you were right, as you usually are.'

'What about the story?' he asks. 'Where are you with that?'

'We know there's something involving Krishnappa Gowda and his men. There's the possibility that the rape thing is a set up. We don't know who wants to get at the Swami.'

'Do you think you can follow up when you're better?'

'Yes,' I tell him. I take a deep breath. No time like the present. 'But not for you.'

'What do you mean?' he asks.

'I quit, Srini. You've been lying to me.'

He sighs and leans back. He's not hiding anything, but he still tries to spin things in his favour. 'I was just trying to give you an extra kick in the backside,' he says. 'Just to help get you straightened out.'

'That might be. But you also got your stooge Vish to persuade everyone to throw me out. And you told me that you were the only one holding them back.'

'That's only one version,' he says. 'You can spin it however you like.'

'Right,' I tell him. 'It doesn't matter. I've had enough of this place. I don't trust you any more. I quit. The paperwork will follow in due course.'

'What are you going to do?'

'Considering you've been trying to get me knocked off, I don't think I want to tell you.'

That gets his attention. 'What?' he says, sitting up straight, thoroughly flapped. 'You must be kidding. I wouldn't dream of doing that.' His voice is plaintive. 'You can't believe that, Bala.'

'I don't know. Someone knew I'd be returning from CV's house that night.'

'You told me, I remember, but I didn't tell anyone else ... I was in meetings continuously for the rest of the day after you left. Check it out if you wish.'

'We'll leave that aside for the time being. But there are lots of things about this story that don't add up. I wondered how you got hold of this story in the first place. Shafiq didn't know a damn thing about it before he got orders telling him to support the TV news guys. So where did the tipoff come from?'

'You're right,' he says. 'I got the tipoff from a friend in Bangalore.'

'Who?' I ask.

He shakes his head. 'Can't tell you that.'

'Was it a cop?' I ask. It was someone who knew the kind of action they were planning, most likely a policeman.

He hesitates a moment, then nods. 'Yes. Someone I've known for years, someone in the Commissioner's office.'

'Okay. Why me? On the story, I mean.'

'You're not going to believe this, Bala, but the guy asked

for you. He didn't insist, but he said they'd appreciate it. I thought of your condition and my efforts to get rid of you and it all tied up nicely. I thought I'd send you there to turn the rocks over with a TV crew to take care of whatever crawled out from under. With your fear of TV cameras, and the booze, I was sure you'd screw up badly – blow your last chance, as it were. Then I could justifiably ask you to leave, and even your acolytes in the company – you still have them, you know – wouldn't be able to say I was the bad guy.'

'Did he know I was on the booze?' Only after I say this do I realize I said 'was', not 'am'.

'I don't know, but I told him you were. He said that was all right.'

'The papers that you got me from Mangalore. Someone had interfered.'

'Yes. That was me having a look, and Jimmy.' Jimmy is a reporter, still learning. 'He must have stuffed the papers back in the envelopes any old how.'

'That was stupid of you,' I tell him. 'Besides being mean.'

He looks straight at me. 'You've been a liability for some time now,' he says, after a pause. 'Whether or not you drink. I want to move into more profitable areas, go public, but you refuse because of your insistence on sticking to reporting in depth. You have enough shares and enough listeners to block everything I do in the direction I want to take.'

'You could just have told me,' I tell him. 'I'd have sold you the shares. Looked for another job. You like empires and profit. I like news ... maybe we should have parted company ten years ago.'

He nods. 'We should have. I could see there was trouble ahead.'

'Why didn't you tell me?'

He's silent, but I know the answer. He thought I'd see his

empire-building ways and extract what I could from him. I give him a moment, then say, 'I've had enough of you and your bloody spin, Srini. I'm going to think about what to do after I'm discharged from here. Just bugger off. Leave me alone.'

He rises and walks slowly to the door. He turns before opening it. 'I wish I'd got rid of you ten years back, Bala. It would have saved both of us a lot of heartburn,' he says. He pauses, and when he speaks again his voice is strangled. 'I always wished I'd been you. If I'd had half your talent I'd have done ten times as much.' Stunned, I see the jealousy raging in him. There's a beast in his belly, too, and it's got me in bad trouble. As he shuts the door behind him I hope I never see him again.

As Srini leaves, Rattan returns: he's obviously been waiting right outside. 'Didn't you go to the canteen?' I ask.

'I came back in ten minutes,' he replies. 'I heard you talking inside, and I didn't want to disturb you, so I waited outside.'

'Thanks,' I say, lying back.

'You look tired,' he says. 'Are you all right?'

'A headache,' I tell him.

'You don't eat enough,' he says. 'Maybe you'd get better fast if you ate well. You're too thin even otherwise …'

I know he's not trying to wriggle out of duty at my bedside – in any case, CV's paying him for it – so I just smile and tell him I can't eat. Quite the opposite, in fact: a wave of nausea comes up, and I make it to the bathroom just in time. Rattan holds my arm as I emerge afterwards. 'Get to bed,' he says. 'I'll get the nurse.'

I get the boss doctor instead, Dr Baliga, with the usual nurse following. He stomps in and looks at the mess of papers on the bedside table. 'Better you keep your papers at your office,' he tells me. 'Avoid colleagues. Colleagues mean work, and no holiday for your brain. Meet only friends and relatives. Relax.'

'I'll try,' I tell him.

'No trying,' he says. 'If you don't, I'll have to make you do it.' He gestures to the nurse, who comes forward, syringe in hand.

Fifteen minutes later, I'm getting woozy again. All the stuff he's said about names and gurus and everything sloshes around painlessly in my mind, as do memories of Gokul's concerns about my using a scooter and what Srini had once said about not facing my fear of TV cameras. I slip off into the dark, and wake with my bladder near bursting: no catheter. It takes all my willpower to navigate to the bathroom, even with Ramnath to hold on to.

Back in bed I doze off again, but come awake sometime in the middle of the night, to the sound of Ramnath snoring gently in his bed eight feet away, and a gentle feeling of disorientation, that nothing matters any more. And then, out of the depths of my mind, comes another thought. 'It's not the TV camera or the audience you're afraid of,' it goes. 'It's pissing in your pants.'

The disorientation vanishes, and in its wake comes another flood of memories, this one from childhood, from well over four decades ago, the first time I ever went on stage, at the age of six, in a school production of *Sleeping Beauty*.

I have two lines to do, as a sentry at the gates of the castle in which Beauty sleeps. The rehearsals have gone smoothly, and I have been delivering my lines well, if shrilly. On the big day, the lady teacher who directed the play is busy elsewhere, and the teacher in charge of operations is a large, gruff, red-faced man. I find him terrifying.

Some minutes before the play is due to begin, the gruff

man booms at us that now is the time to go to the toilet. The next opportunity might come only after the play. Everyone who wants to go should raise their hands. I want to go, and, being too scared to raise my hand alone, look for company. There's none, so I keep shut, hoping I'll last until the end of the play.

As it turns out, I don't. On stage, pretending to be asleep, looking out of the corner of my eye, I notice the gruff man staring at me. It's unnerving. Is my costume all right, I wonder. Very soon it's time to wake up, and then to deliver my first line. The strain of remembering that line and the gruff man's stare together make me forget to keep my bladder under control, and I feel a wetness spreading down my pants just as I open my mouth to deliver the first word.

I flee, in confusion, to condemnation from the gruff man, and, afterwards, on the way home, from my three-years-older brother, who calls me an idiot, the strongest swear word I know, the worst thing I've been called yet. It seemed the end of the world, that one word, and it remains the worst thing anyone has ever said to me.

The hurt is difficult to bear, though there's no reason for any hurt. I know now what Prakash meant about how we skirt around unpleasant bits of our life. What lies beyond? I'm going to try to find out. I know the beast better, and know that it lies.

Is the beast itself a lie, then?

The fear of the camera, of people watching, remains. Perhaps I've to prod deeper in my mind. Perhaps it's something I was born with, a matter of luck. I'm a prisoner, I realize, of chance and of my nature. With that admission comes a kind of peace, and sleep follows as I wonder how they handled the kiss in that story.

Later, awake in the quiet of the night, I find that many

little things are falling into place. I consider them again, and find no inconsistency. There are things I have to confirm, questions I have to ask, but now I know what to do. And then I sink into perhaps the deepest sleep I've had since the crash.

# Chapter Fifteen

ON THE ELEVENTH day after the crash, at noon, Dr Baliga visits my room for the last time, for once without a retinue. 'Be careful for four weeks. Call me if any symptoms recur. Take it easy if you can.' He signs the papers for my discharge and leaves without fuss, and I'm free to leave.

Ramnath, approaching the end of his spell of nursemaid duty, offers to drop me off at the guest house in his dilapidated old car, but I turn his offer down, shake hands, and tell him I'll find my own way. I call a cab to get to the guest house, and as I enter the house my cellphone rings. It's CV. 'Where are you?' he asks. 'Dr Baliga told me you've been discharged, and Ramnath told me you refused a lift.'

'I wanted to be alone,' I tell him. 'I'm back at the guest house for the time being.'

'I'm glad I got to see you at work,' he says. 'If you keep off the booze you should be all right.'

'I'll do my best to keep off the booze. The rest …'

'You'll make it. Your bloodhound nature will ensure that.'

'Thanks for the faith, but it might be misplaced.'

'It won't,' he replies, crowing a little. 'If there's one thing I can do, it's telling a winner.'

The beast rears. Who the hell is he to judge me, it says. Then it settles as I remember Prakash's notes about chance. He only thinks he can judge a winner. Well, let him. It does me no harm. I can understand now why people flock to godmen. If ten people visit, and half succeed in some way, they'll believe in him. They go back, and take another few with them. And so on.

CV breaks into my reverie. 'I called because there's something for you in the mail. A courier dropped it off yesterday but I didn't want to give it to you before you were discharged.'

'Can you send it over?' I ask.

'I think you should come here. Why would someone send me something for you?' He pauses. 'I'll send the car for you.'

'Who is it from?' I ask.

'One Jyothi Acharya,' he says. 'It was sent from Dharmasthala.'

The name is strange but my heart leaps. 'Okay,' I tell him. 'Send the car. I'll be ready.'

What with the traffic and my stopping for lunch it's four when I arrive at CV's gate. He leads me to a patio at the rear, where one of his people serves tea. He hands me the packet, a brown paper envelope, addressed to me in a familiar neat hand. CV leans forward, curious to see what's in it. When I slit the envelope open, a single sheet, two CDs and a pen drive fall out.

'Dear Bala,' goes the letter, printed on a laser printer, 'Raju modified the recording system at the ashram long ago. Even when it's turned off, one mike keeps going. On the CDs are recordings of my last meeting with Ms Smita Sharma, and an earlier one, of a meeting with Krishnappa Gowda and Sadashiv Uchil. These are the CDs on which the recordings were made, just in case someone wants to verify them in a forensic lab. There are copies on the pen drive.

'At the meeting, Uchil said that Gowda had already asked me very politely to let him use the ashram for his own purposes. He was asking once again, and that my continued refusal would lead to consequences I wouldn't like. He also told me that he had a man in the ashram to make sure things went the way he wanted. That must have been Narsimha with his iPhone ... Poor Raju. Raju hid the recordings in my room, thinking he'd be safe. Narsimha on his own wouldn't have been able to poison him. Uchil's man must have prodded him.

'If I had handed the recording of my meeting with Ms Sharma to the police, she would have suffered the most, while Gowda and Uchil would hardly be troubled. On the other hand, if I gave both these recordings to the police, Gowda and Uchil would be tempted to finish me off, because the recording is useless without my corroboration. If I had told you about these things they would have tried to finish you as well. They would have tried to finish you off if they even suspected I might have told you something, which is why I decided to stop talking to you in jail.

'Someday we might have the chance to resume those conversations. Even if we don't, though, you and I have enough to think about.

'I rode a bus for a few hours before sending this to you, and now I'll ride another bus to the place where I'm going, so I won't be easy to find.

'Look after yourself, Bala. Here's some advice I haven't been able to follow fully: let go. Let go the booze, your daughter, your wife, your friends, your enemies, and most of all yourself.

'Be well.'

The letter is unsigned but I know it's from Prakash, and I now understand how he picks false names. I put the sheet and the pen drive in my pocket and tear up the envelope into small pieces. CV is itching to know what's in it, I know, but he'll have to live with the itch. 'Don't ask, CV,' I tell him.

'It's better for you if you don't know.' He doesn't know what to make of this, but he knows that my accident wasn't an accident, and will not pursue it.

'All right,' he says, mildly upset. Then, recovering, 'What do you plan to do with your shares in your present company?'

'Sell them to Srini, I guess. I've had enough of the company, and him.'

'Give me the details. How many shares you have, what percentage, when you got them, and so on. Let me negotiate the price. How much do you expect?'

I tell him and he grins. 'I'll get you much more.'

'I really don't care,' I tell him. It's a small thing, in context.

'I do. He must pay for his treachery. If you won't make him, I will.'

'As you wish,' I tell him. A little extra money in the bank will be a comfort in my old age, which isn't far away. 'Thank you.' Then, 'Excuse me, I have a call to make.'

I call Kamal Srivastava, and tell him I'd like to take him up on his offer, but will join only after a month. 'Sure,' he says. 'We need to meet to discuss terms.'

'We'll do that soon,' I tell him. 'I've got over my little problem, by the way.'

'I heard something like that,' he says. 'Good for you. Heard you had an accident.'

'Yes. Just out of hospital. I need a month's rest before getting back to work full-time.'

'Take as long as you need,' he says. 'Tell me at least a day before you're ready to come over, and I'll email you the tickets.'

'Don't hang up yet,' I tell him. 'I need some help. Your young colleague, Rahul. I'd like him to do something for me.'

'What?' he asks.

It's a bit complicated, but I tell him, and he agrees without question. After I hang up, I call Gaurav. 'You told me to call if I needed help,' I tell him.

'Sure,' he says.

'Tell me how you found out I was going to Mangalore,' I tell him.

'A serving police officer told me,' he says. 'Someone who knows Srini.'

'And how did he know?' I ask.

'Someone asked him to ask Srini to send you.'

'Who?'

He's silent for a moment. 'I owe you one, Bala,' he says. 'That's paid off if I tell you.'

'Of course,' I reply.

He tells me. It's no surprise, but it's good to have a guess confirmed. 'I need something more,' I tell him. 'You might be able to get it without fuss.'

'What?' he's wary.

I give him a couple of cellphone numbers. 'Can you find out where these two phones were some days back?' I ask.

'If the phones were on, and they were used, I might be able to. I know a guy who can hack into systems. But remember that none of this will be permissible as evidence.'

'Good,' I tell him. I give him the dates for which I want those details, and he promises to get back to me in the next day. There's nothing more to do but wait and get well enough for what I have in mind.

Gaurav keeps his promise, for my email next evening contains a tabular column of where those two numbers have been, and whom they've called. I compare the calls and the locations and then it's obvious, though, as Gaurav said, none of this will be usable in a court of law.

Some days later, when I trust myself to take an airline trip without falling down, I call Gokul. 'Got some time free tomorrow evening?' I ask. 'Around seven?'

'Depends,' he replies. 'What's it for?'

'I'm well enough to travel,' I tell him. 'We've got to catch up with the investigation. Get you up-to-date on what's been happening here. I've got a lead you might want to follow up, and I don't want to discuss it on the phone.'

'Sure.' He's happy. 'What do you want me to do?'

'Remember the hotel I stayed in last time?' I ask. 'I'll be in the restaurant at seven, and we'll take it from there.'

My flight is late but I still make it to the restaurant ten minutes early, and sit where I can watch the entrance. Three tables away are two sinewy-looking men in white T-shirts who don't seem to fit, besides having little to say to each other. When the waiter comes, I order coffee. Gokul arrives in his homely jeep, and swaggers into the restaurant a couple of minutes late. I see him and raise my hand in a wave, and he walks across to my table and pulls out the chair facing me. 'We could have gone home, Bala,' he says. 'We don't have to sit here.'

'Bear with me,' I tell him. 'This won't take long.' The waiter places a mug of coffee in front of me. 'What'll you have?' I ask Gokul.

He shakes his head. 'Nothing,' he says. Then he grins, pointing at the mug. 'I'm glad that's not rum.'

I smile back. It hasn't been rum for some days now, but the thought of an infinity of days without even a teeny-weeny bit of a drink still unnerves me. 'So am I,' I tell him. 'I think I've got it licked.'

'Good for you.' As we speak, a large man in a dark safari suit and a youngster in faded jeans take the next table and ask for tea. A third man in a white shirt and black trousers joins them a moment later. 'What's that lead you were talking about?' Gokul asks.

'I'll get to it in a couple of minutes,' I tell him. 'We're

here to close a case, but not the case you think, and not the way you think.'

'What do you mean?' he asks.

I take my time answering. 'I should have figured you out the day we met Uchil and Gowda in that hotel basement. You set it up. You were working with them all along. You're a small fry, Gokul, too small to challenge them the way you did. It was all an act, to convince me That you were on my side.

'You got a pal in the Bangalore police to call Srini with the tipoff, and you got him to put me on the case because you thought I was a drunk and you'd be able to point me whichever way you wanted, and guide the investigation besides. Then you got me thinking Srini was leaking information to the other side.

'You told them I was going to CV's house the night I crashed. It had to be you, because Srini was the only other one who knew, and I confirmed that he couldn't have done it. Your people couldn't do anything to me on the highway in the traffic but they got their chance when I was on my way to the guest house in the rain.

'I thought you were a friend, Gokul, and you tried to have me killed, or scare me off. But none of it was any use, Gokul. It didn't scare me off, and Prakash got away.'

'Where's he hiding?' he asks, a new rasp in his voice, the rasp he uses on suspects. 'If you know and you don't tell me, you could be in a lot of trouble.'

'I've been in trouble before, Gokul, and I have no idea where he's hiding. But it doesn't matter because he sent me a little package.'

'What package?' he rasps.

'Just a letter and a couple of audio recordings on a pen drive,' I tell him. 'One recording is of the conversation at the meeting at which Smita Sharma accused him of trying to rape her: it seems her version is a lie. The other implicates both Gowda and Uchil: they threaten him with consequences if he doesn't allow his ashram to be used as a sort of depot for booze and cash and other goodies that Uchil distributes during the elections, besides a lot of other things.'

His toughness has turned mean. His eyes calculate. He leans back. 'I can still get you done,' he says. 'You might never get home.'

'I've had copies made. They're ready to be sent out to lots of people. One of them is a judge of the High Court, and we can expect the court to take suo moto action.

'You really screwed up. There are other things besides. Remember, you told me you were going for a wedding. You lied.

'I've got access to cellphone records, so I followed up on the number that Narsimha called most often from the phones he borrowed. Then I checked out your number, the one you gave me. You know what? Your phone and that one were in the same cell all the time. All the time. You were somewhere near the ashram that night you were supposed to be at the wedding, and you got a few calls, one on your phone and the other on the secret one.

'There's no proof, but I know you're the guy Narsimha was calling: he called when we were in that toddy joint and you shouted, something I've never seen you do. You had to shout because he can't hear very well, and then you pretended to be angry. You were the one between Uchil and Narsimha and whoever else you have at the ashram. You set Narsimha up to finish Raju.

'I think he asked you for an iPhone as part payment. But then he goes and drops the thing in his hot lunch, and he had to borrow cellphones to call you. That gave him away. That and the Rolex.'

'I thought you were too far gone to notice these things.'

He slams the table with a fist in frustration. I keep still. The two men in T-shirts get up and amble across. Their trousers are khaki and they're cops. 'I knew you were onto something,' he says, 'but I wasn't sure, so I kept some men here. They'll do what I tell them, and afterwards, if necessary, they'll testify on my behalf.' He turns to them. 'Arrest him,' he says. 'He's a reporter trying to bribe me to reveal the details of an investigation.'

'Don't do this, Gokul,' I tell him.

'Get up,' he says, 'or my men will make you. Then you'll tell me where he is. Like it or not.' Now that his backup has arrived, his voice is normal again.

The large man in the safari suit rises from his seat at the next table and walks up, looming beside Gokul. His young friend in faded jeans comes alongside, and then the man in white and black. Gokul tenses up.

'Relax, Gokul,' I say. 'The gentleman in the safari suit is a trained bodyguard. He's here to take care of me. His friend in jeans is a reporter, a future colleague, and he's been recording everything. Behind them is a very good young lawyer. Just in case you get the wrong idea. Your bosses won't like the fallout if you do something stupid.'

Gokul drops back in his chair, breathing heavily. He sees he's beaten, and signals to his men, who move away, and out of the restaurant. Rahul and his two companions go back to their table and their tea. 'I'll find your pal,' Gokul says when they're gone, his voice thick with anger. 'He'll have left a trace somewhere or other. He'll have depended on someone for some little thing. A reference, maybe, or a false certificate, or something of the kind. I'll hunt him up, Bala, and I'll put him down.'

'Prepare for a surprise,' I tell him, the anger building. 'Not everyone lets their friends down.'

He glares at me for a moment, then turns away. All of a sudden I think of the way he used to be and my anger begins to dissolve. 'Why, Gokul?' I ask, very gently. 'Why?'

He clenches his jaw for a moment, still looking away. 'I found I was clearing cases,' he says, 'but failing to prosecute. Witnesses were turning hostile. Experts were declaring evidence ambiguous. People were getting away who shouldn't have been. Then I caught someone who knew enough to bring some big guns down.' He pauses. 'I interrogated him. I got … I got rough with him. He died some hours after I left him in his cell. I'd gone home, and a senior came visiting at midnight. There wasn't time to cover up.

'There'd have been an inquiry, and I'd have been thrown out of the department. Dishonour. No pension, nothing to show for all those years.' He shakes his head. 'Gowda, through Uchil, gave me a way out. No inquiry, no witnesses, a faked autopsy report, no case against me. Instead of disgrace and penury, they said, I could keep my career, have a pension, and, if I wanted, more money than I could hope for if I were straight. But every now and then, they said, I'd have to do as they told me.'

'Does Jayanthi know?'

He nods. 'All of it. She agreed in the beginning, and once I was in there was no turning back.'

'What about Narsimha?'

'His arrest was all theatre. He used to be a clerk in the Transport Office, always looking for bribes, and he jumped at the offer of a Rolex and an iPhone for following instructions. They'll take care of him …' He smiles bitterly. 'Just like they took care of me.'

I try one last time to get through to him. 'Cross over, Gokul. We can go to the top. With what you know, we can hit them hard. You'll have 24-hour protection, the works.'

He laughs. 'If it were as simple as that you'd have had a thousand whistleblowers by now. If I cross over they'll finish me off. Slowly. After finishing off my boys and their families. Also slowly, in front of me. They have sources everywhere.' He shakes his head. 'No, Bala, no. All that's changed is that we know where each other stands. I won't have to go to jail. I'm not at the top of the group but I know too much for them to let me go down. They'll take care of me.' He grins without humour. 'But no matter what happens to me,' he continues, 'you just sealed your pal, the Swami's, fate. If he turns up, he's a dead man.'

'I know,' I tell him. 'He, too, knows that. He won't surface. Impasse, Gokul. Your side won't sleep in peace until you're sure he's dead.'

'I'll be watching you as well,' he says, 'just in case.'

'Go ahead,' I tell him, exhausted. 'Do what you like. I don't care.' At the moment, I really don't. I think I know where Prakash is hiding but he wants me to leave him alone so that's what I'll do. Gokul can follow me as long as he likes but I won't lead him to Prakash.

He leaves without a backward glance, and his subordinates follow quietly. As I watch his retreating figure, I know what to do. Gokul is as much a prisoner of his nature and his circumstances as I am. I won't sit in judgment on him, or anyone else. If we get him and his gang, they'll make sure plenty of innocents go down with them, like Smita Sharma. Justice is a ghost, like Prakash implied. It exists only in the mind. If you want to live in peace you have to let it go, like much else. Outside, Gokul gets into his jeep. His backup men have disappeared. He's alone in defeat.

I wonder how he feels. It's not been much of a victory. There are no winners, really, and we're all alone. I know what Prakash meant when he said that. Pallavi comes to mind then, and I think, maybe not.

I leave some money on the table and follow the man in the safari suit to a white car parked just inside the gates of the hotel. As we wait for a gap in the traffic to pull out onto the road, it strikes me that I might've closed a case but I've also opened up a huge old can of worms.

# Epilogue

THAT CAN OF worms stayed shut: all we got was a brief look at the crawling mess inside. Narsimha's case never made it to a trial. Investigators reached dead ends everywhere. Narsimha's defence turned the tables on the prosecution, claiming that those calls were made in good faith to a person Narsimha thought was an insurance salesman selling policies at a very low premium. If it was a scam, then Narsimha was a victim in a matter entirely unrelated to Raju's murder. As for his hearing, they got an expert to testify, with perfect truth, that deafness need not be consistent. Some deaf people have good days and bad, and on good days they hear things they don't on bad days.

The recordings of Prakash's conversations with Krishnappa Gowda and Sadashiv Uchil were no use without Prakash himself as a witness to offer corroboration, so both remain at large, though not as destructive as before. Prakash himself is still officially a fugitive. The contents of the recordings did become public, though, and the TV channels all made sure that everyone heard them. Gowda lost his seat in the next elections by a large margin. He and his gang continue to be held in check by their fear that Prakash might surface and bring up the old scandal all over again. They've left Prakash's ashram and the trust alone.

Both the ashram and the trust survive, though their

revenues have fallen off. Their school was taken over by an NGO last year, and the hospital closed down. But the old people in the ashram are still there, and as well as they can be, except for one who died soon after Prakash disappeared.

I shifted to Chennai soon after that last meeting with Gokul. Mohini filed for divorce, and the divorce was granted six months later. Thanks to CV, there was no dispute over Pallavi, who stayed with Mohini, in CV's house, where I was free to visit whenever I wanted. Best of all, the house is big enough for me to meet Pallavi without bumping into Mohini, who hasn't got over her anger at me yet, and puts me in my place whenever she can.

Thanks also to CV, Srini paid a surprisingly large sum for my shares, so now I have a car. No more messing around on two wheels.

CV himself is in better shape for his age than ever before. He eats very little, drinks rarely, walks around quite a bit, and has been doing yoga for a couple of years. He's mellowed, but his cutting sense of humour shows now and again. He keeps track of all the gossip, and we have long chats whenever I visit Bangalore.

The belly-beast lives on. It protects its lair as keenly as ever, though it roars less often. Now that I know it lies, I watch out for the lie. On the rare occasion I catch the lie, the beast retreats. What lies beyond I don't know: maybe I'll write it down if and when I find out. Or maybe I won't.

Pallavi has matured. At eighteen, she's a lot more assertive. After high school she took a year off to think, and decided to take to law as a profession. She's earned herself a place at a law school in Delhi. She just spent a few days with me in Chennai and is now on her way to Delhi, where Mohini will pick her up and accompany her to the school. At the airport, we meet a boy her age, Michael, a new friend also off to Delhi to the same school. Out of her handbag she takes a plump wallet to pay off the cabbie – she has plenty of money now, thanks to CV – while the lad trots away to get a baggage trolley. She has two large suitcases while the lad has one, and the cabbie takes them out of the boot and leaves them on the pavement.

She dismisses the cabbie as if he's beneath her notice, though she does tip him well, and when Michael's a little clumsy loading the suitcases on the trolley she snaps at him. He blushes and mumbles an apology, and I see that he's got a crush on her, and she knows it. He flashes me a strange look, and I can see what he's thinking: how could this moth have fathered a butterfly as glorious as Pallavi?

We reach the gate. Pallavi turns after seeing that her luggage is safe and says, 'Take care, Dad.'

'You, too, sweetheart,' I tell her, fighting a sudden lump in the throat. 'And watch out. Delhi's a lousy city for girls.'

She gives me a watery smile as she fetches her ticket and ID out of her handbag. Clutching those, she turns to give me a parting hug and tightens her arms around me for a moment. She steps back, and in the warming glow of the morning sun I see, briefly, Mohini in her stead.

In that moment my feeling for her changes. I've never been able to look at Pallavi without also seeing the baby with whom I used to play, the girl who used to hug me tight when I left town for a night, the vulnerable teenager whom I deserted for some years, and a few others as well. I see her now for what she is, beautiful, bossy, and more like her mother than ever before. Stay away from her, I want to tell Michael, she'll lead you a mad dance, ruin your years of study.

I remember Prakash's time bomb, whatever will be, will be. Let her take care of herself. Doesn't matter what she is, what she does, she'll always be my daughter and I'll always respond to her. But there's a difference now. There's no guilt mixed up in the love, or judgment, or expectations, or plans. I see her for what she is, and a weight is gone, leaving me rich beyond words. I'm all alone now, yet not alone.

The moment passes, and I take a deep breath and smile back at her.

She puts a hand on my cheek. 'What happened, Dad?' she asks. 'You clouded up for just a second.'

'Nothing,' I tell her. 'Nothing that matters.'